D1566296

Acclaim for Huddle

"*Huddle* is a tightly written book packed with action, both on and off the field. Each character's story fascinates as it reveals hidden vulnerabilities, even on the sweaty, testosterone-charged football field. Sharply written with characters that sometimes define but mostly defy the stereotypes of gay men in LA, *Huddle* takes us on a journey of community, discovery, and ultimately, love."

—G. Bruce Smith, Playwright and Journalist,
Venice, California

"An intriguing look at an often unseen side of sports. So much happens on the field—and off—that most people never see. Dan Boyle has opened the door to the closeted locker room, and his readers can walk right in. This book should appeal to all readers, gay and straight, who realize that even macho athletes such as football players can lead lives laced with nuance and can express both lust and love in the most unlikely ways."

—Dan Woog, Author,
Jocks 2: Coming Out to Play

"*Huddle* is a rare debut novel that proves gay fiction is alive and well with complex, compelling, three-dimensional characters, an interesting plot, and beautiful use of language. Dan Boyle is surely a writer to watch."

—Greg Herren, Lambda Literary Award Finalist;
Editor, *Shadows of the Night:*
Queer Tales of the Uncanny and Unusual

"Dan Boyle has used the clever device of a flag football team as a parallel universe to the social lives of nine gay men to explore their relationships, aspirations, insecurities, isolation, and loneliness. Each character emerges as an individual entity and personality with his unique set of circumstances and needs. Boyle's use of various points of view, unconventional presentation, natural and witty dialogue, and his use of the team and it's games to frame the story advances the action effortlessly and creatively. Setting a story about the loves and lives of nine gay men within the traditionally macho, he-man world of football is a wonderfully amusing, tongue-in-cheek touch."

—Jerrianne Hayslett, Writer, Author, Consultant

"Dan Boyle has captured the camaraderie, friendship, interplay, and sex-play that can occur within a bunch of guys who play football together and all happen to be gay. There isn't a character you haven't met, they're all so real, with a series of stories that range from pathetic and tragic to erotic and hysterical. It's one of the most enjoyable reads in the gay literary press in years."

—Mike Szymanski, Movies Editor,
Zap2it.com (Tribune Media);
Contributor, *Frontiers, Advocate, Genre,*
IN LA, Gay Chicago

Huddle

HARRINGTON PARK PRESS
Southern Tier Editions
Gay Men's Fiction
Jay Quinn, Executive Editor

Huddle

Dan Boyle

Southern Tier Editions
Harrington Park Press®
An Imprint of The Haworth Press, Inc.
New York • London • Oxford

Published by

Southern Tier Editions, Harrington Park Press®, an imprint of The Haworth Press, Inc., 10 Alice Street, Binghamton, NY 13904-1580.

PUBLISHER'S NOTE
This is a work of fiction. Names, characters, places, and incidents either are the products of the author's imagination or are used fictitiously, and any resemblance to actual persons, living or dead, business establishments, events, or locales is entirely coincidental.

Cover photograph by Steve Paige.

Cover design by Jennifer M. Gaska.

Library of Congress Cataloging-in-Publication Data

Boyle, Dan, 1959-
    Huddle / Dan Boyle.
        p. cm.
    ISBN 1-56023-459-8
    1. Gay men—Fiction. 2. Flag football—Fiction. 3. Los Angeles (Calif.)—Fiction. I. Title.
    PS3602.O97 H83 2003
    813'.6—dc21
                                                                    2002151039

For the LA Quake . . .
and for Jason

CONTENTS

The Winter League Championship Game

The football soared into the blue sky, above the palm trees, the El Capitan Theatre, and Mann's Chinese Theater along Hollywood Boulevard. Jack Scott—his eyes hidden by dark sunglasses, his graying hair hidden by blond highlights, and his expression hidden by the Botox injected in his forehead—followed the trajectory of the ball as he rubbed the shoulder of his throwing arm. The football rose up and away until the quarterback lost sight of it in a cloud of smoke blown from the nostrils of the dinosaur towering over Ripley's *Believe It or Not!* Museum.

The dinosaur's bursting growl signaled one o'clock. Vince Pastor, the best receiver on Jack's team, was beating his closest defender by four strides as he ran perfectly in timing with the ball. Vince's deep-set eyes were the first to catch sight of the ball as it emerged from the smoke. The motion of the ball had now become part of Vince's own motion as he adjusted the speed of his long, lean gait, preparing for the pigskin to fall over his shoulder and into his arms.

But Mitch Vanowen, with deceptively quick, spindly legs half covered by his knee-high soccer socks, was gaining on Vince. Twisting his neck to peer over his shoulder, Mitch also saw the ball advancing and suddenly he built up speed to overtake it.

Jack held his breath. A wrinkle actually broke through on his forehead exterior. If Mitch intercepted the ball, Jack would again be teased and chastised by everybody on the field. "Can't make the big play," they would say. And this *was* the big play.

All the other players—those in blue jerseys who were on Jack's team and those in red jerseys who were on Mitch's—stopped blocking and running. All of their eyes focused on Vince, Mitch, and the ball spiraling down to greet the two. There was nothing any of them could do. It was now the Vince-and-Mitch show.

As Vince had anticipated, the ball was coming down over his shoulder. But Mitch had anticipated as well; he leapt off his right foot, lunging forward, his arms and shoulder arcing in a forty-five-degree angle toward Vince.

Their shoulders collided. Vince, his upper body twisted back to welcome the ball, fell sideways onto the grass with Mitch tumbling over him. Last to fall was the football itself, bouncing off Mitch's curly blond-covered scalp before landing on the grass.

Vince wasted no time on the ground. He cocked his elbow back and threw Mitch off him. Then, catching sight of the football, he picked it up and slammed it into his defender's back.

"What the fuck!" Vince cried. "Pass interference! That's fucked up, man! Fucked up!"

As Vince watched Mitch brace his hands against the ground to push himself up, he struck Mitch's shoulder blades with his hands, forcing him back onto the grass.

"Damn you, motherfucker!" Mitch cried as he rolled several times along the grass to escape Vince, just long enough to plant himself on his feet. He spit the dirt out of his mouth and pounced on Vince. "If that's the way you want it!"

Both of them attacked with outstretched arms, each trying to lock onto his opponent, fingers twisted together in a battle that appeared as a dance, cleats jabbing into the soft dirt as each man bent his knees in an attempt to throw the other down.

Their teammates, a distance back on the field, ran to stop the fight. But the first to reach the two in battle was Dave Vander Beeken, the quiet newcomer who had agreed to referee this game after his Green Team lost in the semifinals. Dave raced up to the two, but when he arrived at the scene of the fight, he stood silently, staring for several seconds before choking out a nasally chirp from his whistle.

"Um. No fighting in the game, guys," he stated softly, his command having no power of authority. And when he saw that his words had no effect, he placed his hands on his hips and continued to stare, trying to determine whether he should blow the whistle again.

Marcus Taylor, the running back on Jack's team, was the next to arrive. He rushed up to Vince and Mitch and forced himself between them, then pulled them apart with his powerful brown arms.

"Man, what the fuck you two always going after each other?" Marcus yelled at them. "This ain't no wrestling match!"

Marcus turned his head to the referee as he kept Mitch and Vince at arm's length.

"Whatchoo say, David? That was definitely pass interference."

Dave's eyes had a watery stare as he watched Marcus break up the fight, but as soon as he heard his name, he blinked several times.

"It's Dave," he said matter of factly.

Marcus lost focus on stopping the fight for a moment when he heard Dave's reply. He looked back at the referee and cocked his head.

"What!?"

"My name is Dave. Not David."

"Look, I don't care whatchore name is. That was pass interference."

"I didn't see it," Dave answered.

"What are you talking about, you didn't see it?" asked Jack as he ran up to the referee, his scowl creating lines all over his face except his forehead. "You were standing right by the play!"

"I didn't see pass interference."

"What!" Jack exclaimed. "How could you not see pass interference? It was clearly pass interference! Mitch knocked Vince over before the ball was touched. That's pass interference!"

"Hey, Mitch had his head turned," argued Jerry Tollari, the short, dark-haired Italian on Mitch's team. Jerry had redesigned his red jersey by cutting it up so that it now had become a slinky string tank top exposing his model body. "That shows he was going for the ball."

"That don't mean nothin'," Marcus replied. "Shit! You don't know football anyhow!"

"Dave made the call," Jerry argued. "No pass interference."

"Dave doesn't know football either," Jack said. "He wouldn't be able to call pass interference if he saw it."

"I know when it's pass interference." Dave spoke in a quiet monotone, showing no signs of football ignorance, but again, showing no signs of authority. "This would be too close to call. So I can't call it pass interference."

"Then play over," Jack demanded.

"Play over!?" Marcus cried, turning to his teammate. "Jack, whatchoo talkin' about? This would have been the go-ahead touchdown! Fuck that, man!"

Dave blew his whistle a second time.

"Down over," he stated.

"Fuck that!" Vince and Mitch yelled simultaneously. The two had given up their resolve for fisticuffs, and now they both stood with their hands on their hips, their eyes cast down, unwilling to look at each other and somewhat ashamed at how their anger had gotten the best of them.

"OK, OK. The ref's made his decision," Jack said, nodding and clapping. "Come on, Blue Team. Huddle!"

His teammates followed Jack forty yards down the field. Slowly they gathered into the huddle, squatting in a circle, their eyes turned to the quarterback. Before Jack could speak, Marcus nudged the tall redhead to his left.

"Fuck, Tom! Jack had to let go of that ball too soon 'cause you let Curt in! If you had given him one more second to throw, Vince would have been way ahead of Mitch there. Come on, Tom! Be aggressive! You're twice as big as anyone out here, man!"

Tom nodded with his head down, ashamed to look up.

"Sorry," he said. "I just got to focus. It's work, you know. I've got to stop thinking about my job. We're really trying to get this Australian actor to sign on to our agency. His name's Russell Crowe. You heard of him?"

"Dammit, Tom!" Jack yelled. "This is football now! Concentrate!"

Tom felt a nudge from his other side. He looked over to see Al Gillaspie, who had bent his head down to look up at Tom and give him a reassuring look with his wide brown eyes.

"I know Curt, and he's seeing you planting too soon. So he's going around you," Al said with a warm, comforting smile. "Just take a few steps forward. Come up to him, and then square up on him."

Tom raised his head in a smile, feeling his teammate's camaraderie. Al kept reassuring him with his smile until Tom nodded in approval.

"We should go right back to the bomb," Vince said. "Mitch is the only guy they got that can keep up with me."

"Fuck! Why do you think the ball needs to go right back in your hands!" snapped Sam Barkowski, the team's other wide receiver. "I didn't see you making the catch last time. Maybe we should think about some of the other receivers on the team."

"It was pass interference! Are you blind or something?" Vince fought back.

"Damn!" Marcus yelled with a deep resonating voice. "This is the championship, man! What we doin' fighting in the huddle?" Marcus placed his hands on his hips and then hunched his wide shoulders toward the quarterback. "Go on now, Jack. Call the play."

"Vince is right," Jack said. "But I'm using both my wides on this play," Jack looked directly at Sam, giving him a nod. "Sam, you and Vince do a deep cross. Marcus, hit the rusher, then go out for a short pass in the pocket. Now Tom . . . block! Ed, cut to the sidelines ten yards, then buttonhook. Al, just find an opening midfield. OK? Ready . . ."

"Break!" they yelled in unison.

Mitch brushed the remaining dust off his socks as he watched the huddle break. As the offense came to the line, Mitch turned to Jerry, the other defender in the backfield.

"Get ready. I think they're going right back to the bomb."

Jerry responded by swinging back his long black bangs from his eyes.

"Hey, what's with your hair this week?" Mitch spoke again, a bit annoyed. "You keep brushing it out of your eyes."

"They're extensions," Jerry answered. "I thought you knew I got extensions."

Mitch placed his hands on his hips and nodded, turning his attention back to the approaching offensive line. "Yeah, like that's something I really need to know about."

"Hey! It works!" Jerry said. "Got a spread in *Men's Fitness* because of it."

"Just concentrate on the game, will you? Why didn't you wait until after the championship before undergoing this operation? You're losing sight of the ball."

Bill O'Brien cracked a smile as he overhead Mitch's remark. He liked the way Mitch had used the term "operation." Bill recognized it as his own brand of sarcasm, and he felt proud that his friend was emulating his own style of humor. But Bill's smile was short-lived as he saw the offense approach the line. Playing side linebacker, Bill stood near the line of scrimmage. A year ago he played deep on defense, but now, twenty pounds heavier and only four years from forty, he had been relegated to covering the short play on defense. This was the position reserved for the slower-footed players on the team. Despite his age and additional weight, Bill still took solace in the fact that his handsome face still would turn heads, as long as he wore clothing that hid his stomach.

A smile returned to Bill's lips as he found the man he would be covering on this play. Ed Wakeling glanced up, his opaque blue eyes catching Bill's own for a moment. Ed saw the sly smile on his opponent's face.

"I think you'd better move back a few yards," Ed remarked with a wide grin. "You're playing me too tight. I'll run right by you."

Bill shrugged his shoulders.

"Doesn't matter to me. You've dropped every pass that's come your way today. That's what happens when you're too love-smitten."

"Ah, you're just jealous 'cause the romance is out of your life. You two probably don't even have sex anymore."

Bill dropped his smile.

"We do too have sex!"

"Hike!"

Ed's last words had caught Bill by surprise, and this made him unprepared for Al's quick snap to the quarterback. Ed dashed past Bill, and now Bill found himself turning a full 180 degrees and chasing after his man.

Tom Jacobs, staying back to cover his quarterback, caught sight of Curt Lowry's short black curls approaching like a speeding train. Again, Tom had already planted, but he then recalled Al telling him to take a few steps forward to approach the rusher and then plant. Tom sniffed deeply and ran forward to meet Curt, which only caused the rusher to come down on him faster. Tom panicked, wondering how he could plant himself when Curt was already in front of him. He swung out his arm, ready to brace the rusher's contact.

The first contact was Tom's elbow with Curt's eye.

"UOOOOooooh!"

Curt staggered back, his hand covering his face as he fell to the ground.

Jack found Ed wide open fifteen yards down and threw the ball effortlessly into Ed's open arms. Ed picked up another five yards running before Bob, the dreamy-eyed stoner who played middle linebacker and quarterback for the Red Team, pulled the flag.

First down.

Ed trotted back to the huddle, grinning at Bill the entire way.

"Oh, fuck you!" Bill exclaimed. "I hope you two have a big fight and break up."

"I always like it when my best friends are happy, too," Ed replied, holding out the football as though he would allow Bill to touch the pigskin that took part in an award-winning catch.

Their jostling ended abruptly when Al rushed past them and over to the spot where Tom and Curt had collided. Al dropped to his knees and bent over the downed rusher.

"Curt!" he yelled, although only a few inches from his ear. "Are you OK?"

Curt opened his good eye and glanced back at Al. He took a deep breath and then scowled before removing his hand from his right eye. A deep red bump, crescent shaped, had formed below his thick black eyebrow.

Al extended his hand to help Curt up from the ground, but Curt rejected it, planting both elbows on the grass and lifting himself up.

"Fuck!" Curt cried. "Who riled Tom up? Marcus!"

"Hey, man. I ain't taking no shit for what Tom does," Marcus replied.

"Hey, I'm sorry, man," Tom said. "It was an accident."

Curt stared at Tom for a moment and then swiped his arm through the air, gesturing to the blocker to forget about it. But then he looked back at Al and frowned, irritated by the concern he saw on Al's face. Curt moved his eyebrows up and down, trying to determine how much movement he had left in that section of his face.

"What?" he finally asked Al.

"Well," Al stumbled, "I . . . kind of told Tom . . . that . . . he should take a few steps forward to meet you . . . before planting himself, that is. But I did tell him to plant himself. He was just . . . kind of slow at doing that, I guess. But I didn't mean for this to happen. Honest I didn't."

Curt nodded, narrowing his eyes to give Al a cold stare and a close-lipped grin.

"Right. I know what you're thinking. You're glad I got this bruiser. You think it's going to slow me down, don't you?"

"I wish," Al replied. "But I'm afraid all it's going to do is make everybody think you're that much more macho."

Jack approached Curt and looked at his eye.

"Curt, I think you're going to need to put some ice on that right away," Jack said. He turned to the referee. "Dave, stop the game for a moment, will ya?"

Dave blew his whistle.

"Referee's time-out!" he yelled, but both teams had already begun walking toward the sideline benches before Dave's official call.

Jack rubbed his shoulder as he leaned toward his bag, which was located at one end of the bench. He reached into the bag and pulled out a bottle of ibuprofen.

"Oh, Miss Thing," Marcus spoke to Jack in a breathy, sultry voice. "You have some of those little pills for me?"

"Ha!" Jack snapped. "Mother, I don't know how you can be so butch one moment and so nellie the next."

"Well, I'm very versatile," Marcus answered as he extended his palm flat before Jack. Jack shook two pills into his hand, causing Marcus to furl his eyebrows and stare him down.

"Only two?"

Jack shook out another two pills.

"You got ibuprofen?" Bill asked as he watched the pills fall into Marcus's hands. "Can I have three?"

"And hand some over to Curt, too," added Al as he gave the ice pack to the injured player.

Curt lay down on the grass and placed the ice pack over the one eye, his other eye staring up at the blue sky. Suddenly, his view of the heavens was replaced by the hanging braids of Jerry's extensions.

"Bummer," Jerry commented, causing Curt to huff out a breath and then close both eyes. Jerry then moved on, looking for Mitch, who was sitting on a bench and emptying the dirt that had gathered in his cleats. Jerry fingered his extensions aside and walked over.

"So . . . Tom here mentioned to me you might be pairing up with Randy Clayburg, one of the directors of *The Sicilians,*" Jerry said as he approached. "Working on a movie together?"

Mitch sighed as he stared at Tom, who overheard Jerry's conversation. Tom looked away, aware that Mitch had told him not to mention this, especially since the partnership was very tentative at the moment.

"We're in discussions," Mitch replied.

"Well, if you do, you'll think about your old football bud here, won't you? You looking for a New York Italian lead?"

"Jerry, our New York Italian lead would be some guy who could catch a pass once in a while."

"Oh, Mitch and Randy aren't thinking Italian Mafia anyway in their script." Tom had returned his attention once again on Mitch and Jerry. "Are you, Mitch? I mean, the Mafia isn't top box-office draw material right now."

"Fuck! Mafia's always top box-office material!" Jerry exclaimed.

"Well, maybe you're right," Tom continued. "It's hard to tell what is these days. I mean, can you believe of all the movies it was *Lost in Space* that finally beat out *Titanic* as the number-one movie? Hey, did you know Linda Hamilton used to be one of our company's clients?"

"Who?" asked Al, who had decided to join in on the conversation, aware that Curt was getting angry with his overnursing.

"You know—James Cameron's wife. *The Terminator?*"

"Hey, I liked *Lost in Space*," Ed joined in. "That Matt LeBlanc was hot, though I thought he was beginning to look a bit chubby . . . like some of us," Ed again focused his wide grin at Bill.

"Oh, fuck you," Bill replied.

"I used to hang out with Matt LeBlanc . . . back in New York," Jerry said.

"Yeah, yeah, yeah," Sam Barkowski scoffed while directing at Jerry a limp-wristed throw of his arm that diverged with the masculine, chiseled features of his bearded face. "And you hang out with Matt Dillon and *all* those New York actors. You just know them all, don't you? And you think they swing both ways. Yeah, yeah, yeah."

"You know . . . I . . . ." Dave attempted to enter the conversation, but his stammering indicated he was frightened to do so. "I've heard rumors . . . that Tom Cruise . . . swings both ways."

Everyone looked at Dave and groaned.

"Oh . . . not this again," Mitch said.

"Come on, Blue Team!" Jack yelled, jumping off the bench. "Get over here! Let the Red Team gossip Hollywood if they want. We've got five minutes left! Let's concentrate on the game!"

Curt laughed from his prone position.

"Yeah. Coming from the master of concentration," he said.

"Pretty!" Jack exclaimed. "Blue Team . . . get on the field!"

Bob, the stoner quarterback on the Red Team, walked over to Curt and stood over him. He looked down at his own ripped jersey hanging off one shoulder. He grabbed the bottom of the shirt with both hands and then ripped it through. Now the jersey was completely useless, and Bob threw it aside.

"You OK to play?" Bob asked Curt, his eyes following the trajectory of the shirt he had just thrown aside.

Curt pulled the ice pack from his face and stood up.

"You know I'm not missing the end of this."

"Huddle!"

The Blue Team followed Jack's voice to the middle of the field. Again they circled around him.

"OK now, guys," Jack began, "we got five minutes, a first down, and a tie score. We got time to play out the clock. Now let's make some short passes, and only to wide-open men. Let's kill Bob at his own game."

"Now c'mon, you guys! Let's get aggressive out there!" Marcus cheered. "Be smart. Keep your heads up. Let's go now!"

They broke the huddle. Vince and Sam lined up wide, Ed and Al as flankers, Tom as center, Marcus as back.

"Hike!"

Ed and Al crossed in the middle about five yards past the scrimmage line while Vince posted fifteen yards and then ran back in a buttonhook, thereby faking the defender. Marcus and Tom stayed back to protect Jack.

Sam, meanwhile, raced up the sideline to clear the midfield. Sam's tactic worked, as both deep defenders—Mitch and Jerry—went with him. Now Ed, Al, and Vince were all wide open for a short, easy pass.

But Jack never looked at his open receivers. Instead, he cocked his throwing arm way back and shot the ball out deep.

"Oh, fuck it, man!" Marcus yelled as he saw the trajectory of the ball.

Sam had one stride ahead of Mitch, but Jack had thrown the ball short. Mitch, watching the ball in the air, dug his right foot down and then ran back to catch the ball.

"Stop him, man!" Marcus yelled as Mitch ran the ball back ten yards, twenty yards, shifting past Vince, then Ed and Al. Marcus slanted forward and angled toward the sideline, hoping to catch Mitch just in front of the scrimmage line. Marcus wrapped his finger around one of Mitch's flags and pulled it down.

The Red Team had the ball at midfield with just four minutes to go.

"What the fuck was that!" Marcus screamed as he threw the flag to the ground and marched up to Jack. "You had three men open! Short passes! You the only one who don't listen to your own plays?"

Jack hid his shame behind a scowl and his dark sunglasses, but again a line emerged on his forehead.

"But," Jack stammered, "Sam had two strides on him."

"Yeah, a hell of a lotta good that does us when you can't throw it deep enough," Marcus replied.

Bob the stoner clapped his hands as he ran over to where the flag had been pulled.

"OK guys, huddle!" Bob said.

The Red Team huddled, and Bob began by running his index finger around the curves and crevices of his naked chest.

"Let's show them how to slice up the field," he said. "Mitch, you're here . . ." Bob pointed to his own nipple to display where Mitch would line up if his chest were the playing field. He extended his finger up his chest and toward his neck. "Go long. Get Vince out of the picture."

"Curt," Bob touched his other nipple and moved his finger out to his armpit. "Fifteen yards, then cut outside. You're my main man."

Bob fingered the small hairs emerging from the deep of his chest. "Jerry, ten yards and cut inside. If Curt doesn't get open, I'll throw to you. The rest, get open. Five yards and turn around. Let's go!"

The players sprang back from the huddle. As Bill stepped back and turned his shoulder to square up toward the scrimmage line, he bumped against a stationary body. A whistle blew.

With his whistle drooling from his mouth, Dave had come too close to the huddle, enthralled with Bob's nipple playing. Now Bill's movement and an inadvertent whistle had caught him. Dave stood wide-eyed and widemouthed, unable to determine what to say.

"Oh . . ." Dave was finally able to speak. "Sorry."

The rest of the Red Team paid no attention to the referee. Mitch sided up to Curt as they approached the line and then nudged him with his shoulder.

"You got to get open," Mitch said. "Bob's high, saying Jerry's his second man on this play. We don't need any ball being thrown to Jerry at this point in the game."

Mitch then broke from his teammate, and they lined up on extreme opposite ends of the offensive line.

"Hike!"

Curt did get open as he faked Vince by pretending to go deep and then cutting to the outside. Bob threw a soft easy pass. A pickup of fifteen yards and a first down.

Bob then connected on a five-yard slant to Vince. Jerry dropped an easy eight-yard out as he dove on the ground to catch it, then removed his tank top and flexed his muscles as he brushed the dirt off. On third down, Bill ran out of the backfield and caught a ten-yarder straight up the middle for a first. At the thirty-yard line, Curt caught the ball on an inside slant for a twelve-yard pickup and a first down. Jerry dropped the ball on a well-thrown pass. Then Bill caught the ball just past the scrimmage line and ran another eight yards for the first down before being pushed out of bounds.

First down and goal. Ten seconds to play.

"Time!"

"Defensive huddle!" Marcus yelled.

The Blue Team circled around Marcus.

"Fuck, man! They've been doing shorters all day!" Marcus exclaimed. "C'mon guys! Goal line D!"

"They're going to Curt," Vince stated. "He's got the best moves going short."

Jack turned to Al.

"You stay on him. Don't let your boyfriend get away."

"I got him," Al assured his team with a nod.

Al lined up against Curt, whose injured eye now was partially closed. Al stared at the eye, at how the red had turned to purple, how the purple had turned to black. Then for a moment, he felt an overwhelming concern for his boyfriend, wondering whether that eye would ever be the same.

"Hike!"

Curt jabbed his head to the outside. Al backpedaled to the outside. But then Curt jabbed his left foot and ran inside, faking Al in the wrong direction. Al tried to change his momentum, but it was too late.

Marcus saw Curt's fake and ran desperately to intercept the pass. Bob threw a hard, straight pass, the ball rocketing into Curt's gut.

Curt tucked the ball in just past the goal line.

The whistle blew as time expired.

The Red Team had won the Gay Flag Football Winter League Championship Game.

2

Horizontal, Vertical

Al slowly turned the knob of the front door to his Hollywood apartment, hoping not to disturb Curt if he might be sleeping. But as he quietly swung the door open, he saw the flickering light from the television, and he heard the low-volume grunts and sighs from one of Curt's porno tapes.

He walked into the living room to find Curt sprawled on the couch, naked except for an unbuttoned flannel shirt that was spread back, exposing his chest and stomach. Curt's eyes darted from the screen and toward Al, his hand-jerking picking up speed as he saw his boyfriend.

Curt stared back at the television as Al walked toward him. Al saw that Curt's black eye had gone down a bit, now only a small purple-black crescent below his eyebrow.

"Having fun?" Al asked as he walked behind the couch and threw his jacket onto a dining-room chair.

"No, I'm fucking not having fun!" Curt exclaimed. "That fuckin' stupid Tom! Now I gotta jerk off 'cause I'm not getting any with this shiner."

"I'll give you some," Al said with a smile, but Curt did not turn his head around to look at him.

"And you! Trying to give him instructions!" Curt continued. "You know he's a klutz!"

"I'm guessing you didn't make much in tips tonight with that attitude," Al replied.

Curt still did not look at him. Worried that his boyfriend was not aware he had spoken in jest, Al walked behind the couch, bent his head down, and kissed Curt on the forehead.

"You know it's not that big," Al continued. Realizing his words might have been misconstrued, seeing that Curt was still jerking off, he added, "Your black eye, that is. And like I said before, I'm sure there's hundreds of guys who'd find it kind of masculine, thinking how they'd like to get laid by some tough guy with a black eye."

Curt swung his head away from Al, now leaning sideways on the couch while still watching the porn. Again, Al had the sense that Curt did not want to be overnurtured.

Curt finally turned Al's way.

"Well, maybe I just wanted to come home and fuck you. I thought you'd be home, wanting to make me feel better."

Al nervously looked away.

"Well . . . I would have been home, only, you know, I drove Marcus over to Hooker, and he wanted to stay for after-hours, and I couldn't get him to go, and . . ."

"Come here."

Curt was jerking harder as he stared at Al, his mouth open and his Adam's apple throbbing.

"Um . . ." Al looked down at the couch and at Curt's wild look. He then glanced over at the porn, still playing. "OK. Right here? On the couch?"

Curt grabbed the remote and turned off the television. He then lodged his cock between both hands so that it towered straight up.

"Sit on it."

Al tried not to look at Curt's eyes, feeling his stare was once again a test.

"OK, but I've really got to pee first. I'll be right back . . ."

"Oh . . . afraid I'm going to see cum stains?"

Curt had planted the accusation just as Al had turned toward the bathroom.

"What? No! I mean . . . cum stains?"

"It's three-thirty in the morning. You already got fucked, didn't you?"

"No!"

Al turned around nervously.

"I mean . . . what do you mean? You know we agreed. No actual fucking."

"But you fooled around with someone."

Curt had brought his head and arm over the backside of the couch, now staring at Al. Al began to pace nervously, keeping his eyes off Curt.

"Well . . . uh . . ."

Curt grinned, his lips curling up on one side.

"I knew it. I fuckin' knew it."

Curt slumped on the couch, his stare turned toward the television set, looking at his own image and the black eye, now even blacker cast upon the dark screen.

"It doesn't seem fair, does it?" he asked. "I'm the one who scores the winning touchdown, and yet, look who gets laid!"

"Yeah, and you should be happy you won the game!" Al countered, his voice rising. "I'm the one who has to live with the fact that I gave up the winning touchdown! Do you know how that makes me feel? Well, maybe it's the loser who should get some reward, so he doesn't feel so bad."

"Oh, so you got some big reward, did you? Just loved your reward. What did he do ... took you home and fucked you?"

"He didn't fuck me."

"But he took you home."

Al began to pace again.

"Why do you want to know the specifics? I fool around once in a blue moon, and you have to ask for every detail. And you fool around every night! Do I ask you what alley you made out in? Do I ask, 'well, did you finger his ass?' No. Because if I did, you'd spend half the day telling all the details. See, it's not right."

"You did go back to his place."

"Curt . . ."

Curt jumped off the couch and stood face to face with his boyfriend.

"Fuck! What is it with you? You always got to get in bed with them!"

"I can't believe you're arguing about this again. The guy didn't mean anything. OK? I mean, he was only twenty-four."

"Then why'd you go back to his place?"

Al shrugged.

"What did you expect me to do? We were at Hooker, right by MacArthur Park. It's dangerous. I could get killed if I did it there."

"Well, then maybe you shouldn't have fucked. What is it with you, always having to get intimate with a guy?"

Al gritted his teeth and turned to face Curt.

"Then what is the deal?" Al asked. "You say we'll have this open relationship, but then you say it's only OK to fool around if it's vertical. But you know I can't do that. I can't just meet someone and fool around like that in a car or behind a bush or whatever. Not like you. I mean, is that the deal?"

Curt nodded his head rapidly, his lips quivering.

"Yeah, that's the deal. That's the deal."

He stormed past Al and into the bedroom.

Moments went by. Curt reappeared in his clothes, shoes, and jacket.

"Where are you going?"

"What's it to you? You want details?"

"Curt . . . why do you want to do this?"

Curt stuffed his shirttails into his jeans.

"Because I fucking want to show you how it's supposed to be done." He slid his hand against the dining-room table and scooped up his keys.

"It's three-thirty in the morning! It'll be all skanky."

"It's supposed to be skanky."

It was an overcast early March morning, the cloud layer keeping the temperatures in the low fifties. Despite the chance of showers, Curt drove his '67 Mustang with the top down. *Better chance of catching someone's eyes,* he thought.

He shot down La Brea toward Santa Monica Boulevard, figuring at this time of night he'd find someone either near Probe or the Spike. It was late. Al was right. It would be skanky. No prime candidates out at this time. But, fuck, flip them around and fuck their ass. It could then be anyone.

That's the way it's supposed to be done, he thought as he waited at the red light at La Brea and Fountain. And Al plays this game with him, saying he doesn't fool around that often, that he rarely has a one-night stand, and that he just can't cum if it's going to be quick sex in a car or an alley.

It's this intimacy thing, Curt thought. *Al loves this intimacy thing. He loves to meet a guy and know him, love him, and then the sex is so good. Well, how long can Al do that before he's ready to call this relationship quits?*

Curt thought back to when they had met in Seattle. Al was there visiting his family for a couple weeks. Curt had taken a few months off, driving around with a pop-up camper pulled behind his Mustang. Having just made $25,000 off a commercial, he'd decided to see America cheap. Every KOA campground, every gay bar, every cruising spot. In Seattle, at the Neighbors bar, he had met Al. Strange how they both lived in LA but had met in Seattle. They both agreed it was the only way their relationship could have been. It just wouldn't have worked if Al had gone to the Apache nightclub back here in Studio City and Curt had tried to pick him up while bartending there—just no romance in that. Curt had already done that with a thousand other guys.

But Al was the only guy he had ever picked up in Seattle and brought back to his KOA campsite. Yeah, he had done the same with other guys in other cities—John in Portland. He couldn't remember the names of the guys in Minneapolis, Cincinnati, St. Louis, and Oklahoma City. There also were the other guys in Santa Fe, Denver, and Missoula, but they never had made it very far from the bars before they came and went.

It was just something about Al. That sparkle in his eye when they first danced at Neighbors. How that supposed-to-be-meaningless exchange of cocksucking in the bushes of the park nearby had turned into something more. When Al sucked his cock, his eyes would flash up and stare into Curt's. It was so strange. How could someone be so intimate when all he was doing was sucking a stranger's cock?

Then, back in the KOA campground ten miles north of Seattle on the east side of Lake Washington, they went into the rest room and ended up making out in a shower stall. How they laughed when Al got his head wrapped in the shower curtain as he moved around, licking every part of Curt's body. Again, it was so strange. The way Al looked into his eyes. That loving look. And Curt knowing he felt the same way. That same intimacy. He never had felt that way, ever, with a guy. And perhaps not even ever with a woman.

A car whizzed by in the lane to his left. The light had turned green. Curt had not even noticed. Now it was yellow. He threw the throttle into first gear and flew through the intersection.

Fuck that!

His hand grasped the throttle. Second gear. Third gear. Fourth. Whizzing his hand from gear to gear, jamming his leg on the clutch. Trying to forget that whole image. He'd been a fool. He'd been infatuated. He'd been a sissy. Men aren't for falling in love with. They're for sex. For play. How had he let Al reel him in like that?

Al can just fucking keep on playing with men, falling in love with them. Then I can go back to being myself, fucking around with guys, Curt thought. *Because women are for loving. Guys are for fucking.*

He turned the corner fast, a right onto Santa Monica Boulevard. Time to slow down. At this speed, he wouldn't pick up anyone.

Close to 4 a.m. on this Saturday night, or Sunday morning. Amazing how quiet it was. The clouds up above caused a vacuum, letting no sound escape. Just a few other cars on the street. Mostly just pavement, streetlights, and dark buildings.

The faces through the bright windows of the Yukon Mining Company coffee shop were a warm welcome. He trotted his Mustang by, getting a rush whenever a head in the coffee shop turned his way. A guy held off on taking his next bite to watch him pass by in his car. Yeah, he still turned heads, even at age thirty-two. Al might be one of the best-looking guys in LA, but something about Curt made heads turn. A sex appeal; he knew it. That's how he always scored: pure raw sexual energy.

He raised his head and looked at himself in the rearview mirror. Then he saw it again: the black eye. That's what they had been looking at—not at him, but at his black eye.

Fuck that!

He sped to the next light.

A twenty-four-year-old, huh? I can't see a younger guy fucking Al. But maybe Al fucked him. Hmmm.

He recalled the first time he allowed Al to fuck him. He had fucked Al so many times before, but then Al wanted to be in him. Curt had allowed himself to become so vulnerable, to let himself be fucked. He remembered the half-dozen times he'd been fucked before, but that had been in his teens and early twenties. Now he was a man, and being fucked meant being the passive one. Still, he let Al fuck him. And for one moment, seeing Al on top of him, looking into his eyes, fucking him with such passion, Curt had actually felt content to have a man inside him, to have someone be in control, to have this man watch over him and take care of him. But after he came, Curt had shivered at allowing himself such thoughts during a moment of passion. He feared his desire, however brief it might have been, of wanting to surrender to another human being. What had made him even more afraid was that now he knew Al was just as passionate, just as intimate when fucking as he was when being fucked. That meant fucking another man had to be as much off limits in their open relationship as was being fucked, which meant Curt had to stop fucking others as well. That had to be part of their rules—that is, if rules even mattered anymore.

"I'm fucking someone tonight," Curt declared to himself.

A car pulled up alongside Curt's Mustang at the light. Curt looked over to his right, knowing the intention of the driver beside him. The driver was already staring at Curt, his crow's feet accentuated as he smiled. His thinning hair had been gelled and sprayed, and he wore a tight T-shirt that rose up to a long, bony neck and chinless face.

Turn him around, and he could be anyone. *Ah, but it's too soon. Still got a few blocks until Spike.*

Curt sped through the intersection as the light turned green.

An older man stood in the recesses of the porn theater near Spike as Curt drove by. A few other men were staggering slowly out of the bar, pausing in their tracks to watch Curt's cruising eyes, then looking above the bar door at the dim lightbulb, which was much too bright for them, exposing all their imperfections, which had been hidden inside the dark club.

Then, out of the bar came a short, younger guy in faded jeans and a yoked Western shirt, unsnapped to the bottom of his chest, his blond hair disheveled and his eyes not completely focused.

"Mmmmm," Curt throated.

The blond looked up, his sad mouth an image of innocence—or as much innocence as one could expect from someone coming out of Spike. His eyes then fell onto Curt's deep stare and upturned grin. The blond looked both ways, making sure no one else was the object of Curt's affection. A sweet smile formed on the guy's face.

"Mmmmm."

Curt turned right and parked on a street on the opposite side of Santa Monica Boulevard, then hopped out of the car, his eyes leaving the blond for fifteen seconds at most.

The blond was still there.

This guy wants to get fucked, Curt thought as they exchanged smiles.

He crossed the street on the way to fuck that boy and to fuck up the only relationship he ever had with a guy.

It was like the last time he had crossed to other side of the dance floor of the Vogue Disco, a very "mixed" Austin nightclub, to the men's rest room in the back—the nightclub's very "gay" rest room—to have a quickie in a stall before returning to his girlfriend Saundra. He was in love with Saundra, but gay bathroom sex was dirty and fun. Never could he feel that thrill with Saundra, who was aware of his past gay escapades but not the current ones.

It was on that day that he told her everything—the glory holes, the quick crotch feels when she had turned away from him in a crowd, even the times he fucked the third party—always a male—of one of their several ménage à trois very quietly after she had fallen asleep. He did love her, but after three years with her and with his graduation only a month away, it was time to break loose and head for Los Angeles. It had been at that moment that he had made a choice. It was great being in love. But what he really wanted was deep down dirty fucking with men.

"Where you off to?" Curt approached the blond.

"Home," the guy said, looking down at his feet.

"Where's your car?"

The blond motioned his head toward the side street.

"About a block back."

Curt eyed the doorman, then stepped up to the blond and whispered in his ear, "You want to get fucked?"

Curt didn't watch the blond's face react. Instead, he watched the swell in the guy's jeans.

He heard a sort of laugh-grunt come out of the blond's mouth, and so he looked up at his blue eyes. The guy froze, looking into Curt's eyes, then closed his own for a moment as he felt a hand cup his crotch.

"I'd . . . like to fool around," he whispered back. "At least."

"At least," Curt repeated.

Oh, so easy. Is there anyone in the world better at this? He loved the feeling he had when the guy submitted. He felt so powerful. It's like nothing he could have felt with Saundra. Women submitting was one thing. A man submitting was another.

They walked around the corner and onto the side street.

"What did you do to your eye?" the blond asked. Curt looked at him, raising a grin.

"It doesn't matter. I won."

The blond breathed deeply in, his shoulders rising.

"You did?"

Curt placed his hand on the blond's shoulder.

"Come over here."

Curt motioned over to the back alley. The blond's eyes widened and he looked around.

"Here?"

"Yeah."

Curt brought his face down and started kissing the guy's neck. As he sucked the sweet skin, he heard wondrous sighs from above. Oh, if any sound could be as satisfying as to have a man sigh from the ecstatic warmth of his tongue.

But these sighs felt shallow—sighs seeking only the dominant foreplay of a man. Sighs wanting, not loving. They could not compare to Al's sighs—sighs seeking some higher reality, seeking oneness with a man.

Curt pulled his head back. He placed his arm over the blond and led him behind a garbage bin hidden in a recess of the alley.

"I'm going to fuck you," he said.

The blond looked stupefied, eyelids heavy, bedroom eyes, wanting Curt to the point that he wished to forget all else.

Curt unbuckled and unbuttoned the blond, feeling the guy's crotch before pulling down his own jeans.

"But," the blond interjected, "I live just a mile down—"

"Kiss it."

The blond looked deeply into Curt's eyes. Then he lowered his gaze, and then he lowered his head, obeying Curt's demand.

Feeling that warm, wet mouth slide up and down his cock, Curt closed his eyes. He was in total control of this guy.

If only he could have total control of Al. Then Al would without a doubt be his greatest sexual conquest. But then—would he love him?

Curt pulled out a small packet of lube, ripped it open, and squirted it in his hand. His index finger slid into the blond's ass. The blond closed his eyes, returning to his sighs, now more anxious.

"You're going to be fucked like you've never been fucked before," Curt whispered, exclaiming his sentence with a deep thrust of his finger.

Curt displayed a condom before the bent-over face of his prize. The guy looked up at Curt longingly and made a high-pitched, airy sigh.

The best feeling always came when the tip of his cock pushed into the hole. Nothing, as long as he lived, could ever feel better.

The blond emitted a rasp of pain through clenched teeth. Curt waited patiently, cradling the guy's balls, pushing ever so slightly at first.

And then he began.

Total control. When he had his cock fully up a guy's ass, then he had total control. Curt felt the rhythm, his teeth clenched, breathing heavily.

Why was it, the question crept to his mind, that he never felt fully in control when fucking Al? It was as though they both had control. Why did such a thought thrill him, much more so than when he was fucking a guy like this?

Because he wanted Al to have control, too. He didn't want to love someone who submitted. He wanted another man.

He recalled their three-month anniversary last October, how Al had orchestrated a candlelit dinner, making all of Curt's favorite foods, playing Vivaldi's "Four Seasons," and how they had not made it halfway through the meal before they were spread out on the floor, how Al had stripped him naked, how he had let Curt tear off his shirt, and how, with those huge, powerful legs, he had pulled Curt down to him, and into him.

Curt opened his eyes, seeing this blond guy so obediently bent over, taking it from behind.

He had fallen in love with Al, and now he was some wimpy, jealous boyfriend, afraid that Al would find the same intimacy, the same passion, the same love with someone else.

Curt hated himself. He hated what he had become. He was so much cooler when he was single. But he had fallen for someone—fallen hard. And now he didn't know what to make of himself. Everything he felt for Al was the complete opposite of who he actually was.

He knew he couldn't blame Al for what Al had done tonight. It was who Al was. It was what he loved in Al—and what frightened him most.

He pulled away. The blond looked up, still bent over.

Curt stared at the sky, into the cloudy white, as he buttoned up his jeans. He then looked at the blond, so desperate, so wanting.

"Sorry," he said. "Game over."

3

Sunday Morning Hangover

I got wasted again last night. I'm trying to figure out what's wrong with me, why all week I say I'm going to stay home, get things done, finish my novel, and then Saturday night comes around, and I've got to go out, and when I do, I get so depressed that I just get drunk off my ass.

Of course I would have to bump into Ed and his new boy-friend—what's-his-name. I really didn't find him all that great. His eyes are too sunken in. Yet all Ed ever talks about is Trent this and Trent that, like he's completely infatuated or something. I should have expected going to the Revolver that I'd meet people I know. But hey, I'm not going to any dive bar like Rafters or something just so I don't see anyone. I haven't stooped that low. Yet.

Anyhow, I told Ed I was sorry about yelling at him and walking off the field during our practice yesterday. I mean, I know he didn't mean to trip me. That's not why I got angry at him anyway. And Ed, he's such a sweet guy; he probably doesn't even realize why I was so angry. Probably didn't even care. He's so infatuated right now.

Anyhow, I'm glad I said I was sorry. And then I got the hell out of there. I mean, what was I going to do, being there with Ed and his boyfriend and really not knowing anyone else? So I would have had to stand around with those two. That's just way too uncomfortable.

But what really upset me is that I didn't know anyone else! Five years ago I would walk into Revolver on a Saturday night, and I would know half the people in the bar. I was Mr. Popular then. Now I'm Mr. Has-Been.

Anyhow, I was pretty juiced up by the time I left, and I figured a few more gin and tonics at Mother Lode couldn't hurt. I mean, what's the worst that could happen? I could get in a traffic accident and die? Now that would be pretty gruesome, being pinned against the steering wheel, the car mangled around my body, and I'm in agonizing pain, and yet I can't even move enough to grab a gun from the glove compartment and blow my head off.

Like I'd ever really own a gun. But a bullet to the head would be a much better way to die. It's instantaneous. At least it seems like it would be. But then, what if, after you pull the trigger, time just slows down? A second seems like a year. And so while everyone else believes the pain was instantaneous, you really are agonizing over a very long death in your own time-mind. It's like what William James said about how a hummingbird conceives time as longer than we do because it flaps its wings a thousand times a second, so it can conceive a thousandth of a second while we really can't. Well, maybe God likes to punish us for committing suicide by slowing down our perception of time.

Or how about pain for eternity? Hell, that is. Sounds gruesome, but I don't know; if I woke up and found myself in Hell, I'd let out one big sigh of relief. Of course, I'd be upset that I didn't make it to Heaven, but I would just be glad to know that I still "exist." Then there would at least be some meaning to life, although that meaning might be meaningless.

Anyhow, I've been thinking about death a lot lately. I mean, how can I not when I've come to a dead end in my life?

Hopelessness.

Now there's a word. Is that how I feel? Funny, when I was young I never thought of hope. I was too confident for that. I just *knew* something would happen, that I'd become rich and famous. How many times I practiced my speech for when I won the Pulitzer, or the National Book Award, or the Nobel Prize? I knew it was going to happen.

But it didn't. So if I never felt hope before, why do I feel hopelessness now?

I saw Tim the other day. He's now a soap opera star. Anyhow, Tim, as usual, was talking about himself and his career and how everything is just falling in place and how he's going to New York to star in a

one-man show and how Tom Hanks's manager is seriously considering him and how Robin Williams's agent just loves him and how Brad
Pitt's stylist just adores his hair, and then he puts in a comment that
just floors me. Now how did he put it? Something like: "I really believe that there are people born to be someone. I've been blessed, but I
believe I was born to be so." A complete fatalist.

Funny, how I used to think that same way when I was a kid. I
thought I was born to be famous . . . William the Great. I liked to
think I would be called that one day, although I'd hate to be called
William. But it sounds better than Bill the Great.

But anyway, as I've grown older and wiser (ha ha) I've become so
much more of the free-will type of guy, which is cool. It's trendy. It al-
lows us to understand that life is meaningless, which is cool and
trendy, too. I'm just like a real cool and trendy person, but no one really cares, because what do I have to show for it?

I don't have anything . . . except for this nagging fear inside me that
it's just too late, and so all I can really think about is dying, and that's
scary. But hey, as Tim says, there's some people who are born to be
important and the rest are peons. I've figured out I'm just one of those
peons, and so the nerve of me to even think that my existence should
go on forever.

I keep thinking how I really should face my fears. And I have been,
thinking of death all the time. In fact, I've actually been kind of fasci-
nated with this fear. There's certain times when I'm really depressed
and I'm pondering my wasted life and my inevitable death and then,
all of a sudden, I get this overwhelming dread. Something drops in
my stomach and my whole body shivers. At first, when I felt this
dread, I would hop out of bed right away, try to shake it off, put on
some music or watch some silly TV show. Anything to dispel that
feeling. But now when I get that feeling I try to keep it going. I just lie
there, not moving a muscle, trying to savor that complete terror, see
how far I can sink into it. Then, when I can't get any further into it, I
like to think real decadent sexual thoughts about men and torture and
bondage. Mostly it's me getting tortured, because, well, I'm working
with this sense of dread, and so the lower, the more demeaning I can

get, the more fearful and sexual it becomes. And then I get off. In fact, at these times I cum harder than I do at any other time.

I figure I probably would have done it—knocked myself out—by now if it wasn't for football. I've been getting such a rage inside me, hating the world, especially hating anyone who makes more money than I do—which is, of course, most of my friends. If it wasn't for football, I'd have no outlet for that rage. I'd burst from the inside.

But it's football that keeps me from getting that far off. I get all this aggression out on the field, and to think I'm pretty tame on the field compared to others. But I figure that's likely to change. I'm catching up and ready to pass them on the rage scale, especially seeing how I acted yesterday.

Funny. Mitch was actually proud of me, how I lost my cool on the field yesterday, thinking I was so aggressive. That is, he was impressed until I told him to fuck off. But I'm feeling bad about that, too. I should call him, tell him I'm sorry. But then, he'd probably think I'm a wimp for apologizing. Then, of course, I'd have to go through his whole spiel about me and how he can't understand how I'm not more successful than I am, and that it's all due to Larry, how Larry has drained me of my ambition, that I'm not the same guy I used to be. It's people like Mitch that make me want to escape LA. To be forgotten. To move to some unknown hillbilly section of the country sitting around in a rocking chair on the porch all day long eating pork rinds and not having a care in the world that I could have been somebody once.

How long have I been in LA now? Twelve years? I got here when I was twenty-four. That's right. And when did I start the novel? I remember I had just turned twenty-nine. I figured I'd be famous by the time I turned thirty. Where is the novel now? I should really finish it, but what do I do? I go to work every day to my twelve-dollar-an-hour job as an administrative assistant—I can't even say the word *secretary*. Then I come home and Larry and I go to a cheap matinee or drink margaritas during happy hour. We watch TV, and too often it's the old stuff on Nick at Nite that I've seen a hundred times before, and then I go to bed, thinking, "Well, there's another completely wasted day."

OK, why don't I change the subject? Like maybe I should stop concentrating on everything I did wrong in the past and start thinking about what I can do now. 'Cause it's now or never, baby. I mean, look, I'm thirty-six, almost middle-aged, and all I can think about is how I can't be around anyone who's doing better than I am. Who I really don't want to see are people like Matt Damon and Ben Affleck expected to win the screenwriting Oscars and being so young. It's like when I'm at work and some vendors or lawyers come in and they're wearing really nice clothes and just seem like real cool guys, got everything together, and they're five or ten years younger than me. Here I am sitting at a desk, and they know I'm the CEO's administrative assistant, and they're just laughing at me behind my back, thinking about what I loser I am. I really hate that.

But all will be different once I finish this novel. I mean, in one day everything can change, from being a nobody to being the talk of the town. I'll finish that novel, an agent will see it, say it's the most amazing thing he's ever read, sell it to Doubleday, and it will go into print, a hundred thousand copies, top of the *New York Times* best-seller list. I will go around the nation signing my book, talking with Oprah, David Letterman, Jay Leno. Everyone will adore me, and I'll no longer worry about some stupid nine-to-five job, and I'll be so thankful, say humble things like: "I'm amazed that so many people have suddenly taken an interest in me."

Oh, I should get back to reality. I mean, let's face it. I'm thirty-six, and I've been thinking a lot about why I haven't finished the novel and why I'm an administrative assistant and why I'm not making any money. Maybe I should just accept the fact that although I might have delusions of grandeur, I have no talent.

I guess what I might fear even more than death is that perhaps I really just don't have any creativity, that I can never really be a good writer, no matter how hard I try. I mean I look at young people who I really think are creative geniuses, such as Thom Yorke of Radiohead. When I look at people like that, I think of them as Mozart and me as Salieri, just like the movie *Amadeus,* and how I really haven't any talent at all. Or I feel like that fat guy who lived with Joe Orton in *Prick Up Your Ears,* and how he killed both himself and Joe because he realized he didn't have any talent and Joe was the real genius. Now that's a real feeling of dread for me. That's just too terrifying. Unlike death, I can't even start to contemplate it.

So then I think, *Why am I even wasting my time writing this novel when I really have no talent? Why don't I just enjoy the moment? Why don't I focus on simpler things anyone can do to enjoy life more?* Of course that's when I think about sex—the great cop-out. So you're a loser, you're uncreative, you have no talent, and you're stupid. What can you do? Sex! Because other guys who want to fuck you don't really care about those things, just as long as you have a good body and you're good in bed.

But look at me. I can't even lose this stomach. I'm completely pitiful. I don't even have sex as a last resort.

Last night at Mother Lode, before I was too soused, I was standing on the upper deck of the bar, all by myself, and I remember staring at this one good-looking guy on the lower deck. A black-haired Italian boy, nice wide smile, really animated as he talked to his friends. Wearing a tank top. Big muscles. Not too overdeveloped. He was probably twenty-eight or so. Anyhow, I was feeling pretty good, and of course, I was thinking, 'cause people always say I look much younger than thirty-six, that perhaps he would like what he saw if he looked my way. I wasn't wearing my T-shirt too tight and so I thought he might not notice the roll. But he didn't look. So I sucked my gin and tonic and thought inside of how nice it would be to savor his naked body in bed, and we would laugh and talk and kiss and then perhaps make some love.

Then the guy walked to the upper deck to get a drink from the bartender in the back, and he looked right at me as he walked. One quick look, however, and he turned his eyes elsewhere. Now there was a reality check for me. Any elation I might have felt instantly went out the door. I just felt depressed and stupid because all he saw in me was some old man drooling over him. He acted just as I had when I was twenty-eight and there were middle-aged men looking at me, and how I thought, "Yeah, like you got any chance at all." But now I am that middle-aged man, and he is who I once was.

Larry keeps telling me that all of us in football cling to the game because it's the last refuge of our youth. I mean, if we're able to be these speedy, strong, macho athletes running around on the field once a week, we'll always be young, right? I hate it when he keeps putting down the game. I guess I especially don't like it because there's some truth to what he says. I *am* getting too old for this game. I'm getting hurt much more often now. That sucks. And I am slowing down. I'll admit that to no one, but it's true. However, once I realize I can no longer play, what does that mean? I'll never be able to play football again ever in my existence? Like I'll never be able to catch the big wave again? I'll never be able to downhill ski again?

That's the problem with life. As soon as you're born, you just start the dying process. Now at thirty-six, I'm more than half dead. So why don't I just get it over with? The way I figure it, when we're born it's just like one big bang—a burst of energy. Then, through life, all this energy just dissipates until finally there's nothing. Everything we are and everything we know is part of this big bang of energy. As we grow older and we think we're learning new things, or believe we have suddenly come up with a creative idea, really it's just a memory of what we already know. Nothing but memories—that's all we're made up of. No creativity. No new learning. Just an understanding of a memory is the most we can muster.

That's not true. The most we can muster is the interaction of memories with others. That's why no matter how hard I try to believe that I can exist on my own I really do need others.

I remember last weekend, when Al and Mitch and I were all stoned at Hooker, and what Al said: "Life is energy. You focus your energy here. You focus your energy there. Life is how you focus your energy." I was so elated just hearing that, thinking of Einstein and all. You know, $E = MC^2$ and how that means each minute object of mass is millions and millions of bits of energy, and therefore energy is the one true thing in life. When we die we weigh fifteen ounces less, and perhaps those fifteen ounces are millions of millions of billions of bits of energy that constitute our soul, and this energy flees our dead bodies and flies into the universe, ready to continue thinking great thoughts and creating new concepts. For a moment, after hearing that from Al,

I felt perhaps we're not just a bunch of synaptic impulses running up a string of neurons. Maybe we're something more—something spiritual rather than physical.

But by the end of the night I had twisted Al's concept into something else. I figured that once I die, my energy flows out of me. Each particle of energy goes its own way and perhaps combines with other particles of energy that never were part of *me*. So my energy has scattered all over the universe, but who I was cannot comprehend that because my energy is all torn apart. I have no consciousness. Therefore, I do not exist—at least not in any form close to what I was. There's no connection.

Enough worrying about this. A person who is so afraid of death really should be a success in his life so he doesn't have to contemplate suicide.

What I really need to do is make some drastic change in my life. Like leave LA. The problem is, leaving LA is such a cop-out. It's as bad as going to Rafters on a Saturday night.

But isn't that what I'm trying to do here? Cop out? Escape? I mean, take your pick—leave LA or suicide.

As though I have no other choices. I do have another choice. Frankly, it really is the only choice I have.

I need to leave Larry.

It is unfair of me that I've come to blame Larry for my own actions, my own insecurities. I've often felt a bitter resentment of Larry because of my own inability to jump on possible opportunities, like the nine months that Ed was single until this Trent came along. Again, it is unfair that I've allowed Larry to always be secondary to Ed, especially without ever letting him know this was the case. But Larry has to know. He probably had to know the state I had been in, the nervousness, when Ed and Mark had split up. I had been thinking, *Now here's my opportunity, if only Larry wasn't in the way.*

You know, I blanked out just now—all thoughts and everything. I was recalling a memory. It was six months or so after Ed and I met on the football field. We had really only seen each other on the field up to this time. We didn't have any common friends. But we both saw each other at Studio One one night, and I think we both had a nice little buzz, and I said to him, really without thinking of anything, that we should go dance.

This song came on, and it was fast, and I remember we were doing this rub-your-dicks-close-together-and-get-down kind of dancing, and I was oblivious to everything, being so into the music, and then the track slowed down for a moment, and I kind of laughed, realizing how much I had gotten lost in the music, and I looked up at Ed. And he looked at me at the same time; all of a sudden, our eyes locked. He stared at me with those beautiful light blue irises under his long, curled lashes. Well, the muscles in my cheeks dropped all of a sudden, and I thought for a moment that this could just be the perfect guy for me. I also thought that at that instant, he was thinking the same of me.

The music got faster again, and I tried to drown that thought, guessing I had imagined it all, and trying to return to the rhythm I had before. So I tried to get back into the music for the next hour or so, keeping my eyes off him; I was just too embarrassed. Then, on the drive home, all I could think about was the way we had looked at each other. In fact, for the next couple weeks, it was the only subject on my mind.

Just another one of my missed opportunities. Ed was out of a relationship for nearly a year until this Trent guy, and I never had the guts to break up with Larry and try to make something with Ed and me. What did I fear? Rejection? Of course. How could Ed ever love me? Frankly, he deserves someone better.

I can't get this thought out of my mind, how I acted on the field. Doesn't he know it wasn't him? It was me. Of course he knows that. That's why I don't have the right to have someone like him anyway.

But you know, if it wasn't for Trent I would go up to him right now and tell him exactly how I feel. How I love him.

Love him? I'm actually admitting it, that I love him? Even though I can't have him?

I will tell him. I will. Just as soon as he gets over this infatuation stage with Trent. Because I can't really tell him when he's so infatuated with Trent. It just wouldn't sink in. But later. I'll tell him later.

Or will I? When will that be? Trent's a pretty good-looking guy, and I probably would have liked him and his dry sense of humor last night if he hadn't been Ed's date.

Anyhow, I see it's finally noon, and I've been lying in bed all morning with this hangover. Larry finally got up, and so I'm spread out on the mattress, sweating the booze onto the sheets. They say when you're really down on yourself, thinking bad thoughts, you should just hop out of bed really quickly and start the day. But there's no sun out today, and I really can't concentrate on anything, like writing the novel. Not with this hangover. So I'll just hang around for a while, maybe watch TV. In a few hours they start the beer bust. I'll just have a couple. They say the best way to cure a hangover is with a couple of drinks. Besides, beer will help me forget about these ridiculous thoughts I have about suicide.

To tell you the truth, a drink sounds good right now. I do need a drink. I really do.

❧ 4 ❧

The End of Hanging Out

A high pitch hummed against the rocks, the sudden rise in temperature forming a thermal that sang through the passes of the huge boulders, skirted up the lifting crags, scraped against the cacti's thorny leaves. On this mid-March day, the high desert had been cold and frozen in the early morning, but now the land of Jumbo Rocks sweltered.

Ed wiped the perspiration from his forehead with the back of his hand as he trekked up the side of a rising, jagged slab. He welcomed the heat, the outpouring of sweat, seeing it as a ritual to release the impurities within him. He reached the top and kicked off the drying black-and-brown mud from the soles of his hiking boots. He then raised his head and surveyed the lay of the land: nothing but rocks and sand and cacti for miles on end. He could not even sight a fellow hiker or climber. Ed closed his mouth, standing silently, listening to his breath whistle through his nostrils, smelling the dry, dusty air . . .

He was alone.

Trent's voice spoke again. What he had said last night repeated itself for the hundredth time.

"We never were really going together, you know. We were just hanging out."

Oh, to be so cool as to just hang out with someone, while all the time the other was loving him, desiring him. But for Trent, all it was was hanging out.

Ed sniffed in the dry air. He shook his head and started down the other side of the boulder. He had to move. He had to stop this current way of thinking. He had to forget that he had been so vulnerable, so controlled, so infatuated by someone whose only emotional depth was to hang out for a while and then move on.

"So are you saying you want to stop hanging out with me?"

He recalled this question he had put to Trent. He hated himself for asking it, as though he had agreed with Trent that all they had been doing was hanging out. At that moment, he had conceded, agreeing that their relationship had never meant anything in the first place.

"Yeah." He saw again the image of Trent, his deep brown eyes, under those dark, thick brows, attempting to look sad as he nodded slowly. "Yeah, that's what I'm trying to say."

Ed came to a pebble-covered decline on the rock, which then dropped thirty feet to the mud below. He welcomed this new challenge, however small, that allowed him to concentrate his mind on something else. Carefully treading sideways down the rock, he leaped to a boulder three feet over and continued his descent.

He now was close to the ground, the sun hidden by the rocky hills to the west and the south. He had been hiking in Joshua Tree National Park for several hours, but still he could not fight off a chill in his shoulders as he trudged in the shadows.

"It's just . . . right now I'm not ready for anything heavy. And you . . . well, I know you've been getting more serious with me."

Trent had not even given him the chance to debate that. Trent had just stated it as fact. Every time Ed replayed these words, he felt anger, an emotion he disliked so much.

It's just like some stuck-on-himself guy to make that kind of statement, that I was more into him than he was into me, as though this mades him more important, Ed thought.

Tears formed in his eyes. Ed now was walking next to a trickle of a stream along a firm mud wash on the desert floor. He could not recall having stepped off the stone and onto this path, but here he was all the same, walking northerly into a wide expanse past the current outcropping of boulders. A brown-orange light glowed beyond the rocks, shining on the sand, the shrubs, and the dim green cholla. It was the ideal setting for a Western movie shoot, for a cowboy to go riding into the sunset in pastoral isolation—solitary, independent. The perfect home for a man who does not judge the actions of others, because their actions do not concern him. He can live with them or without them. It doesn't matter. For he is able to live by himself and be complete.

He had been nothing of the cowboy sort last night. He had come back from football practice yesterday nervous and excited. He could not figure what to do with himself as he waited for that night. He spent an hour flipping channels, but he could not stay with one program. He tried to take a nap, but his mind was spinning. So he drove down to Melrose and walked along the sidewalks, looking at everything, thinking of small presents for Trent, trying on new shirts to wear for this special night.

He started getting ready for their date early—showering, picking out what he would wear, recombing his hair—even before 8 p.m., although they were not scheduled to meet at Campanile until 10 p.m., the time when Trent finished his waiting shift. From the way Trent spoke the night before, Ed had conjectured that something special was happening tonight, that they would finally make love in the full sense, that they would lie together, intermingled, consummating their union, and they would be one.

He was ready to leave by nine. Another hour. He could not bear it. He sat down at his computer desk, placed his elbows on the desktop, his hands on his cheeks, and looked up at the ceiling, envisioning Trent's face during this evening of intimacy, how their eyes would look softly at each other as lips touched sweet lips.

Then they would proclaim their love for one another.

Ed closed his eyes, grimacing. The path was smooth, with cholla and Russian thistle several feet back from the wash of mud and sand. He could keep his eyes closed while he walked. But for how long? It was like his dreams—when he ran away he would close his eyes, believing that by being free of sight's restriction he could run faster.

He reopened his eyes. He then recalled the first time he had seen Trent last night.

"You're early," Trent had said as he entered the bar, his waiter apron tied with a folded lip halfway up his white, buttoned-down shirt. Ed had not known Trent was there until he had spoken. Ed placed his beer bottle down on the counter and looked over at Trent with a wide, happy grin. Trent did not return the smile. Instead, he stood there, staring with his dark, gothic eyes. Then Trent looked away, turning to the bartender.

"Bob, two Absolut martinis up with a twist of lime."

Ed looked back to his beer bottle, nodding his head.

"Yeah, yeah. I know I am. It's just, you know, it's Saturday night. I'm kind of excited to get it started."

Ed raised his eyebrows for Trent's acknowledgment. He was still wearing his huge grin, but Trent did not return the smile. He just parted his lips a bit and looked up in the air.

"Well, I've got at least another twenty minutes here. So, you OK waiting?"

Ed nodded. "Sure! I'll just talk to Bob. Besides, I wasn't doing anything at home anyway."

Ed now had passed the rocky crags on both sides and had reached the warmth of the open expanse. He looked both ways. The next closest set of boulders was half a mile ahead and to his right.

That had been the nail in the coffin: his eagerness and anticipation of seeing Trent again, of being with him. Trent had looked befuddled at that moment. He was almost sure of it now, although Ed had not been aware of it then. Behind his always-so-cool exterior, Trent was befuddled, thinking, *This guy is wanting me just way too much.*

Ed recalled some of the moments when they had lain together in bed. Trent's face was a vision of perfection—a rugged outline with a square jaw. A smooth, high forehead. Thick, wavy, brown hair so dark it was almost black. Dark, thick brows and big brown piercing eyes. When he contemplated that face, Ed could not believe he was with someone of such beauty. In fact, he felt as though he had cheated somehow, to have such a man.

But then, when they lay naked together in bed, he felt so much warmth, such tenderness for this man, for as perfect as Trent's face was, his body had flaws—the skinny legs, a lack of definition in the chest and the stomach. Ed loved each and every flaw, for it made Trent human. It allowed Ed to embrace this man, to cover him with tender kisses.

He had come to know every inch of Trent's skin, every wave of his hair, every curve and wrinkle of his lips. Trent had once returned that same desire. Ed knew it from the way Trent had caressed his body, which was more defined—not overbuilt and the shoulders and knees a bit too bony but his muscles hard and strong, full of wiry tension, like a cat ready to pounce.

And Ed had wanted to pounce. So many times he had wanted to take Trent in his arms, to feel inside him. Also, when Trent was on top of him, his smooth belly rubbing against Ed's own, so often Ed had closed his eyes and envisioned a moment of complete relaxation, complete abandonment, of surrender, as he allowed Trent to come inside him.

"I know that you've wanted me to come inside you," Trent had said to him once, "but, you know, things begin to change between two guys once that happens."

The conversation had occurred three weeks ago. Trent then had told his story about a guy he had recently dated. After their one and only night of intercourse, this guy had become extremely possessive, even driving by Trent's apartment at night to see if his truck was on the street, making sure Trent was at home. Trent stopped hanging out with him soon after that. The lover, rebuked, got even by pasting bumper stickers that read FAGGOT on Trent's truck.

"I do want to be inside of you," Trent had said to Ed. "It's just—it has to be the right moment, when we both feel comfortable enough with each other."

Ed looked up. He had been staring at his feet as he walked, one leg on each side of the trickling creek in the wash, watching the water sparkle in the sun and then turn dark under his own shadow. The boulders now rose in front of him—orange and brown, drenched in sunlight. Ed sought the shadows of those stones, knowing they outlined the best paths to the top.

Ed felt envy for Trent's former mate. He had the honor of having Trent inside him before he was rebuked. Ed had not even gotten that far, as though his hang-out time with Trent had never been as special for Trent as had been Trent's hang-out time with the previous guy.

Perhaps Trent's infatuation stage with this other guy had been stronger, or at least longer.

Because Trent *had* been infatuated with Ed. Ed knew that. It's just that Trent's infatuation receded faster than Ed's own. It's like when watching a comedy, when there's a scene that causes a big belly laugh in the audience. Some members of the audience end their belly laughs sooner, and others just can't control them. Their insides will not let them. Ed always was part of the audience that laughed longest, so long that when he finally got the laughter out of his system, a dull pain was present inside.

Ed now felt that pain.

The new outcropping before him started out with smaller stepping-stones about three feet wide that rose up to a pebbly trail angling steep between huge boulders stacked one upon another. He looked up, trying to envision where the paths had been that he had previously spotted from a distance. He began climbing the pebbly trail.

He could not believe he would not see Trent again soon. Trent had been his whole life these past two months. Not a waking minute had gone by during this period when he had not thought about him. Until last night, there had never been any conversation about ending their relationship. In fact, last night's conversation had seemed too surreal. There had been no transition between hanging out and not hanging out. Ed tried to take comfort in this, thinking that there had to be some type of transition. By transition, that meant that he would see Trent again.

"Look, I'm going up to Malibu tonight," Trent had said at the end of their conversation. "Carl's having a couple of friends over at his parents' house, so I thought I'd chill out there, hang out at the beach tomorrow or something. Are you going to be OK?"

Ed now wondered who these other couple of friends might have been. He had not even considered them when Trent had spoken last night. He had been too numb, thinking that Trent was leaving him. He had no thoughts then that there might be someone else.

Trent's previous lover must have been hanging out with Trent up to the time that Trent had met Ed. The whole issue of the bumper sticker—Ed recalled that happened less than two weeks after he had met Trent. Had Trent possibly stopped hanging out with this guy not because the guy had become possessive but because Trent had found a new infatuation?

Ed was staring with heavy brows, grinding his teeth, hardening his jaw, when his foot slipped on the pebbles. He instinctively reached out for a jutting crag, grabbing the stone with his four fingers as they scraped against the rock. Now having a firm hold on that rock, he pulled himself up enough to catch his feet on firm ground.

Trent had met someone new. The sudden realization of this, the knowledge that Trent had become infatuated with someone else while still hanging out with him, infuriated him, which had led to the fall. To slip, to risk injury due to Trent's actions—Ed could not allow that again. He had to let go of Trent, forget about him and forget about this infatuation. Because that's what it was and nothing more. There never had been any love involved—just mindless, irrational infatuation.

Two months of this relationship and yet he could recall so few special moments with Trent. There was that weekend they had stayed at the country-club vacation home of Trent's father in Palm Springs, how during the night they had slept in the master bed and how during the day they tried to sneak in moments of lovemaking while the real estate lady was showing the home during an open house. There was one moment when they had been in the Hancock Park guesthouse of Trent's boss, when they had danced slowly and kissed in complete abandonment to a Sinéad O'Connor song.

Ed could recall little else about their two months together. It had been a fog—two men loving mindlessly in limbo. This infatuation had been his lotus leaf, yet he wanted so much to consume another.

He had never felt such an infatuation, such a high, for a man before. He looked up at the blue-white sky above the rocks, recalling the elation he had felt. It had been like a drug, like speed, and now he was coming down . . . hard.

The sky seemed so unreal next to the browns and oranges of the desert. The sky appeared to him now as life, and the desert land as death. Light and dark. Color and colorless. He watched the narrow wisps of white clouds form in the eastern sky, one on top of the other, appearing in waves, as though alive, as though beckoning to him, singing to him.

No. He had been wrong. He had felt this high once before, if only for a brief moment.

He could envision that night as if it were yesterday, although it had been four years ago—that night at Studio One when Bill had said they should dance. Ed had come to LA only nine months before. He knew Bill from football, knew that he had a boyfriend, but still, he had a secret crush on him. Bill was witty and good looking, and yet Bill always made himself the brunt of most of his own jokes. He was a bright, intelligent man with an inferiority complex. Ed liked that combination. Again, perfection and flaws. He had thought of Bill that way, as he had with Trent. He loved the flaws in Bill. That made him so human.

Bill had said they should dance. It wasn't a question. He had just said, "Let's go out and dance," like a friend saying it to a friend. Still, he had felt an exhilaration by planting in his mind the idea that Bill really was trying to get him out on the dance floor for reasons other than dancing. But then, when he saw Bill dancing, jerking his head around as he did, closing his eyes, being so in tune with the music and his body, Ed realized it was a hopeless hope. That is, until that one moment—such a short period of time and yet an eternity—when Bill opened his eyes and caught Ed staring at him. Then his eyes, his whole expression had just changed, had grown so soft, so caring, had just melted into Ed's own expression. It was a connection, and in that brief moment they were one.

Then Bill had turned away, had closed his eyes, had lost himself in the music and the dance again. Why? Out of embarrassment? Ed had hoped that had been the case, but over the next several months he had allowed himself to believe that what had happened had really been just his imagination.

Even though that brief moment might have only been a dream, it did generate two realities. The first is that after that night Bill and Ed had become very good friends. The second . . . from that moment on, Ed had begun an unrelenting search to find that elation once again.

He searched for it every time he met any guy he liked. Finally, he had found it when he met Trent.

He had moved above the pebbly trail and was now stepping from one flat rock to another like a game of hopscotch, his arms spread out for balance. A stone to the left. A stone to the right. He became aware of his dancing from rock to rock, and he let out a short chuckle, thinking that he had often danced this way when he was in his silly infatuation.

Trent understood this game of infatuation, while Ed had been a novice. Trent had been infatuated with him, just as he had been infatuated with the guy before who ended up plastering FAGGOT bumper stickers on his truck, and just as he had been infatuated with countless guys before. Trent knew that infatuations couldn't last forever, and so once he felt one infatuation waning he had to move on to the next.

But Ed, having experienced his first infatuation for only a brief moment, wanted the next to last forever.

Trent had infatuations at approximate two-month intervals, with these infatuations overlapping so he was never really out of the high, just throwing away the old while gathering in the new. Ed so envied Trent.

The top of the mountain rose straight up. From that side, the top could be reached only by a true rock climber with rope and pitons. Ed therefore descended the east side of the mountain to find another route. He had not realized the physical exertion he had put his body through until he began descending along this easy trail in the shade, sweat now feeling cold against his skin. He shivered, hoping to re-enter into sunlight soon.

Just last night he had returned with Trent to his Hollywood apartment, and now he was hiking several hundred feet above the desert floor more than 100 miles from his home. The sun would be setting in a few hours, and he still had to drive home so he could be at Warner Bros. at 8:30 tomorrow morning to finish up that merchandising contract before lunch. The contract was the specter that made him realize he had to return to LA.

He recalled how last night had ended, after Trent had told him he was leaving for Malibu and asked whether he was going to be OK.

"Yeah, I'll be all right," Ed had answered him.

Then there had been an embarrassing silence, as neither of them knew what to say next. Ed had felt numb and was unable to look at Trent. After nearly a minute went by, he glanced Trent's way. Trent could not return his gaze. Ed could not breathe. He felt so still, thinking that he would pass out. And so he shook his head, paced his feet, started walking, jerked his shoulders. . . . Movement! He need to move, to remove that numbness.

"Look, Trent. Maybe I'll just get out of here," Ed broke the silence. "I mean it's Saturday night. It's still early. I guess then I'd better make some other plans tonight. Maybe I'll go to Revolver or something."

Trent nodded. "Yeah, that would be good. You've always got one or two of your friends there."

Ed nodded back, his eyes locked on the front door. He took a deep breath, looked at Trent with a nervous smile, and then cupped his hand on Trent's shoulder.

"Well, see you."

He went out the door, straight to his car, never looking back.

He rounded the mountain and saw another jumble of rocks several hundred yards farther east. He figured those rocks would be the last destination of his hike, and then he would have to return home. He stopped for a moment, looking at the dusky blues of the eastern sky. Dark and silent, except for a strange, distant howling. Perhaps a coyote, he thought.

He had not gone to Revolver. Although numb and shocked by Trent's change of heart, Ed had been able to muster a clever word as a means of testing Trent. Revolver had been the bar where they had met two months ago. Ed had been there by himself, hoping to find someone that night. Not someone to sleep with, but someone with whom eventually he would fall in love. That always was his plan when he went to the bars alone. If he didn't find it, then a one-night stand would be better than a night alone. So he put out the name Revolver as if to say to Trent, "Well, I'll just go over to the bar and pick someone else up then."

His simple and inept plot did not work. Trent had not been troubled at all by his words. And why would he be? The night they had met at Revolver, Ed had spent nearly an hour looking Trent's way, yet he never approached him. Trent eventually had to make the move. Trent knew that Ed was shy and that he was not smooth at picking up guys. Probably just mentioning Revolver had made Trent laugh inside at that moment.

Even worse, maybe Trent didn't care if Ed picked up someone that night.

Flat and jagged stones crackled under Ed's boots as he climbed the eastern slope. The trail ended at a boulder rising vertically fifty feet before him. The only way now to reach the top was to sidestep along a six-inch ledge that angled up to the top of that rock.

Ed stopped for a moment. One slip and he would be done for, but there was plenty of room to maneuver. He did not fear the challenge. It was second nature to him. Besides, he had other things on his mind.

He had begun to drive toward West Hollywood, but he could not fathom the idea of facing others at that moment. What would be best was to go home and sleep. Once he lay in bed, he could not keep his eyes closed. Instead he lay on his back, staring at the ceiling, replaying over and over what had taken place.

Time passed so slowly that night. Finally, he could lay there no longer. At four in the morning he got in his car and drove to Joshua Tree National Park.

Sliding along the narrow ledge was easy enough. The rock curved inward at eye level, and Ed was able to place his hands against the stone for leverage. Within a minute he had reached the top, which was nothing more than an oblong spire, barely enough room to stand. So he sat and looked out to the east, to the next challenge before him.

Everything grew quiet, and his ears were able to focus on that faint howling sound. "Ep . . . ep." It came in steady bursts, as though there was some logic to the noise. When Ed heard it, he could not conceive of it coming from a coyote. An opossum? No, something larger. It didn't sound dangerous. It was a mystery to him.

Perhaps I should end the day by solving a mystery, he thought.

The mystery would put off his inevitable return to LA. He dreaded that so, because as the day wore on he realized that he did not run out here to escape the pain of last night. It was primarily to escape the aftermath, the moment in which he would have to tell his friends that all his happiness had crashed in one second, that he had finally come to the pitiful fact that he had been a fool in love.

Of course Bill will know what happened the moment he catches my eyes as he steps on the football field next week, Ed thought. Ed could hide nothing from him. He had announced yesterday to Bill that he and Trent would finally spend the night joined in sweet bliss. How could he face Bill now?

Ed always discussed his relationships with Bill. In doing so, he sought Bill's approval, hoping that Bill would see in one of Ed's short-time boyfriends what Bill had in his own longtime lover. Yet Ed never felt he could win Bill's approval—until Trent came along, that is. Because Bill had conceded yesterday that he could see how Ed now appeared truly happy. Finally, the approval came.

As he stepped off the rock, finding an easier path down on the south side, he knew he soon would be trekking easterly along the desert, farther away from LA. That thought gave him some satisfaction—to leave LA; to start over. But how would that help matters? He would still be the same person. As much as he tried to blame Trent for this breakup, he could not help but think it was his own fault.

He had been able to attract Trent with his easygoing nature and quirky sense of humor. He had a bit of an understanding of how others saw him—an athletic and solitary type, which often was interpreted as very masculine, a concept that Ed never saw in himself. In fact, he often laughed to himself about his newfound, macho status—just because of playing football.

Ed never had been sure what Trent had liked in him. Perhaps Trent also had considered Ed masculine—perhaps good looking as well. And nice. Always nice.

Ed was painfully aware that people always saw him as a *nice* guy. Everyone always said that to him, but he never was sure if they meant it as a compliment. He truly believed that Trent saw it as a defect.

Trent, on the other hand, was a spoiled Beverly Hills-raised actor-slash-model who always hung out with the right crowd and who would often use his sarcastic wit to put down others that were not part of that crowd. After getting over the infatuation stage with Ed, Trent was able to see the reality of the situation: Ed was not part of the right crowd. He was just too nice.

Ed jumped off the last boulder onto the desert floor once more. He would have to walk in the shadows of this mountain for a quarter mile before reaching sunlight once more.

Again, the pain of thinking that he had been at fault in the breakup due to his personality overwhelmed him. He felt something rise in him, admonishing him, telling him to let go.

He screamed.

The scream came back to him, bouncing off the rocks. He just had to get it out as he lurched forward faster. These thoughts. This agony. What he could not handle thinking about again. The reason Trent left him. The realization that he was just some nerdy jock who could never be loved by anyone of consequence.

"Why do you do that?" Trent had asked suddenly one night, changing his entire demeanor as he lay on top of Ed. Just a moment before he had been tenderly kissing Ed's neck. Now he raised his body up, his arms locked on both sides of Ed's body.

"What?" Ed asked.

"Why do you laugh like that when I go down on you?"

His silly giggling. A laugher. Ed was a laugher. How unromantic. He was unaware that he had been giggling during the lovemaking. He could never be a good lover with this stupid, idiotic, nervous tittering. Now he could see why Trent broke up with him. He was just a nerdy, unsophisticated nobody who could never be on the same level as Trent.

He ran. The thoughts still crowded his brain. So he ran faster, into the sunlight, getting it out until the sweat ran into his eyes.

The adrenaline rose inside him as the orange rocks rose higher and higher. Running was the cure-all, letting in the air, letting out the sweat, showing him what he could do, refusing to set limits.

"This mountain before me. I shall conquer it," he exclaimed.

But then he stopped. There it was again, mixed with his own heavy breathing—the howling, now closer.

It was human.

Ed looked toward the rocks, from one end to the next. He cupped his hands to his mouth.

"Hello?"

"Here! Here!" he heard the voice, louder now, followed by a cough. "Over here!"

Ed ran in the direction of the voice.

"I'm here!" Ed called. "Yell so I can find you."

"Over here!"

He reached the mound of rocks and entered a narrow sandy trail between two huge boulders.

"Where are you?"

"Up here, next to the pine tree."

Ed slowed down, surveying the pass.

"I can see you," the voice said, coughing once again. "Look up . . . to your right."

Ed turned his head. He spotted a gnarled, dead pine hanging over one edge of a sheer rock rising vertically 100 feet. His eyes dropped lower.

There, hanging only by his own rope, was a young man, no older than twenty years of age. He was staring at Ed, his face almost completely white and his shoulders rising as he wheezed out a dry sob.

"I . . . uh . . . think I broke my leg," the climber exclaimed. "Last night."

Ed looked up in disbelief. The guy was hanging vertically fifty feet off the ground. Three pitons were locked into the rock above him and three more below him, allowing him to create his own shelf as he sat on the rope folded over three times. He had on only a long-sleeved T-shirt, shorts, and climbing shoes. His right knee was caked with a mound of dried blood.

Ed noticed a day pack at the bottom of the rock.

"Your bag!" Ed exclaimed. "Do you have more rope in there?"

"Yeah," the climber muttered in pain. "I think . . . My feet. I can't feel my feet."

Ed hurried over to the bag and zipped open the pouch. There he found a thin fleece jacket, toilet paper, some rope and pitons, and a bottle of water.

He grabbed the rope and pitons and looked up at the climber.

"Look . . . what's your name?"

"Carl."

"Carl, I'm Ed. Look, I've never rock climbed like this before. So you got to help me, OK? You got to help me if I'm going to get you."

Carl nodded, his shoulders heaving as his dry sobs began again.

"Good. Good," Ed stated as he returned Carl's nods. "Then . . . we'll work together on this."

Late that night, Ed sat in the waiting room of the Joshua Tree Emergency Clinic just a half hour north of the park's borders. He had been sitting there for more than an hour, a solitary figure in an empty space, waiting to learn of the climber's condition. Finally, a nurse entered and walked over to him.

"Ed Wakeling," she stated, her eyes focused on him. He perked up and raised his head to see her.

"The boy . . ." She paused for a moment. "We set his leg. It was broken. However, he suffered major frostbite. He . . . we have to remove the small toes on his right foot. Three of them. He'll be transported to the hospital at Twenty-nine Palms."

Ed looked up, feeling the tears well in his eyes. She looked at him, then squeezed his hand with her own and gave him a warm smile.

"You saved his life," she said. "You know that, don't you?"

The nurse walked away. Ed watched her exit through the door. He then turned his head, looking once again between his legs, down at the murky gray tiles of the floor.

He placed his face into his hands, thinking of no one else but of Carl, of a life changed so dramatically because of one incident, one moment of time. And that entire day Ed had wallowed in his own self-pity because of a matter so inconsequential.

He forgot all else, thinking of his own selfishness.

Suddenly, he felt a hand touch his shoulder.

"Hey : . . hey now."

The nurse had returned. She sat down next to him, putting her arms around his shoulders. "You should feel good. There's a young man here who's alive today because of you."

Ed looked at her with wet, red eyes. He dropped his head into her welcoming embrace and cried, waiting for release, for a return to peace.

◆ 5 ◆

The Culver City Centurions

Dave Vander Beeken heaved a sigh, releasing his anxiety as he walked onto the fields of Fairfax High School. At the same time, he felt proud to be wearing his new blue mesh jersey, signifying that he was a member of the LA Quake. He had asked Marcus less than three weeks ago if they still needed players to fill up the roster. Marcus had said, "Sure, Dave. I mean, you know, I can't promise you a lot of playin' time, but you can be a Quake." Now, walking on the field during the first day of the West Los Angeles Flag Football Spring League, Dave felt anxious about the passes he might drop, but also he constantly imagined that one spectacular play he would make which would change how his teammates regarded him. He had never been able to make that play back home, his last chance of having such an opportunity dashed when he was cut from the University of the Pacific football team in Stockton while a freshman.

Jerry walked beside him, his shoulders jutting out in his usual cocky attitude. Unlike Dave, Jerry chose not to wear the Quake uniform while making his entrance. Instead, he hid the jersey in his backpack while sporting a tight gray tank top designed by Malibu Body Wear, one of the country's premier weight-lifting clothing companies. This article of clothing was his gift from the editors of *Men's Exercise* magazine for posing for the "Ab Work-Out" article in the February 1998 issue, not to be confused with the "Awesome Abs" article in the March 1998 issue.

The West Los Angeles Flag Football Spring League brought together teams from Culver City, the Crenshaw District, Hollywood, West Hollywood, West Los Angeles, Santa Monica, and even the San Gabriel Valley. It was a major step up for Dave, Jerry, and the rest of the gang, who had previously relegated their football talents to pickup games at Hollywood High School on Saturday mornings. These pickup games had recently become more formalized into a gay league, but still the rules were simple and the referees were only volunteers. But in the West Los Angeles Flag Football Spring League, referees were paid fifty dollars a game, and the rulebook contained forty-eight pages.

Unlike Dave, the rest of the Quake members were not intimidated by playing in a *straight* league. They did not know how good the other teams were, but they were confident of their own skills. What concerned them most was not the players on the straight teams, but the players on the other gay team.

Because so many players from the gay league had expressed interest in playing in the intercity league, two teams were formed—the Los Angeles Quake and the West Hollywood Warriors. How these teams were chosen had led to a bitter rivalry between Vince and Marcus. Three Saturdays ago Vince had suggested that the teams be chosen by the captains—Vince picking one player, then Marcus picking two players, then Vince picking two players, and so on. Marcus argued that this wasn't any pickup league, and players should have a choice of which team they would like to play for. A majority of the players agreed with Marcus, which led to Vince storming off the Hollywood High School football field. Within two hours Vince was on the phone, persuading guys to play on his team. He had a group of loyal followers on the field, and they too began making calls. But Jack and Marcus were making the same recruitment calls, and so within a week, the Quake and Warrior teams were formed.

The league was set up so that two games were played at 11 a.m., followed by two more games at 12:30 p.m. The first two games of the season had just been completed as Dave pointed at the far field.

"There's our team."

"Look at the team we're playing," Jerry responded. "See! They're wearing tank tops. I mean, I'm not against the design of our jerseys—Marcus did a good job—but we really should wear tank tops. That would make us seem more imposing to the other team, showing our muscles and all. See! There's Vince's team, walking off the field. Fuck!

They must have won. Look at Vince smiling like that. But look! Tank tops, too. And they got nothing to show off. Fuck! We made a mistake with these jerseys."

Wearing white tank tops with large red numbers, the West Hollywood Warriors walked toward the sidelines separating the two chalked fields. Marcus and Bill stood in the far field, staring at Vince as he shook the referee's hand.

"Look at him over there," Marcus said with a moan, placing his hands on his hips. "Butterin' up the ref. Always trying to find a way to win, trying to get on the good side, so when there's a controversial call, it'd be called his way. But no way is his team going to beat these Santa Monica Seahawks. Mmmmaaan! Did you see them?"

Bill nodded, his hands on his hips. He looked over at the Culver City Centurions, the team the Quake would play within the next thirty minutes. They were a young team wearing red tank tops and a variety of shorts and sweats. Bill looked down at his own uniform, at the Quake emblem of a football soaring off a Richter scale, and at the bright yellow mesh shorts that accompanied the blue jersey.

"Yeah, the Seahawks are good, but we sure look the best," Bill said, slapping Marcus on the chest. Marcus nodded, staring over at the Centurion team, recognizing Bill's compliment of the insignia he designed and the uniforms he chose.

"These Centurions must just be outta school," Marcus said. "You noticed that one boy, the blond with the short hair in the back and those cute long bangs in the front?"

Bill's wayward eyes answered that he had. He watched the tightening of the blond Centurion's hamstrings as he stretched out one leg. The object of Marcus and Bill's affections then suddenly turned their way and caught their stares. Embarrassed, the Centurion turned his eyes away and said something with a laugh to a nearby teammate.

"You think he possibly could be?" Marcus asked.

"I don't know, but I know Curt is working on it."

They turned their eyes at Curt, who was staring intently at the blond guy. Curt was stretching next to his boyfriend. Al, aware of Curt's prowling, laughed and hit him on the shoulder.

"Hey! It's the opening game!" Al scolded. "Don't you think you ought to focus on the game instead of boys for once?"

Curt shrugged his shoulders.

"Some people can walk and chew gum simultaneously. I can score a touchdown and a trick at the same time."

Curt turned his gaze away from the blond and looked over at Al. "Of course, I'd have no problem with us sharing him either," he added.

"Hey everybody!" Marcus yelled out toward the field. "Curt! Al! Quake! Huddle! Come on now! This is it, guys!"

The team gathered over to the sidelines, Curt trailing a bit as his eyes kept darting back to the cute blond on the other team. Marcus scanned each of the players, making sure they were coming to the huddle.

"Where the hell is Ed?" asked Jack, who surveyed the field as he stood next to Marcus.

"I was wondering the same thing," Bill replied.

The team gathered around Jack and Marcus. Each player placed his hands down on his knees; eyes focused on their captains.

"I just wanted to say to the Quake . . ."

Marcus's pep talk was broken up when Vince peered his head over the slouched backs of the Quake players.

"I just came to wish you all luck," Vince said. "And to say . . . great uniforms."

Dave stood up and looked at Vince.

"Great uniforms . . . for . . . for a great team," he stammered.

"Hey, that's a good one," Bill remarked. "Well said. You're right. The Quake deserves great uniforms."

"Well, thanks for the encouragement, Vince, but we're just going into our pregame huddle, ya know," Marcus said. "You gonna be watchin' or you scoutin' the other game?"

"Oh, I'm scouting the other game, but I'll be turning my head every so often, rootin' you on."

Vince walked away. Al watched him leave and nodded in appreciation.

"See?" Al remarked. "Vince really is a pretty nice guy overall."

"Man, whatchoo talking about?" Marcus argued. "Vince wants so bad to see us lose. Now come on! Get into the game! We're talkin' just eight weeks! Eight weeks of our lives we're gonna dedicate to the Quake! No drinking on Friday, y'all! No movie-making deals on Saturday until after the game! No preppin' up for Saturday night parties till after the game! This is football! And we're thinking and living football! We got a great group of players, and we got a great team!"

"Yeah!" the Quake responded in unison.

"Now it's fifteen-minute quarters and the clock don't stop except during a time-out, which both teams get two of each half. So it's gonna be a fast game, so we can't slip up on any plays. Every play counts."

"Especially the two-point conversions," Jack added. "Vince's team made every one. That's what we got to do."

Marcus nodded.

"Yeah, now Vince's team got an easy first round, but I can't tell you what these Centurions are going to be like. They're pretty young. So I expect they'll be fast. That little black guy over there, Wesley's his name. He's supposed to be real fast. At least he's been shooting off his mouth that he is, trying to psych us out. But we'll just play our regular D, man on man at first, and if we need to adjust, we'll adjust. I'm going to start as rusher to begin with, so we got Mitch and Curt on the wide receivers to start with . . ."

"Hey, guys!"

Once again, Marcus's attempt to inspire his teammates was disturbed by someone trying to break into the huddle. All the players turned their heads to find their missing teammate slowly nudging into the huddle.

"Sorry I'm late. My car broke down," Ed explained.

Ed looked over at Bill, but once he saw his friend's eyes upon him, he looked down at the ground.

"Oh, that's right," Bill commented. "Ed told me he was finally getting laid last weekend by his boyfriend. Or was that last night? Slept in a little, ay?"

"No," Ed corrected. "Just . . . are we playing a game or what?"

"You're right, Ed, we are," Marcus added. "We only talk football till it's over. Save the bed talk for later, y'all."

Marcus finished his pep talk, and the players went back to the bench as Jack and Marcus met with the referees and the captains of the other team. As Al walked toward the sidelines, he spotted two women looking down at his bag. The taller woman, a dark brunette with large breasts packed into a black sports bra, bent down and pulled out an old T-shirt from the bag. As she caught Al's eyes, she raised the shirt's sleeve to her nose and sniffed deeply. The other woman, a striking blonde with long hair, turned Al's way and laughed at her friend's gesture.

Al smiled back at them, but then he nervously glanced at Curt, who was walking by his side, hoping his boyfriend had not seen the shirt-sniffing scene. Curt was busy staring down the cute blond boy on the Centurion team.

"Holly! Brenda!" Al exclaimed as he approached them. "I didn't know you two were going to come."

He hugged and kissed Holly, the blonde woman whose tanned and slender arms and legs appeared even longer due the scantiness of her apparel—a tank top exposing her navel and very short cutoff jeans. Meanwhile, the brunette twirled his T-shirt around her index finger. As she did so, the shirt swiped against his head once or twice, causing him to break the embrace with her friend.

"You won't smell a pit stain in that shirt, sorry to say," Al now responded to Brenda, and his words seemed a substitute to also embracing her as he backed away from the swinging T-shirt. "You know that shirt is probably cleaner than anything you have in your closet."

"Oh, you already know me too well," Brenda replied.

"I told Brenda we had to come to the first game of the season," Holly said. "You playing that team over there? They're just boys!"

"It looks like a game of men versus boys. Pederasty, if you ask me," Brenda added.

"I know, and Curt won't take his eyes off that blond boy over there," Al replied.

Holly pointed to the blond.

"That boy there? The one looking over at us? I think he's very envious of you right now." Holly suddenly sent out a lip-smacking kiss toward the blond, who caught her action and laughed, only to shyly turn back toward his teammates.

"I tell you," Brenda said, "I think Holly here is a gay man in a lesbian's body. She's always flirting with cute young boys. Holly, I've never seen you flirt with a real man before."

Holly laughed and put her arm around Al's shoulder.

"Oh, I always flirt with Al."

Brenda smiled slyly at her girlfriend.

"And what would you do if I started kissing you right here in front of all these straight boys? What if we dropped all pretenses and just did it here right now?"

Holly hugged Al tighter.

"Oh, you wouldn't do that. You're enjoying the attention from these boys too much."

Al laughed.

"You two. Could you even be more lipstick lesbian?"

Al looked out onto the field. He swallowed anxiously and began hopping up and down.

"I tell you, I'm so nervous. I just hope I don't let my team down."

Holly and Brenda each took one of Al's hands.

"You're going to be great," Holly comforted him.

"More than great," Brenda added, and with her other hand she pinched his butt.

Al quickly took two steps back.

"Well, better get on the field!" he responded immediately, his shoulders shuddering. "See you at halftime!"

The Centurions won the coin toss and would receive the kickoff. Mitch, the best kicker on the team, soared it back into the end zone, and so the Centurions would start at their own twenty-yard line. The Quake set up on defense.

"Pick a man! Pick a man!" Marcus yelled. "Al, you got the runner! Ed and Bill, take the insides!"

Bill trotted over to Ed.

"You decide. Which side?"

Ed shrugged. "I don't care. Whatever you want."

"Well, I don't care either," Bill answered. "I'm very versatile."

"I'll take the right then."

Bill nodded and walked to the left. But then he stopped and turned once more to Ed.

"So . . . consummated it yet?"

Ed took a deep breath. "Bill, will you forget it, OK? It's over, OK? You glad? Like I can hide that from you. He . . . you know. Let's just play the game."

"Come on, D!" Marcus yelled. "They're coming to the line!"

Wesley and the cute blond on the Centurion team lined up as wide receivers at each end of the offensive line. Curt, seeing that the blond was lining up on the opposite side, ran over to Mitch.

"You take the other side, Mitch. I got the blond here."

"Bro!" Mitch exclaimed. "Get ready then! They're up to the line!"

"Hut!"

The two wide receivers ran ten yards out, then crossed in the middle. Curt stutter-stepped and reacted to the cross, staying on the blond, playing such tight defense that he grazed the blond's rear with his pelvis. The blond picked up his step, trying to get free, but as he did he hooked his teammate's leg as they crossed, and both receivers fell to the ground just as the ball was thrown. The ball ended up over everyone's head. Pass incomplete.

Curt bent his shoulders over the blond receiver and offered him his hand. The guy clasped Curt's forearm and pulled himself off the ground.

"Thanks, man," the blond said. He momentarily caught eyes with Curt, who gave him his signature grin.

"No problem," Curt responded. "It was a good pattern, you two just played it too close."

Al caught his boyfriend with the blond. He placed his hands on his hips and shook his head, then let out a laugh. Sam walked up to Al and nudged him with his elbow.

"Oh, this is going to be easy," Sam said. "They can't even stand up on the field. And look at who I'm covering. The center starts a huffin' and puffin' after a ten-yard trot."

Marcus walked back to the defense. As the rusher, he had pressured the quarterback to throw early during the previous play. Marcus now clapped his hands, his head nodding.

"That's right, D! Good job, Quake! Now that's just one play. One play. Don't get soft!"

They lined up for the second play of the game. Curt, who usually stayed about ten yards off the wide receiver, closed in to five, again trying to make eye contact with the blond, who was staring at the ground in front of his feet, waiting for the hike.

"Hut one! Hut two!"

The ball was hiked. Wesley ran directly at Mitch, jabbed with his right foot, and then flew left and up the field. The sudden jab at his face momentarily threw Mitch off balance, and when he finally changed directions with his man, Wesley was several strides ahead of him.

"Curt!" Mitch called, desperately trying to catch his man, who had run over to Curt's side of the field. "Open man! On your side!"

Curt, who had been too busy shadowing the blond, turned his head to see Wesley run past him.

"Shit!" he cried. He swung around and ran full force to try to catch up with Wesley.

Marcus flew toward the quarterback, but the wide-shouldered center had planted himself directly between the rusher and the quarterback. Marcus chose to knock the center over rather than go around, but his impact was muffled by the center's belly, and by the time he slipped around, the quarterback had sailed a long bomb.

Mitch and Curt could do nothing except hope the ball had been thrown off target. Instead it flew directly into Wesley's arms.

Touchdown.

The Quake stood silent, all of them in shock, while an uproarious Centurion team ran to the end zone, giving Wesley high fives. None of the Quake moved, except Marcus, who walked over to Mitch and Curt.

"So c'mon, Quake! How'd we let that happen?" Marcus yelled.

Curt, still dazed as he watched the Centurions celebrate, turned to Marcus.

"Mitch let his man get by him."

"Damn!" Mitch yelled. He turned to Curt and threw out his arm. "If you weren't fooling around with that blond boy, playing five yards off the line, you could have helped me out! This is a team, and we're only two deep! Fuck! We don't even have a safety!"

"Hey! Come on now!" Marcus replied, his voice calming down. "It's just one play. It's early in the game, man. We don't know nothin' about this team, and we'll adjust to how they're playing. I say we stay on the man to man, but we'll drop Sam back as safety. That center's not gonna do nothin'. Bill, Ed, stay on your men, but watch the center. He ain't gonna do nothin'."

The Centurions brought the score up to 8-0 by successfully executing the two-point conversion from the five-yard line.

The Quake now had the ball on the forty-yard line after a short kickoff by the Centurions. After a quick first down, Jack called a play in the huddle to overload the right side after seeing that the Centurions were playing a zone defense. Curt again smiled to himself, knowing that he would be running on the side of the blond boy he liked so much.

Within seconds after the hike, Curt, Marcus, and Bill were running deep on the right. The blond boy, who defended that area, became confused, not knowing whom to defend. By the time he began running after Curt, Curt was several strides ahead of him.

Jack threw a perfect pass to Curt, who was all by himself. The ball fell perfectly into Curt's arms . . . and then through them.

Pass incomplete.

The blond defender approached Curt.

"It was a good pattern," he said, his voice deeper than Curt had expected, "you just dropped the ball."

Curt sneered at him. "Funny! Putting my words back at me."

The blond laughed and nodded to himself, congratulating himself on his joke. Curt returned the guy's jesting with a sly grin.

"So," Curt looked at the blond face to face, "what are you doin' after the game?"

The blond looked up at Curt, his smile turning to a confused grin. "Huh?"

Curt took a step closer. "We win, you buy me a beer. You win, I'll buy you a beer."

"Curt! Fuck, man! Get over to the huddle!" Marcus yelled.

Curt noticed his teammates were waiting for him back at the line. He looked at the blond and at his confusion. Curt ran proudly back to the huddle, feeling he had taken control of this recent exchange.

"Fuck, you were wide open!" Marcus yelled. "We got to execute now! Whatcha doin' talking to that boy when you dropped the ball? C'mon now, Quake!"

"OK, Curt, Bill, both of you go fifteen yards and cut right across the field," Jack called the play. "Marcus, you roll out to the left sideline. Mitch, Sam, you both go long to clear up the short field for Marcus."

"Fuck, man!" Marcus complained. "It's second and ten. We don't need the wides going long. There's a big hole between their short and their deep. Let's get the flankers to buttonhook past the short, pick up the ten or fifteen, and we got the first down."

Jack placed his hands on his hips, saying nothing at first, just staring at Marcus through his dark sunglasses.

"And you've been calling such great calls on defense, I see."

"Guys!" Mitch interjected. "We only got so much time in the huddle."

"Fine!" Jack answered in a high pitch. "Bill, Curt, buttonhook for a first down. Marcus, veer out to the right. Al, stay out to block. Wides, just . . . get open."

They ran to the line. The ball was hiked. Curt and Bill ran perfect twelve-yard buttonhooks and found open pockets, waiting for the throw. The defensive backs paid no attention to them as they ran with Mitch and Sam toward the end zone.

"C'mon, Jack. C'mon, Jack," Bill said over and over to himself. But Jack did not look at him or Curt. Instead, he sent the ball soaring toward Sam and the two defenders right on his tail.

The ball was thrown short. Wesley leaped into the air.

Interception.

"Damn!" Mitch shouted out. "What are we? A bunch of idiots!?"

This Centurion possession ended up the same as before. The quarterback threw a perfect pass to Wesley, who caught it over Sam's outstretched arms for another touchdown.

The Quake's only consolation came when Mitch deflected a pass to ruin the Centurions' chance for a two-point conversion.

"That's it, Quake!" Al yelled, clapping his hands, trying to fire up his deflated teammates. "That's the turning point right there! We got them now!"

By this time, Jack had learned his lesson. The flankers, and the short field, were now in his field of vision. On first down he threw a ten and out to Bill, who dropped the ball. On second down he threw a five and in to Curt, who dropped the ball.

Third and ten. Curt walked off the field, calling in Ed to replace him as flanker.

"Come on, Quake!" Marcus yelled. "We ain't catchin' no balls!"

Al looked wide-eyed at his captain.

"Then let's run it!"

"Yeah!" Bill exclaimed. "Al's right. I've been watching. The deep's playing pretty deep. The guys playing close aren't all that fast. And the flanker on my side isn't too big. I'll get a good block on him, and Marcus has got twenty yards, easy."

They ran to the line. The ball was hiked. Mitch and Sam ran deep to the left side of the field, taking the three defensive backs with them. Marcus veered to the right. Jack pitched it to him. Al took out the center linebacker with a block.

Now the play was only Marcus and Bill and the short right defender. Marcus came barreling behind Bill. Bill stared squarely at the defender's waist, never focusing on the man's eyes, knowing that eyes can fake a blocker out.

Bill plowed into the defender, blocking him inside. Marcus ran outside him. Now all that was left between Marcus and the end zone were the deep defenders. The blond ran back toward the right side of the field, but Mitch, having anticipated the defender's move, ran in front of him, squarely blocking him and allowing Marcus to run up the sideline.

Touchdown.

The Quake's elation was short-lived. Bill ran the wrong way on a pattern for an unsuccessful two-point conversion. On the Centurions' possession, Wesley made a tough catch on a misfired throw in the middle pocket and then the blond turned a short catch into a twenty-five-yard gain for a touchdown. This time the Centurions executed on the two-point conversion for a 22-6 lead.

Jerry started to complain that he had not seen any time on offense. Halftime was less than a minute away, and so Jack brought in both Jerry and Dave. In the first play, Jack threw an easy pass to Dave, who dropped it, causing Jerry to complain again, saying he had been wide open. Mitch, meanwhile, was arguing that Jerry and Dave, the two weakest players on the team, should never be on offense at the same time.

At halftime the Quake walked dejectedly to the sidelines with their heads bowed.

Bill sat on the edge of one of two benches given to the Quake, trying to isolate himself from the other players. He had dropped a pass, had turned the wrong way on a pass pattern for an important two-point conversion, and he had allowed his man to fake him out for a fifteen-yard gainer.

He felt he had no right to be a Quake.

Bill saw Mitch throwing his hands in the air, arguing about the game with some friend in street clothes. He knew what Mitch was saying. He was telling his friend how much his teammates were screwing up—how Curt had dropped all those passes; how Jack had his regular "telescope eye" going, passing always to Sam, his boyfriend, despite others being open on the field; how Dave, as usual, dropped the ball; and how Marcus hadn't adjusted the defense properly.

Bill then recognized Mitch's friend, with his round glasses and short, just-starting-to-gray brown hair. It was Randy Clayburg.

He had met Randy a few evenings earlier at a coffee shop on Beverly. Randy, a director of the acclaimed HBO series *The Sicilians,* had mentioned how much he liked the *Ally McBeal* spec script Bill had recently finished. Having someone of Randy's caliber like his spec script certainly could be a huge opening, Bill had thought on that evening. But today he had forgotten about such an opportunity. Instead, focusing too much on his own poor performance on the field, Bill had again reverted to his loser-status thoughts. His recent errors on the field stuck to him like glue. Mistakes he could never rectify. Regrets he would live over and over in his mind, like the dozen or so serious mistakes in his life that never left his mind for long, that persisted, that clung to him.

But now he again saw Randy, who glanced momentarily his way and waved his hand and smiled, which seemed an inappropriate act while Mitch was in the middle of complaining about his teammates. Mitch, seeing Randy's brief inattentiveness to his arguments, also looked Bill's way. Bill gave both of them a nod and a smile, which caused Mitch to suddenly stop his chattering and stare at his friend in confusion.

Bill looked the other way and saw Ed, standing on the field with his hands on his hips, pivoting at his waist to limber up for the second half. It was Ed, Bill thought, that caused his errant playing. He was thinking too much of this man, of whatever troubled him at this moment. Of his relationship with Trent. Was it truly over? Ed seemed crushed by it, and Bill needed to be there for support. But over? Ed was single again? Could that really be true? He wanted to ask Ed more questions, but he was afraid he'd look too eager. What Ed had said immediately brought back to mind Bill's greatest regret of never telling Ed his own feelings for him. Oh, the possibilities that could have arisen if he had just told Ed before, if he had just gone with his instincts at Studio One or the events after that, rather than going home and analyzing everything to death without ever taking action. The Hamlet in him. With every pass he dropped and every play he did not execute during that first half, he felt Ed was to blame. Why hadn't Ed made a move, if Ed really cared for him? Because he didn't. Or did he?

How could Bill ever know unless he took some kind of action? Now he had that chance.

Bill studied his friend, his sad eyes, appearing only to go through the motions as he swung his arms and ran in place. Bill returned his glance to Mitch and Randy. Again, they caught Bill's nodding and smiling, more prominent than before.

Marcus stood up from the bench. He heaved his chest in a big stretch, then pivoted at his waist, first to his left, then to his right, surveying his team.

"All right, Quake!" he called. "Let's get together."

Al was the first one to the huddle. The rest of the team staggered over as they relived their mistakes in the first half.

"OK now, Quake, we've had a horrible first half, but we're going to change that," Marcus began. "This is it. This half could determine the play-offs. Now forget about the first half and think about the potential we've got. We're only down two touchdowns. That ain't nothing. So c'mon. And Curt, stop cruisin' that blond. You can't score on the field and with a guy at the same time, ya know?"

Al elbowed his boyfriend.

"Now we're going to change to a zone," Marcus continued. "I'm going to safety. Ed, you be rusher to start. Curt, you and me will play off that Wesley, and Mitch will stay on the blond. Curt, I ain't gonna let you on that blond no more."

The halftime huddle broke. The players took the field, running short sprints and stretching. Bill walked up to Mitch.

"Hey, Mitch," Bill began. "Fuck, I played like shit the first half."

"Shake it off, man," Mitch replied. "Think of what we're going to do in the second half."

Bill nodded.

"Yeah. Yeah. I have been thinking about it. You know, I just want to say . . . thanks for showing Randy that script. It sounds like he likes it."

"It's a good script. I told you that."

Bill nodded again.

"Yeah. Thanks. You know, Mitch, I can't tell you how much I appreciate you . . . for having that kind of confidence in me. And . . . I've been thinking, everyone has so much confidence in me. Everyone but me. And I've got to change that. I'm thinking . . . there's only one other person who hasn't shown that confidence in me, and . . . it's Larry."

"Hey, man, just show that confidence in the second half. That's all you need."

"You're right. You're absolutely right."

Bill looked over at Ed.

"I'm going to do it. I've decided," Bill said, speaking as if to no one, his eyes glossy. "I'm breaking up with Larry today. As soon as we get back. I should have done it long ago. It's time. I'm starting over, Mitch. This is it."

"Whoa! Bro!" Mitch exclaimed. "Just think about the game first, will ya?"

"Oh, I'm thinkin' 'bout it, Mitch. I'm thinking about it all so clearly."

The second half started with the Quake receiving the kickoff. Marcus and Mitch played deep, but the ball was kicked short to Bill.

Bill caught the ball. The defensive line rushed him.

"I'm following you, Ed!" Bill yelled.

Ed ran ahead. Wesley was the first one down the field. Ed watched his waist and blocked him head on.

Bill saw the entire field before him. Run to Ed's right. There's four other defenders on that side. Mitch would block the quarterback to the left. Al would block the blond boy to the right. Bill would run to his right then shoot straight up the field between Mitch's and Al's block.

It was textbook. They made the blocks. All that was left between Bill and the goal line was the overweight center and the one flanker who had not seen much action yet. Bill ran straight for the flanker, thinking the defender would plant his feet to pull the flag, and he did.

Bill waited to see those feet square off, and then he jabbed his own left foot, changed direction to his right, and left the defender in his tracks.

Now there was only the fat center. Bill felt twenty pounds lighter as he galloped down the field, then changed direction toward the left flag, laughing at the puffing defender as he ran into the end zone.

Touchdown.

It was now the Quake's turn to rejoice as they passed by the defenders to praise Bill's return. Ed ran up to Bill and leaped, butting Bill's chest.

"Frickin' A!" Ed yelled. "What a run!"

Bill brought his arms out and gave his friend a big bear hug.

"That's just the beginning!" Bill yelled back. "The Quake's got this game!"

They made the two-point conversion: 22-14.

It became a whole new game. Bill, Al, and Sam on defense stopped the short passes, while at safety Marcus played strong on Wesley's side so that he was double-teamed. Curt kept his eyes off the blond and focused on playing against Wesley. Ed learned to fake around the fat center, his rushing causing the quarterback to throw early.

On offense, Bill became Jack's number-one receiver. Bill kept on slanting up the middle, getting fifteen- to twenty-yard pickups. The Quake scored their next touchdown when Bill ran across the middle to the right side of the field, caught the ball, then pitched it off to Mitch, who ran unopposed up the sideline. With an unsuccessful two-point conversion, the score was 22-20, the Centurions still ahead. But the Quake no longer were concerned. They felt they had this team beat now.

The Quake's sudden overconfidence created their first mistake in the second half, however, as the Centurion quarterback pitched to his running back. The Quake had stopped considering the running play at this time and, in shock, several of the short defenders rushed the line. The quarterback ran to the middle field, and the running back threw a loft to his open man, setting up short yardage to the end zone and ultimately to a touchdown three plays later.

This mistake only caused the Quake to refocus, and Ed rushed the quarterback with a new determination, successfully deflecting the throw to stop the two-point conversion.

28-20, Centurions.

"Give it up to Bill now," Marcus said to Jack as they went into their huddle. "He's in a zone."

Bill slouched in the huddle with glossy eyes. He felt a pat on his back and turned to see Ed looking at him with an encouraging smile. He smiled back and returned his stare at the small round patch of grass surrounded by his teammates' feet.

Al scored the next touchdown. But again, they failed to make the two-point conversion, and the Centurions were still ahead 28-26 with two minutes to go in the fourth quarter.

"Fuckin' A, man!" Curt yelled out. "We needed that! C'mon guys! There's only two minutes left!"

"We got it, Curt!" Bill yelled back. "We got this game! There's no way we don't have this game!"

The Centurions brought the ball up the field on short passes, two of the catches coming off Bill's man. But Bill was always there to pull the flag right after the catch was made.

"Hey man! Play tighter!" Jerry scolded Bill. "I got the guy if he gets past you."

"You're right!" Bill replied. "They think they've got a weapon here. It's now time to play tighter."

Two plays later, the quarterback saw Bill's man open, thinking Bill was playing a loose zone. The quarterback cocked back his arm. Bill caught the quarterback's eyes and instantly shifted, running toward his man.

The ball was thrown. Bill leapt in front of his man, tipping the ball with his right index finger. As his feet caught the ground, his eyes still on the ball, Bill dashed over to the tumbling ball and fell down with it in his hands.

Interception.

A minute left. Jack called in his first team. They had forty yards to go to win the game. "This is it, guys!" Jack revved up the Quake. "It all comes down to this possession."

The Centurions played straight up man to man. The blond played ten yards back on Curt. Wesley played tight, five yards back on Mitch.

The ball was snapped. Curt and Mitch ran out, their defenders hugging them. But as they crossed, the blond stumbled, allowing Curt to catch a couple strides on him.

The pass was thrown short to Curt. Curt brought his hands close to the ground, and cut down his speed. The ball floated and fell into his hands.

This time Curt would not fumble it. He waited until the ball was firmly grasped, and then he kicked up the speed just as the blond was ready to pull his flag.

Touchdown.

Curt danced in the end zone, staring at his man. He galloped back to the blond.

"You buy the beer!" he exclaimed.

The blond returned a nervous smile.

The game ended. The Quake had won 32-28. The players went their own ways, now able to focus on the night ahead. Bill went home ready to take one of the biggest actions of his life. Ed had felt a rush during the second half, but now alone the thoughts of last weekend came back to haunt him. And Curt and Al dashed off to the Melrose Cantina, where Brooks, the blond boy, had reluctantly agreed to buy them a beer.

By the end of that day, Curt had scored twice, and he brought his boyfriend along for the postgame celebration.

6

The Perfect Couple

I

Mrs. Terrence G. Hoffman III looked proudly once again at the antique silver samovar she had polished the day before. It was showcased on an ornate teak table that stood in the entrance hall adjacent to the living room of their Bethesda residence. For so long the samovar had been hidden in a box in the attic of her Little Rock, Arkansas, home. But on the day the Soviet Union dissolved, Mrs. Hoffman firmly pulled down the folding steps from her second-floor ceiling, climbed up the staircase with sobs she choked back into her throat, and victoriously returned with the samovar. As she unpacked the samovar she had inherited from her grandfather, she mused over whether she could now introduce herself as Ms. Paulene Fedorovna, a maiden name she had packed away as well for the sake of her husband's political aspirations.

The congressman's wife walked over to the samovar, next to the white porcelain teacups and the packets of Earl Grey. She was carrying another dozen powdery Russian tea cookies, which she had so lovingly baked that afternoon to complement the family heirloom. The other desserts—tiramisu, chocolate mousse, crème brûlée with Grand Marnier sauce, and sweet potato pies—were showcased on silver plates on the dining-room table. Most of these desserts were purchased at DC's most renowned bakery—all but the sweet potato pies, that is. Congressman Hoffman himself had driven to a soul food restaurant in Virginia to obtain these pies—which were a reflection of the home-style values he attempted to instill into his politics.

Most of the guests had now arrived. President Clinton and the first lady had written their apologies, stating their regrets that they could not attend this gathering the night before Amy Hoffman's wedding, but they added that they were looking forward to tomorrow's ceremony.

Mrs. Hoffman surveyed the reception as she placed the cookies next to the samovar. All the seats on the living room's two couches and four chairs were occupied by guests engaged in conversation. In the dining room, a dozen guests were eyeing the desserts while speaking cheerfully to one another. Mrs. Hoffman smiled approvingly to herself. No one planned to leave, not before the groom had made his entrance.

The hostess walked toward the dining room to enter the kitchen as she sought her husband and daughter, but she stopped momentarily when her eyes caught upon our hero, Mitch Vanowen, who had flown in from Los Angeles to attend Amy's wedding. She watched the tight curls of his blond hair bob up and down as he spoke avidly to Mrs. Franklin Kessler, a fellow Arkansan who was one step above Mrs. Hoffman in societal circles, since she was a senator's wife. Mrs. Hoffman stopped and contemplated Mitch's style and confidence as he spoke.

"Mother."

Mrs. Hoffman broke out of her trance when she heard her daughter's deep female voice—void of expression, only statement. She turned and smiled at Amy, who stood straight and tall, never a slouch, her face cast with deep brown eyes—almost black—and short, straight hair that exposed her small and round white ears, which appeared to never have been touched by sunlight. Amy looked seriously at her mother, but not as seriously as normal, which allowed Mrs. Hoffman to glimpse the affection for her that her daughter hid so well. Amy's eyes darted over to where her mother had been looking, catching Mitch in conversation with the senator's wife. Mrs. Hoffman glanced in that same direction, then placed her hand on Amy's shoulder.

"It appears your old beau has made himself a friend tonight," Mrs. Hoffman smiled as she spoke to her daughter.

"Friend?" Amy replied matter of factly. "I think not. More like a business acquaintance."

"Yes." Mrs. Hoffman nodded for several seconds, pondering Mitch and Mrs. Kessler again. She then broke out of her daydream and looked squarely at her daughter. "You know, I often think how we were fortunate your father never won the senator's race."

"Mother."

Mrs. Hoffman nodded again, a thin smile spread over her lips.

"Do you know," Mrs. Hoffman began, "back in Roman times, during the reign of Caligula, senators' wives were forced to take part in a brothel?"

"Mother," Amy said, and for the first time she provided expression in her voice, stressing the second syllable in the word she had just spoken. She placed her hand on Mrs. Hoffman's back and led her into the kitchen. "Perhaps this conversation is not appropriate in such company."

Mrs. Hoffman and Amy disappeared from the room, leaving our hero unwitnessed as he continued his networking opportunity with the senator's wife.

"In the past, movies had to have a leading man and a leading woman, but now, after the success of such films as *Pulp Fiction* and *Boogie Nights,* audiences have accepted movies with ensemble acting."

Mitch brought his head and shoulders closer to the sixty-year-old woman with the mink-lined jacket as he provided his expert film analysis to the wealthy Arkansan.

"In *Boogie Nights* and in many other movies, most notably those directed by John Sayles, there will be a camera shot that lasts for ten minutes or more, never a cut or break, which is a style I want to include in my film. During this extensive shot, the camera will follow one character. Then suddenly that character crosses paths, literally that is, with another character, and the camera then follows this other character. A film that sustains such movement creates a sensation within the audience, providing a mood that our various lives are interconnected. Robert Altman has attempted this in many of his ensemble pieces, but it wasn't really accepted then. I believe it is now. Therefore, my idea is really on the cusp of a trend. It has to be capitalized upon at this moment."

Mrs. Kessler looked at him with her soft gray eyes and warm smile, holding her chardonnay close to her breasts. "Those movies you mentioned—*Pulp Fiction*? Oh, there was just too much violence in that."

"Those are just examples," Mitch nodded. "I agree that the violence in films doesn't reflect society in general. However, the film was a breakthrough in . . ."

"And that *Boogie Nights*," Mrs. Kessler continued. "Of course, I never saw it. I understand it was pornographic."

Mitch stopped and stared, taken aback by her comment. Realizing, however, that his stare had a condescending demeanor which would not be fruitful to this conversation, he attempted a smile that portrayed friendliness.

"Well, the movie was not pornographic, but the story was about the pornography industry . . ."

"Frank and I just saw *Good Will Hunting*," Mrs. Kessler spoke with her eyes on the ceiling as she envisioned the film she had just seen. "Now that was a darling movie." She returned her gaze upon Mitch. "And of course that Robin Williams, such a talented man." She laughed. "Oh, did you ever see that movie where he pretended he was a woman? *Mrs. Double . . . Mrs. Dobner—Mrs. . . .*"

"*Doubtfire*," Mitch helped her along. His smile now stuck so heavily that it began to wobble on his face. Our hero had come to the conclusion that nothing of significance would come from this conversation with the senator's wife, so he raised his head and surveyed the crowd, analyzing who else at this reception might be more appreciative of his ambitions and could provide some investment into his project.

Mitchell Solomon Vanowen had arrived last night for his weekend stay in Washington, DC, with three purposes. The first purpose was to attend the wedding of Amy Hoffman, his former girlfriend and the woman whom he had loved and perhaps still did love to some degree. His role in this wedding was to be the man who got away, who would have been the one in her life if there hadn't been that issue about his sexuality.

The second purpose was to tap into a new market that, as of yet, had not yet been capitalized upon, that is, the nouveau riche Arkansan society in DC that rode on President Clinton's coattails. This aim, of course, was secondary to the primary one, and Mitch had no expectations that he would be successful in this endeavor. But as long as he was in DC, it would behoove him to tap into this resource, since Amy's family did provide a connection to this group. After his conversation with the senator's wife, however, Mitch had determined that perhaps this society was just a little *too* nouveau and therefore still naive to networking's intricacies, that is, of successfully mixing business with pleasure.

Then there was his third purpose, which our hero understood was perhaps the most important because it would have the most immediate impact on his life. That aim, that intention, was to decide whether to break off his yearlong relationship with Paul Harris.

"That's it!" Mrs. Kessler exclaimed. *"Mrs. Doubtfire."* She chuckled to herself. "He is such a funny man. And yet he is such a good serious actor, too. Don't you agree?"

"Hmmm?" Mitch quickly corrected himself for straying off for a moment. "Robin Williams? Oh yes. A very good actor. Uh-huh. And quite successful, too."

"Oh, you know who would love to hear your ideas is Thomas Gulick, one of Frank and Terry's major campaign donors. He actually is flying into Washington tonight for the wedding."

"Oh. Thomas Gulick?"

"Yes. A very interesting man. Of course, he inherited his father's ranch, but you would never expect him to be a cattleman. He's always talked about filmmaking being his first love, but of course everything depends on what cards you're handed, and his cards are cattle."

"Which doesn't necessarily mean that you can't cross into other markets," Mitch responded.

"Well, that is true."

"I certainly would be interested in meeting Mr. Gulick. Could you perhaps introduce us tomorrow?"

"Oh dear, I am so sorry, Mitchell, but Frank and I won't be able to attend the wedding," she said, placing her hand on his forearm. "We have to fly back to Little Rock. You know how busy a senator's agenda can be. But do have Terry introduce you. He would love to do that for you. Terry and Paulene speak so highly of you."

"Well, thank you, Mrs. Kessler," Mitch said, looking down at her hand, which remained on his forearm. "I do appreciate that."

He raised his head once more to view Mrs. Kessler's soft eyes, now studying his face in quiet contemplation.

"This must be a very bittersweet moment for you, seeing your college sweetheart marry someone else," Mrs. Kessler said with her comforting smile.

Mitch nodded, his eyes lowered again as he feigned humility. He was proud that the senator's wife viewed him as Amy's former beau, as a missed opportunity who would have been her life partner, if only their ambitions had not taken them down different paths.

"Oh, I know this sounds funny, Mitchell, having met you just now," Mrs. Kessler chuckled while squeezing his forearm. "I've tried to accept it, but I just can't picture you as being a homosexual."

Mitch fell back against his chair seat.

"Oh . . ." he said, stunned. "I didn't know you were aware . . ."

"I hope I wasn't out of line. But truly, I see nothing wrong with that. I know you must think us Arkansans a bit backward . . ."

"Oh, no. Of course not."

Their conversation was disrupted by the rising voices of guests standing in the entrance hallway. Mrs. Hoffman exited the kitchen and shuffled over to the front door, her arms out in a readying embrace. The guests then made room, and into the Hoffman's home appeared the groom, displaying himself next to the samovar to an expectant crowd. He stood tall, about six feet, two inches, and he wore a rich coffee-colored leather jacket around his very broad shoulders. Seeing his future mother-in-law eager to greet him, he lowered his handsome head, with the thick black hair and the prominent square jaw, and placed his big arms around Mrs. Hoffman.

"Oh, Matt, I love feeling your big bear hugs," Mrs. Hoffman spoke merrily as she let go of his embrace. She then took his hand and turned with him to face the guests.

"Everyone!" she exclaimed. "May I have your attention? May I introduce you all to my future son-in-law, Matthew Marezza?" She then gave him a side hug. "And what a son-in-law, am I right?"

Many of the guests rose up to introduce themselves to the groom, including Mrs. Kessler, who provided a little sigh to Mitch and squeezed his arm once again to show her sympathy to what she believed was a sense of melancholy within him. Mitch remained seated, feeling slightly betrayed by Mrs. Hoffman's affection for the groom. He had always thought that he had been Mrs. Hoffman's favorite of the men Amy had dated, but now he had to reconsider this belief.

This was the first time he had beheld the groom. Amy had told him that Matt was very handsome, but he didn't expect him to be *this* handsome. He noticed that he was disturbed that Amy was marrying this man to a certain degree because of his physical appearance. Certainly their relationship was much different than had been his own with Amy. She had always appeared too rational to allow sexual attraction to dominate any of her relationships. Yet while he was disturbed, Mitch was pleased by Matt's beauty, for it created the notion within him that his own relationship with Amy had been more intellectual—much deeper, that is—and that as they all aged and Matt's looks withered, Amy's fond memories would then be of the times she had shared with our hero.

Of course, Matt was an upwardly mobile Wall Street man as well. Amy had relayed to Mitch an interesting connection between her former and current beaus, that while Mitch's middle name was Solomon (his mother had determined that her son should not completely hide his maternal Jewish ancestry), Matt was a rising prospect with Solomon Brothers in New York.

Our hero now observed the groom as he amiably provided one firm handshake after another to the male guests and hugged the women of the Hoffman clan. Mitch had attempted to dispel the intimidation he had of Matt's Wall Street success, and now by watching the groom's extroverted style he felt somewhat comforted by his new opinion that this success had been achieved primarily by Matt's outgoing personality and physical appearance rather than by any certain cleverness on his part.

Amy had stood back in the dining room, allowing the guests around Matt to disperse before she approached her fiancé. She then appeared in the hallway and took Matt's hand—doing so more as a formality than as a sign of affection—as she turned to the guests and smiled. She then raised her chin up and looked over the crowd to see Mitch, still seated in his chair. As she locked eyes with our hero, she nodded to him, indicating that she was ready to introduce him to the groom.

Mitch sipped the last of the bourbon in his tumbler. Our hero understood that the initial introduction to the groom was just one segment of the entire wedding process, and perceiving it as such provided him with some relief from his anxiety. That and the bourbon, that is, because he did not fare well with anxiety. It was an emotion that he realized came upon him much less than it did upon others; because of that, he was unused to it when it did appear. However, when anxiety did betray him, he prided himself that it never intruded upon his reasoning as he spoke to others, and with this in mind he assured himself that he would make a very good impression with Matt.

He walked through the living room toward the bride and groom. Amy had pressed on Matt's hand when the groom turned away to receive a distant congratulations from a guest in the dining room. Amy then whispered in Matt's ear, and the groom turned with a big smile as he saw the former boyfriend approach.

Matt let go of Amy's hand as he stepped forward to greet our hero. Mitch returned the smile, seeing that the groom was ready to introduce himself without allowing his fiancée to act as the intermediary, thereby making the greeting much less formal.

"Mitch!" Matt exclaimed, pushing out his hand and shaking our hero's own with exuberant swings. "Finally we meet! I can't tell you how much Amy has talked about you." He turned to his fiancée and laughed. "So much that you'd think I'd be jealous."

"Matt, it's great to finally meet you as well," Mitch spoke cordially. "You know I've been nervous to see who Amy finally does marry, but from what I've seen and heard, she couldn't have picked a better guy."

"Other than yourself, that is," he laughed, placing his huge hand on Mitch's shoulder.

Amy stood tall, her dark eyes darting back and forth between them, her mouth set in a permanent, thin-lipped smile.

"Matt, Mitch is fully aware that you have been told about his sexual inclinations," she stated frankly. "There's no need to make that civil of a comment."

Matt laughed again and released his hand from Mitch's shoulder to place it around Amy.

"Always the voice of reason, isn't she?" he spoke to Mitch, then turned slightly to view Amy from the corner of his eyes. "What I inferred in that comment is that I understand how close you two have been. And knowing the depth of your relationship just makes me like the both of you more." He laughed again. "I'm just fortunate that the old boyfriend turned out gay, now aren't I?"

Mitch looked around the room, making certain that no one had overheard Matt's comment. He then turned back to the groom.

"Well, actually, I consider myself bisexual," he stated in a quieter voice.

"Oh?" Amy raised her eyebrows. "So after the wedding tomorrow night, you plan to first hit a straight bar and then a gay bar, or vice versa? It must be nice to be able to choose from the entire human population, now isn't it?"

"Oooh!" Matt raised his eyes. "She's tough."

Mitch lowered his eyes and smiled to one side. He was concerned that Matt misunderstood the connotation in Amy's last comment, in which he thought she actually spoke bitterly or even sarcastically about his bisexuality, when in fact it was her way of displaying a sense of humor.

Mitch decided to change the subject. "So, I understand Amy's marrying a Wall Street stockbroker. I guess that means she finally decided to choose New York over LA. You have any inside tips you might want to share?"

Matt laughed and slapped Mitch's shoulder again with his big hand.

"Oh, want some insider trading? Maybe another time. Don't really want to talk business this weekend, you know what I mean? But yeah, Amy got this great job with Thomas, Moore, and Jankovich. Securities litigation. Now can't you see her hauling me into the courtroom for security breaches that I provided to you the night before our wedding?"

Amy looked up at the ceiling.

"One aspect of Matt's personality that I have not informed you about," she said flatly, rubbing her lower right eyelid with her ring finger as she spoke. "He enjoys coming up with the most preposterous possibilities. I've said to him before, he'd make the perfect studio pitchman."

Matt looked at Mitch and brought his head down, closer to our hero, his eyes widened in inquisitive anxiety.

"And you're in the movies?"

Mitch laughed. "I thought you didn't want to talk business this weekend."

"Oh, that's just Amy talking. If only I was that creative. I've never considered entering the entertainment business. I mean, there is a lot of risk in stocks, but there is a certain logic to it. But the movie business . . . I'd be a fish out of water."

Mitch nodded, raising a smile but unsure of the proper reaction to Matt's comment, trying to determine if the groom was displaying genuine humility.

"Well, like any business, you just have to know the ropes," our hero replied.

"And you?" Matt continued his inquisitive stare. "Any prospects at this time?"

"Well, as a matter of fact," Mitch began, "there is. Are you familiar with *The Sicilians* on HBO?"

"*The Sicilians!*" Matt's eyes brightened. "Am I not Italian? Of course! I love that show!"

"Well, Randy Clayburg, one of its directors, is partnering with me on a potential premier movie deal. Randy recently won an Emmy for directing the 'Aunt Lucia' episode."

"You mean, you can win an Emmy for directing just one episode?" Matt shook his head and looked at Amy. "You guys out in Hollywood really know how to honor yourselves. Wouldn't it be nice if we won a golden statue for starting a run on pork bellies?"

"Randy has been wanting to break out of television, and I have connections in film, having worked with Sayles and Tarantino."

"You know Tarantino!" Matt exclaimed.

"Yeah. I was an assistant director on *Reservoir Dogs.*"

"No kidding!" Matt shook his head. "You know, I've heard that about Hollywood. It's more about who you know than what you know."

Mitch stood frozen for a second, feeling that the groom's comment was inappropriate, especially as it was voiced by someone who clearly used his own extroverted demeanor to get ahead in his field.

"Well . . . certainly there's a networking procedure in the entertainment industry that must be mastered, but believe me, my friend, you have to know what you're doing out there."

Amy stared darkly at our hero, realizing that the conversation always turned for the worse whenever Mitch started dropping "my friend" into his comments.

"Yes, Matt, Mitch is a very savvy . . ." Amy raised a smile as she leered at her old boyfriend, "negotiator in the industry, as they refer to it in LA."

"Oh, I can see!" Matt responded, his eyes inquisitive, appearing unaware of Mitch's negative reaction to his earlier comment.

"Hello, Matt!"

Terry Hoffman, wearing an open-collared shirt, a sport coat, and slacks, suddenly appeared before them. Only the gray hair and the three deep lines across his tall forehead gave away the congressman's true age of fifty-eight. Otherwise, he appeared tall and youthful as he returned Matt's firm handshake. The congressman then raised a friendly smile to Mitch and his daughter.

"Oh, I see we're having a momentous occasion here, the two beaus—old and new. It seems they have hit it off, am I right, Amy? But I'm afraid I'll have to break it off for the moment. Matt, I have several guests I need to introduce you to. And as you can see, there's only one piece of sweet potato pie left, which means the reception will soon be ending. Excuse me, kids, as I borrow the groom from you."

Congressman Hoffman placed his arm around Matt's shoulder and led him into the dining room. As they left, Mitch overheard Congressman Hoffman speak.

"I especially want to introduce you to Thomas Gulick, a good friend and one of the major donors to my campaign. He just arrived. Didn't think I'd see him until the wedding tomorrow, but he rushed here straight from the airport. Been asking to meet you."

Mitch stared at them with his mouth open.

"Thomas Gulick? He's here?" he asked the betrothed.

Amy had lifted a tea cookie and taken a small bite. She now was attempting to catch the powdered sugar that fluttered off the cookie and floated down on her blouse.

"Uh-huh," she affirmed, letting the cookie melt in her mouth before she spoke again. She pointed to a man in a ten-gallon cowboy hat. "There."

"Well, he certainly looks like a cattleman to me," Mitch said. "Amy, you need to introduce me to him this weekend. Mrs. Kessler said . . ."

"Mitch, I am not mixing business either during my wedding. And I believe your reaction to Matt's comment on 'who you know' was inappropriate. He feels no competitiveness toward you."

"I'm sorry," Mitch replied, now turning his eyes away from Matt shaking hands with the cattleman. He gazed at his former girlfriend, then smiled as he saw the powdered sugar on her chin. He tapped a finger on his own chin as a sign to her. She stared back at him, understood his gesture, and then took a cocktail napkin from the table to wipe her chin.

"It was just an involuntary reaction that I would have made to anyone who said that," Mitch concluded. "Believe me, Amy, Matt has made a very good first impression on me."

"And as you can now see, there would have been no alarm if you had accepted my invitation to stay at my apartment during the weekend. There was no reason to get yourself a hotel room."

The bride had indeed invited our hero to stay at her residence, but Mitch had considered it inappropriate. He understood, of course, that neither of them had any intention of sleeping together before her wedding. However, the reaction of the groom or members of Amy's family would be less than approving if they were to know that the bride and our hero were sleeping in the same apartment.

Mitch had declined her invitation, stating that he wanted to stay in the city rather than in Bethesda. Amy's reaction to his decline was twofold. First, she had teased him, stating his need to be close to Dupont Circle. Second, she told him that her parents agreed with her that Mitch should stay with her for the weekend, especially since she would only be at her home on Thursday night and that for the most part Mitch would have the apartment to himself.

Mitch did not change his mind, however, and so he began researching hotels in Washington to determine where he should stay during this weekend trip. He decided upon the Peabody, which was rated just below the four major hotels in Washington. It was expensive, but he believed it would make the best impression if it ever came up during his conversations with others this weekend. Besides, it was only one Metro stop from Dupont Circle.

"I told you before, I just wanted to stay in the city."

"At two-hundred dollars a night? Well, I'm sure you have your reasons." Amy then took her dark eyes off of our hero and surveyed the crowd.

"So have you called Paul today?" she asked while she continued her survey. "How's he doing?"

Amy's sudden change of the subject disrupted our hero's thoughts. Due to his conversation with Mrs. Kessler and then his meeting the groom, he had forgotten about Paul. Yet now that he thought back on the happenings of the last half hour, he realized that that was not truly the case. Every time he had spoken about his current project or mentioned Randy Clayburg's name, he had thought briefly about Paul.

"No, I haven't spoken to him today," Mitch responded. "It's just after six in LA. He's catering right now."

Amy nodded.

"Oh yes. What actors must do."

"He's being considered for a recurring role on *Friends*. And you know what that often leads to . . . a major role in a new series."

"Darn," she stated flatly. "Does that mean I'll have to watch the show now? You know how I detest a series about a group of beautiful people in Manhattan."

Mitch waved a finger at her, laughing.

"Oh, Amy. You know that's what I miss about you. Your ironic sense of humor."

Amy looked over Mitch's shoulder.

"I am getting eye contact from Aunt Marilyn. I suppose I am being rude giving all my attention to you this night. And what would people say?"

Mitch let out a playful sigh.

"It appears they're saying nothing."

Amy placed a light kiss on his cheek, her eyes still gazing at her aunt.

"Bye. Go on. Network with someone else. And I'll speak to Dad about introducing you to Tom Gulick."

Our hero now stood by himself in the hallway, watching Amy as she approached and hugged her aunt. A sense of melancholy fell over him, and he realized to break the gloom he had to find another potential investor to shake him back into the present. Before he did, he turned to view the silver samovar. He smiled to himself as he lifted one of the porcelain cups and dropped a tea bag inside. He then turned the spout of the samovar, releasing the hot water into his cup. As he closed the spout, he recalled that day, so many years ago, when he had visited Amy and her parents in their Little Rock home, and how Mrs. Hoffman had brought him up to the attic and had showed him the samovar. She then had told him the story of how her grandfather had presented it to her as a gift when she was only six years old and living in Moscow. Her grandfather was a member of the upper class before the revolution, and at the age of twenty-three he had accepted an officer's post in the Caucasus. Before Grandfather Olenin's trip to join the Cossacks, his father had presented him with the silver samovar to ease the long, arduous journey.

When Paulene Fedorovna was twelve, she accompanied her parents to London for the first time. Her father had just become the English ambassador for the Soviet Union. Since this would be a long journey by airplane, Paulene said she had to bring along the samovar, just as her grandfather had done on his journey so long ago. Within a year of their stay in England, Paulene's father had requested political asylum, and now the samovar was one of the very few remnants of Paulene's brief life as a Russian.

At that time, Mrs. Hoffman entrusted this story to very few; to those she was endeared to. Our hero understood that, and now as he stood staring at the samovar with a teacup in his hand, he thought of his own brief life as the potential son-in-law of a member of the United States House of Representatives, and he pondered what he might have lost by leaving that life and whether any remnants of it remained.

II

Our hero arrived early at the site of the wedding. The ceremony was to take place in a large white gazebo on the main lawn of the Brookside Gardens, a half-hour's drive north of Bethesda. Mitch had been in Washington for more than a day now and still he had not come to a conclusion regarding his relationship with Paul. Understanding that he needed quiet, solitary time to make his decision, he had arrived at the gardens early for a half hour of contemplation.

The elms had just begun to sprout soft green leaves, appearing as shiny crystal jade reflecting the noontime sun on this cool, crisp day. Mitch was walking down a beaten dirt path, now mostly clear of the moldering leaves that had covered the earth in the earlier months of winter. He had chosen this trail because it was the most wooded . . . and the most untraveled. There he would be undisturbed by the gathering wedding party.

Last night he had mused too long on memories and on what could have been, but now Mitch understood that he must determine, based on his current path, what decisions he should make to benefit his future.

He understood that, at this current moment, his best opportunity was to partner with Randy Clayburg. Five weeks ago they had met at a small party of mostly industry people (and mostly gay men) at the home of Tom Jacobs, an acting agent and Mitch's comrade on the football field. Mitch, recognizing the director of HBO specials and *The Sicilians,* had approached Randy and subtly plugged in his own credentials while conversing on such subjects as HBO, recent movies, the filmmaking artistry of John Sayles, the shallowness of Hollywood, the recent acceptance by New Yorkers of Los Angeles as a major metropolitan area committed to the arts, the future opening of the Getty Museum, and Randy's own recent coming out.

Mitch had scored a major coup when Randy stated that they should consider working on a movie project together, since they appeared to have similar ideas on the future of cinema and since Mitch had a foot in the door with some midlevel yet respected producers at Warner Bros. and Paramount. Mitch had met these producers once or twice at parties similar to this one, but his association with them was much less formal than what he had alluded to in his conversation with Randy.

Despite his success in winning Randy's collaboration, Mitch also was disturbed that this future "partnership" was brought up immediately after Randy had confided to him that he had just begun dating men only two months ago. Unlike Mitch, who attended these parties primarily for networking opportunities, Randy had come to satiate his long-repressed sexual longing for men. Mitch, therefore, was rightfully concerned that Randy's professional interest in him might actually be more of a personal interest.

Mitch's suspicions proved correct the next morning when they met for breakfast at Swingers on Beverly Boulevard and Randy asked Mitch whether he was in a current relationship. Mitch had artfully kept Paul's name out of the conversation the night before, realizing that his boyfriend could only prove a hindrance to any professional partnership he might have with Randy. Mitch had been taken aback momentarily by the question, but he realized the subject would have to be broached at some point.

Mitch then went on to speak about Paul Harris, how they had been in a relationship for more than a year now, that the relationship had never really gone beyond the physical and that a breakup was forthcoming. He elaborated, saying that while he has enjoyed the spontaneity and creative side of his partner, he has come to the realization that Paul is simply another actor with no real drive, and that he does not believe their relationship is allowing either of them to improve upon himself.

By speaking of their relationship as such, Mitch felt that he had betrayed Paul. Of course, he had provided enough of Paul's attributes to make it appear that our hero had not completely waylaid his career for an entire year due to an unprofitable relationship. However, the primary intent of his speech was to prove to Randy that he, too, would soon be single and would soon be looking for someone else to "grow" with personally and professionally.

At this moment, as they had breakfast together at Swingers, Mitch had no intention of starting an intimate relationship with Randy. However, he now saw that Randy was considering such an option, and to continue their professional partnership, Mitch did not want to indicate that it was entirely out of the question.

Now five weeks had gone by and Mitch had slept with Randy six times. The sex was passable. Randy seemed intent on experimenting and on learning from Mitch. Mitch was certain he did not love Randy, but he did ask himself often whether he could "learn" to love him.

At the same time, Mitch considered whether he still loved Paul. Despite the overwhelming *yes* that came from his heart, Mitch dispelled the notion, instead focusing on every trait he disliked about his lover. And they were many, such as Paul's total capitulation to his one acting agent, allowing her to schedule all auditions for him while he never sought opportunities on his own; such as Paul's often-repeated excuse that he had to stay at home to wait for a callback, thereby allowing himself to lie on the couch and watch the afternoon talk shows, when he could be more productive on his computer or making his own callbacks; such as the time he sat on a pen he had left in his back jeans pocket and the ink ruined his pants. It wasn't that this accident would upset Mitch, but two months later the same accident occurred, proving that Paul was unable to learn from previous mistakes.

The sunlight struck down on our hero as he left the woods and emerged on the massive rolling lawn of the botanical garden. He approached the large pond, full of regal white swans, and crossed over the Japanese bridge on his way to the grand gazebo to join the wed-

ding party. It was now time for him to return to his role in the ceremony, to stand quietly on the edge of the gazebo, hands crossed at his
waist, as he watched the only woman he had ever loved marry another
man. It was time again for him to escape from his present conflict to
relive the moments he had with Amy, and to wish her and her husband all the best for the years to come.

The actual ceremony was only a small gathering, about the same
number of people who had attended the prewedding reception the
night before. Mitch had been the only guest on the bride's side who
was not a family member or a government official. Again Bill and Hillary Clinton had sent a letter of regret, stating, however, that they
would attend the dinner afterward at the Occidental Grille.

The gazebo was intricately adorned with filagreed woodcarvings. It
was a popular site for spring and fall weddings, although rarely used
so early in the year. The wedding atendees had been charmed by the
lovely weather, yet there was a feeling of nervous anticipation. The li-
lacs, lilies, and cockleshells had lifted up their stems and begun to bud
prematurely, although unable as of yet to release their fine scent due
to a chill that had not yet receded this early in the day.

A string quartet began a serenade, and the guests, in their suits and
long dresses, stood tall and turned their faces in an attempt to spot either the bride or groom. They all faced in the same direction once they
located Matt, who had rounded the crest of the hill between the parking lot and the gazebo. He was laughing merrily with his father and
mother as he walked toward the wedding party. Looking up and seeing the guests' eyes upon him, he examined his tuxedo coat and, seeing it open, closed it with two buttons, thereby displaying the
massiveness of his chest, so well adorned by the silk black vest and the
wide black-and-white striped tie. He pushed his hair back with the
wide palm of one hand and again laughed with a big, happy grin, now
placing his arm around his mother's back.

Mitch felt very small as he leaned against a railing inside the gazebo. He looked to his left and viewed the guests. Each of the couples
held their hands together and wore sweet smiles while watching the
groom approach. Mitch's gaze was observed by the middle-aged
woman next to him. She had placed her arms around her husband's el-

bow to her left, perhaps in recollection of her own wedding. But now she released her hands from her husband and leaned toward our hero.

"Are you here as a friend of the groom or the bride?" she asked him.

He bowed his head slightly to her.

"The bride. We attended Berkeley together."

She nodded back with a smile.

"Ahh. College chums," she spoke with a gravelly voice that displayed an earthy wisdom. "They do seem blessed, don't they? She an up-and-coming attorney and daughter of a congressman. He a successful Wall Street broker and so handsome. It's almost sickening, isn't it? Ah, if it had been so easy for us when we were young. They just seem too much the perfect couple."

Mitch looked more seriously at this woman to his left, now realizing that he had caricaturized the wedding party, not allowing them to have lives of their own. This woman was playful and so willing to provide that sense of play to a stranger who happened to stand next to her. Yet she spoke what others thought. She definitely was speaking what he had been thinking.

"Yes. That does seem true," Mitch replied. "I'm just very happy for Amy right now."

She looked at him under her black-mascaraed lashes, her lips parted as she studied the truth to his words.

"Yes, I'm sure you are," she said. Then she turned back to watch the groom approach. "But then, as we all know, looks can be deceiving."

"Honey. Shhh," her husband whispered to her. The woman gave Mitch a long look as if to say, "And now my husband shushes me," and then turned her attention to the quartet.

Mitch's eyes also fell on the strings vibrating to the crossing bows. It had been on his mind, but he had dared not accept the fact that, indeed, Amy and Matt made the perfect couple. He now attempted to envision the reaction of this crowd if, instead of Amy and Matt, he and Paul stood at the center of this ceremony—groom and groom—as they shared their wedding vows to love each other for life. Would this crowd, if being gay was not an issue, also be thinking to themselves how they made the perfect couple?

But this crowd could never think it. They would only look at how the two matched externally. They would not be able to conceive of the internal connection between he and Paul. They could not conceive of the moments when Paul, completely on the spot, would draw his arm around Mitch's back and instantly pull him down, look into our hero's eyes with such sweetness, and plant his warm lips upon him.

Mitch raised his eyes up from the strings. The groom had entered the gazebo and was walking firmly to the front of the guests, next to the celebrant in his white and green robe.

Mitch turned his gaze back to the woman at his side. He considered her words again. Now she spoke differently, but with similar words in his mind, speaking now of Randy Clayburg and himself:

"They do seem blessed, don't they?" she said in his mind. "He an up-and-coming screenwriter and producer. He a successful television director with an Emmy to his name. It's almost sickening, isn't it? Ah, if it had been so easy for us when we were young. They just seem too much the perfect couple."

Mitch tried not to recall the words she had said afterward, but they came all the same: "But then, as we all know, looks can be deceiving."

Now the bride appeared—magically out of nowhere—at the steps of the gazebo. She wore a beaded silk gown, and her black hair appeared to have an added sheen, as it was contrasted with a crown of baby's breath. Amy Hoffman wore a smile that seemed to arise out of her embarrassment—either of having to wear such finery or due to the realization that she was the center of attention. This humility fit her well, creating a beautiful pastel rose color upon her high, round cheekbones, which contrasted brilliantly with her black, intense eyes. She stood so straight and lean. The beauty of such a sight caused the guests to forget the lankiness of her gait as she walked down the aisle.

Mitch could not recall ever seeing her as lovely as now. He felt so proud of her at this moment. Yet at the moment when he felt so much pride, she was no longer his.

It had been only two and a half years ago when they attempted to start where they had left off. She was then a law student at Georgetown and had taken an internship at O'Melveny and Meyers in Los Angeles for the summer. It had been only two years previous to this when they had agreed that their relationship should end, that he had to explore his feelings for men, to determine whether they did in fact dominate his sexual interests or whether they were just a passing interest, a curiosity that had to be explored.

Being the pragmatist, of course, Amy was more certain that Mitch's inclinations were toward men and that, if he was honest with himself, he would come to the conclusion that he was indeed a homosexual. Mitch, on the other hand, had attempted to convince both her and himself that, since no good could come from being gay, his curiosities were merely temporal in nature and that once he had explored these prurient fantasies they would no longer be a distraction that was impeding his goals in life.

Which is not to say that Mitch had not explored his homosexual fantasies before this moment. Mitch had indeed slept with several men during his visits to the yuppie gay bar named the Alta Plaza while he lived in San Francisco. However, he had accepted the belief that one, he had taken such actions because of a demented thrill in being "bad," in cheating on his girlfriend. And two, this was San Francisco and he was being too affected by the culture of the city. But once he and Amy graduated and moved to Los Angeles to begin their careers, all these distractions would end, and their style of living would improve.

But the distractions did not end. Mitch had been in Los Angeles for well over a year before Amy had arrived for her summer internship, and his affairs with men continued. He had attempted to persuade her to relocate to UCLA, but her goals and commitments to her career were on par with his own, and she continued her second year of law school at Georgetown.

During Amy's second year of studies, Mitch had begun to realize that a large gay culture existed within the Los Angeles entertainment industry and that it existed even at the top levels. He began to understand that his own sexual interests in men could create opportunities for him. At last he was able to substantiate his semibisexual lifestyle, and until Amy arrived for the summer he would use this lifestyle to his advantage.

Amy had completed her walk down the aisle, and a complete hush fell over the wedding party. It was a beautiful sight seeing the brilliant silk train of the bride and the wide back of the groom tapered down into classic tuxedo tails, the celebrant raising his hands and then touching the shoulders of the betrothed against a backdrop of brilliant rolling lawn and a sun-drenched pond containing a half-dozen swans creating a glimmering wake as they swam toward the wedding party.

Again Mitch looked to his side. The entire wedding audience was of one mind, one thought, as they all gazed at the betrothed, their eyes glassy with joy, with a sense of peace that existed for this one moment, as the celebrant began the ceremony.

Mitch's eyes focused on the bride, hoping that her face would turn so that he could see her eyes once more before she could no longer be his.

Mitch had never really given up on the thought that they would be together again, someday, perhaps. Certainly he had never been in a relationship that had been as strong as theirs. Perhaps the passion never had been as strong as he had felt for Paul, but the intellectual side, the sharing of dreams and goals, had been deeper with Amy. Perhaps he had a better opportunity of meeting his career goals through Randy, but he could never love Randy as he had Amy. His relationship with her had been the perfect balance—love and learning, passion and progress. Now she would give her lifelong vows to another man.

He recalled that fateful day—August 21, 1995. Amy had just finished her internship at O'Melveny and Meyers. She still had three weeks before she had to return to Georgetown. They had spoken earlier in the summer of traveling together at the end of her internship—either to Hawaii or the Caribbean—nowhere far, due to the short time period, but no real arrangements had been made, due to both of their understandings, although never shared with each other, that they had no vision of a future together.

"Mitch, I have loved you like no one before," Amy had said. "But we must be sensible here. Nothing has changed, and you need to admit that to yourself."

Mitch could see that her opinion was steadfast, and he would be unable to change it.

"Amy, you know I will never admit that."

"Can you admit that you're bisexual?"

He had grinned nervously at that moment.

"Perhaps."

She nodded. "Good. At least that's a start."

There was an awkward moment of silence then, much like the hush during the wedding celebration today, but without such a beautiful landscape. Then Amy had spoken again.

"Look, I think I'm just going back home tomorrow. I already have the ticket to Little Rock. We . . . Mitch, we really have to start living our lives. I'm sorry. But you know I'm blunt. It has been a wonderful experiment between us two, but now we've got to move on. You do understand, don't you?"

Mitch nodded.

"I do."

Amy's face had turned, allowing Mitch to see her dark eyes. But only after she had said those two fateful words, making her Matthew Marezza's wife.

III

The portraits of the presidents, from George Washington to William Jefferson Clinton, welcomed the guests to the burgundy-carpeted and oak-walled hallway of the Occidental Grille. With the restaurant located only two blocks from the White House and with the Secret Service inside the hallway and outside the building, the guests nervously anticipated the entrance of the president and the first lady as they walked into the banquet room and noticed the five adjacent table settings reserved for the Clinton family and the bride and groom.

The banquet room, with six round tables and seating for forty-eight, featured the same burgundy carpet and dark oak walls. The restaurant had reserved two waiters and one bartender for the wedding guests. As our hero entered the room, the waiters were passing out bacon-wrapped scallop hors d'oeuvres and champagne to the guests. Most of the guests had already entered the banquet room, although the two couples of honor had not yet been seen.

The woman who had talked with Mitch at the wedding caught our hero's eye. She again left her husband's side and, carrying a fluted glass of champagne, walked toward Mitch. Mitch now saw that she was younger than he had previously thought, and the heavy, dramatic mascara she wore was an act of rebellion against the mores of this social circle.

"Ah, now I know who you must be," she exclaimed as she sidled up next to him. "You're Mitch Vanowen, Amy's old boyfriend, am I right? The gay one?"

Our hero jerked up in response to the woman's statement, causing a waiter who had been approaching them with a tray featuring the fluted glasses of champagne to abruptly stop.

"I'm right behind you!" the waiter exclaimed. Then catching his composure, he extended the tray to them. "Champagne?"

The woman traded her empty glass for one that was half full.

"Perhaps you need one, too," she told our hero.

He reached for a glass, then, after waiting for the waiter to continue his rounds, responded.

"I'm having a strange phobia that all of the wedding attendees gathered together before my arrival this weekend to discuss my sexuality."

The woman laughed a high-pitched laugh, then dropped her hand on his forearm with a playful slap.

"Oh, I'm sorry," she replied, still chuckling. "Perhaps I should introduce myself. I'm Julie, Matt's aunt. I know it seems strange, me being his aunt and all, although we're only eight years apart. Matt had told me about you. Not that he's telling everybody, but you see, we're the best of friends."

Mitch looked at her closely and smiled. An unusual sense of comfort came upon him. Here was a stranger to him, and yet he felt no need to establish himself with this person in any way other than in friendship. He could consider no ulterior motives to striking up a conversation with her, other than to get to know her, befriend her, and have a good time. Yet she was Matt's confidante, a chance to gain information on how Matt and others in his circles perceived our hero. But for some reason, Mitch now had no interest in finding out what impression he had made with the groom and his entourage. Instead, he wanted only relief from his week's constant agenda. He wanted only a cordial conversation with someone such as this woman.

"So someone else has mentioned your sexual inclinations?" she asked while staring at the fluted glass.

"Senator Kessler's wife. Then tell me how in the world would she know?"

"I understand she and Amy's mother are very good friends. Paulene does know, doesn't she?"

"Well . . . yes. Perhaps that's it then."

Julie looked around, rocking her empty glass, searching for the waiter. Now out of the coat she wore at the wedding, she sported a short, red silk dress that draped well on her small, lean Italian body and exposed her sheer white stockings up to her middle thighs.

"So . . . you here alone?" she asked.

"Well . . . yes, I am."

She gave up her waiter search when she recognized the stammer in his reply.

"Didn't feel right bringing your lover. I got it." She then sighed. "Well, you're lucky. Jack—my husband—is just a complete bore at these ceremonies. You know what he did? He bought the Waterford crystal bowl listed in their wedding registry at Saks. Five hundred bucks! Just to impress this Washington crowd. He hopes they open the gifts before the Clintons leave, you know. Ha! Fat chance. You know I have to explain to Matt that the bowl was Jack's idea. I'll just say to him, 'You know, the perfect bowl for the perfect couple,' and he'll die with laughter. That's Matt for you."

Mitch nodded approvingly.

"Matt seems like a very cool guy. Amy is a lucky girl."

"And you?" Julie interrupted herself as she caught a waiter nearby and snapped her fingers. In doing so, she obtained the response of both waiters, one walking toward her with brie-filled phyllo puffs and the other with the champagne. As she grabbed first the puff and then the glass, she finished her question. "Who's this boyfriend you left behind?"

Mitch was raising his hand to grab a puff when she asked this question. He looked up and found the waiter was giving him a naughty gaze. Mitch's face had reddened when he realized that a third party—the waiter—had obtained information about his private life. However, proud of his analytical skills and his ability to adapt under pressure, he was able to return to his normal pinkish beige when he realized that this young man was almost certainly of the same persuasion as he. Mitch, now determined to project his own naughtiness as he gazed back at the waiter, raised one side of his mouth in a sly grin.

"Paul?" he answered in a question form, still staring at the waiter as if speaking to him. The waiter walked on, only to turn his eyes back for a brief moment to catch Mitch still watching him. But our hero realized that such flirtations were inappropriate at this party, especially with a servant, and so he returned his attention to Julie.

"Paul Harris. We've been together over a year now."

Julie nodded while raising her teeth above the puffy top of the pastry and gently biting down.

"And are you happy with him?" she continued.

He did not answer her at first. Instead he stared at her for a moment, although his eyes were not focused on her. Instead they were focused inside her pupils. For a moment, in fact, they were focused on his own reflections in her pupils, until those reflections gradually disappeared as he went into a trance within her eyes, contemplating her question.

"I'm not sure how to answer that," he said, finding her before him once again, believing perhaps he could find some answer within her. "How do you answer that?" he rephrased. "You and Jack. Are you happy with him?"

She blew out a "wheee!" and turned her eyes away for a moment. "Jack! He's a complete mess. Look at him over there."

Mitch followed her eyes over to her husband, who was younger than his premature gray made him appear. Jack was by himself for the moment, circling one table to read the names on tiny cards placed on the silver cardholders at each setting. Then Jack would look up to the ceiling, moving his lips as he memorized—apparently with some difficulty—the name written at each setting.

"Oh, my God. Now that's embarrassing. You see what he's doing? Like no one will notice that!" she exclaimed. As though believing her husband's actions required additional alcohol consumption, she drained her third glass of champagne. Upon finishing and taking the glass away from her lips, her eyes glistened with a squinty mirth. She laughed, looking at nothing but the wall at that moment.

"That Jack. You see what I mean? Happy? You're right. It's just too relative a term. But I do know I'm crazy about him. I'd have to be. Sure he's an unsophisticated mess, but I tell you, I wouldn't trade him for anyone in the world."

She looked back at Mitch.

"My luck, huh?"

"I think we have the same luck."

"Of course you do. All happy relationships do."

Mitch gazed at her, asking himself whether she had just said something very profound or just provided an instinctive response as a means of continuing their conversation. He wondered if this discourse, which had not been on his agenda, might actually be most effective in accomplishing one of the three purposes he had set upon himself during this trip. He smiled at her, then looked down at the bubbles upon the last sip of champagne in his glass.

"One time a good friend told me that he felt the perfect relationship would allow one member of the couple to take off a year to pursue his or her dreams, while the other person paid the bills. And then it would be the other person's time to take off, to pursue a dream. A symbiotic relationship. A win-win situation."

Mitch laughed to himself. "That idea has made quite an impression on me." Our hero then shook his head. "But Paul . . . I just don't see that happening in our relationship. Paul lives too much day to day."

"It's a nice idea," Julie replied. "But for it to work, someone needs to make the first sacrifice."

Mitch looked up at her, his mouth open in wonderment, realizing the truth in her comment. Sacrifice? Commitment? Had he ever thought of taking the first step? He had been so enraptured by his own success that he had never taken the time to help Paul with his own dreams? Paul was such a slacker that he appeared to have no goals. To be the perfect couple, though, Mitch realized it would be his commitment to provide Paul with such goals, or more appropriate, allow him to understand that he does have such purposes in his life.

"Hello, Mitch."

Our hero turned around to see Congressman Hoffman standing next to him. He was accompanied by a gentleman whom Mitch did not recognize. Mitch quickly realized that his current undisciplined state of mind had to be immediately altered in the congressman's presence, especially since he was accompanied by a guest whose well-tailored clothes and fine Swiss gold watch demanded more formal attention.

"Hello, Terry," Mitch greeted him. For years he and the congressman had spoken to each other by first name, but at this moment, our hero felt unwise to have done so within the presence of the gentleman. "I have to say it was a beautiful wedding. And Amy . . . when she walked down the aisle . . . well, it's hard to tell you how I felt, but I definitely felt very proud of her."

The congressman tightened his lips, as if to suppress an emotion too overwhelming to display before such an audience. He then placed his big arm around Mitch's shoulders.

"And you know, I always thought it would be you, Mitch, who would be my son-in-law. But fate, if you believe in such, often takes strange twists, doesn't it?"

Congressman Hoffman then turned to his side to acknowledge the gentleman.

"Mitch, I wanted to introduce you to a good friend of mine, Tom Gulick. Tom here heard you're in the movie business, and he wanted to meet you."

Mitch instantly stood to a more ceremonial attention, his shoulders squaring to greet the cattleman, and by doing so, causing the congressman to release his arm from our hero. At this moment, Mitch was scolding himself inside for not recognizing Mr. Gulick, but he no longer wore his cowboy hat and instead was sporting round, silver-rimmed glasses that brought on a much different appearance from his first impression upon our hero. But Mitch also was congratulating himself from within, for it was this well-respected Arkansan who had sought him, proving that our hero was highly regarded himself.

Mr. Gulick reacted first, reaching out his hand and shaking Mitch's own vigorously.

"I'm happy to make your acquaintance, Mitch," he spoke passionately. "I was able to hold a short conversation with Maude Kessler, who mentioned you to me. And, the sweet old gal, she couldn't remember the director's name, but from inference I recognized that you had worked with John Sayles."

"Yes. Yes, I have," Mitch replied, able to carry the same enthusiasm that was displayed by Mr. Gulick, with a style all his own, with an air of confidence, showing himself as one who was on top of his craft.

"Was it during *Lone Star*?" Mr. Gulick asked, taking one step closer to Mitch, which allowed our hero to recognize just how big this man was in his six-foot, three-inch, 220-pound frame. "I actually met John Sayles on the set there. Quite a visionary."

"Actually, I was an assistant director during *The Secret of Roan Inish*," Mitch replied, making sure he did not provide the full information, that is, that he was actually just the second assistant director. "And yes, I agree. A true visionary."

Julie had stepped back once the three men began their conversation. She had been placed in that embarrassing position of not knowing how to make her departure, since she had not yet been introduced to the congressman and Mr. Gulick. But never one to play shy, she reached her hand between the two new members of the circle and pulled down on our hero's tie.

"It was nice meeting you, Mr. Vanowen," she stated. "I believe I'd better search for my husband."

"Julie!" Mitch exclaimed. Again, his emotions contradicted himself, as he realized he could no longer go back to the intimate style of conversing that he had adopted with this woman. He quickly controlled the enthusiasm that was marked on the last word he had spoken. "Let me introduce you. Terry, Mr. Gulick . . . this is Matt's aunt, Julie . . ."

"Fennell," she said, raising her hand. "Like the herb."

"Julie! Of course!" Congressman Hoffman exclaimed, using both hands to shake her own. "Amy and Matt have spoken so much about you. And you're his aunt? My my. I can't even see an older sister in you."

She laughed and slapped him on his tuxedo coat.

"Oh, you are a flatterer."

Congressman Hoffman then placed his arm around her shoulders.

"Follow me for a moment. There's someone I want you to meet."

Julie was escorted away by the congressman, leaving our hero and the cattleman alone to begin their important conversation.

The timing could not have been less perfect. Two minutes into their conversation, Mitch and the cattleman were disrupted by the entrance of the guests of honor. Not only did the bride and groom appear, but they were accompanied by the president and first lady . . . and Chelsea, too. Amy appeared as lovely as she had in the garden, with her long, thin hand resting on Chelsea's shoulder. Chelsea, who stood a few inches below the bride's tall frame, was looking up at Amy with a happy smile as they finished their short conversation, and then they both turned to greet the party. Everyone in attendance placed their champagne glasses on the tables in unison and began clapping to honor the guests. President Clinton and Matt Marezza, who were of the same height, stood side by side, and each raised one hand in response to the crowd.

As the ovation ended, Mitch turned back to Mr. Gulick. However, he refrained from starting up where he had left off, believing that the cattleman might think it inappropriate, that perhaps this major donor to the Clinton campaign would need to turn his attention to other matters he considered more important.

"Now what were you saying?" Mr. Gulick asked, still staring over at the newly arrived. He then returned his focus on our hero. "*The Sicilians*. Yes. Yes. I've heard of the show, but actually, I'm not as interested in television."

Mitch suppressed a smile, realizing that the cattleman was more interested in their conversation than the arrival of the president.

"Yes, but the director, Randy Clayburg, and I are working on a major movie premiere. And I must say, if anyone has inspired me to make this movie, it's John Sayles."

Mitch's last comment captured the cattleman.

"Tell me more!" Mr. Gulick exclaimed.

Our hero went on to tell of his proposal, enough to arouse the Arkansan's interest but not enough to allow a potential benefactor to plagiarize without compensation. Mitch was at the top of his game. He knew how to present an idea. Yet he felt a bit awkward speaking of his ideas in such a setting.

After a few minutes, however, he became distracted. Our hero's eyes would dart out momentarily to catch a view of the Clintons, or of the bride and groom. So often the fivesome were standing together in a circle, with champagne glasses in hand.

"What was that you just said?" Mr. Gulick said.

Mitch realized that he was not making himself clear. His mind was playing tricks with him. At times, a vision of himself and Amy drinking champagne with the president and first lady would appear, and then he would have to backtrack to remember what he had just said to the cattleman.

He realized, to focus on his pitch, he now had to consider how to move his body to Mr. Gulick's left—without being too obvious—so that he could not see the Clintons and Marezzas in conversation. But when he finally proved successful in repositioning himself, he then was disrupted by the cattleman himself.

"Well, Mitch, I think you'll have to finish your story later in the night," Mr. Gulick told our hero. "You ever met your president before?"

Mitch turned his head to see the first family approach. Although he was aware that the first family was coming their way to greet Thomas Gulick, one of their major donors from well before Mr. Clinton's term as governor of Arkansas, our hero now felt great pride that he would soon be among a small and intimate circle featuring the president of the United States.

"Hi, Tom," President Clinton greeted Mr. Gulick with a firm handshake. "Good to see you in Washington. How're those long-horns?"

"Howdy, Mr. President. Hi, Hillary . . . Chelsea," the cattleman returned the greeting. "Well, they're still out there in the fields, just chewin' up the grass."

Chelsea had taken an instant interest in our hero, her eyes gazing upon him.

"So, you're Professor Vanowen's son?" Chelsea asked. "She's my psych teacher at Stanford."

Mitch nodded with a smile. "My mother mentioned you were in her class. It's a pleasure to meet you." He then extended his hand to Chelsea.

"Did your mother say she's been studying hard?" the first lady smiled, indicating she was speaking in jest. "Hi, Mitch. I'm Hillary. Terry and Paulene have spoken very highly of you."

Mitch extended his hand to the first lady.

"Hello, Mrs. Clinton," Mitch said, now realizing that the unbecoming nervousness he had felt last night when meeting the groom for the first time had now settled upon him once again. He then turned his eyes to President Clinton. "It's an honor to meet you . . . and you, Mr. President?"

He had ended his speech in the form of a question, since President Clinton's attention still was turned to Mr. Gulick. Our hero now scolded himself from within once more for having introduced himself so ineptly to the president. Mr. Clinton, however, appeared not to notice this awkwardness, perhaps because during his first five years in office he had experienced it so often. He shook Mitch's hand.

"Well, Mitch, it's a pleasure to finally meet you," the president said. "I've heard such good things about you from Amy and her parents."

Our hero could barely refrain from raising his eyes wide in amazement, feeling a sense of joy and satisfaction inside, to receive such a greeting from the president and first lady, as if they were honored to meet him more than he was of meeting them.

"Well, thank you very much, Mr. President."

"Call me Bill," the President requested as he finally released his grasp of Mitch's hands. "Now, I hear you're out there in Hollywood making pictures. I guess that's why you got ol' Tom's ear here."

"Mitch has been working with John Sayles," Tom responded, almost proud to tell our hero's own tale. "But now he and his boyfriend are working on a movie of their own."

Words could not describe the sense of dread that now attacked our hero. His shoulders slumped in a thud. His racing heart seemed to fall like a rock in his stomach. His lower lip, quivering, sagged down as if ready to sob. He opened his mouth in an attempt to defend himself, but he could not utter a word. He could barely breathe.

"Uh . . ." he stammered for much too long, "my boyfriend?"

He had to speak again. He had uttered as though he had just confirmed that he indeed was working with a boyfriend . . . in front of the first family.

Mr. Gulick continued without taking into account our hero's emotions. "I wanted to tell Mitch here how much I envy people like him and Randy—a couple working together on such a creative project as a major motion picture." The cattleman nodded his head in a proud smile. "What I wouldn't give to be in a relationship like that. But you know Jeffrey. I can't get him the least bit interested in my cattle business, let alone my vision of producing films."

Mitch stared at the cattleman, his eyes wide and horror-stricken. Mr. Gulick looked at him with a warm, even proud glow.

"But . . ." he could only utter.

"Randy?" Hillary asked. She turned to our hero. "Mitch, I recall that Amy said your boyfriend's name is Paul."

Mitch looked over at the first lady. Her words were like daggers twisted into his heart, killing all opportunities he had hoped for in his life.

"Mitch, are you all right?" Mrs. Clinton asked. "You seem a little pale."

Our hero shook his head.

"Randy Clayburg is nothing more than a business partner," he finally was able to breathe out a full sentence.

Mr. Gulick turned to our hero.

"You mean you and he aren't . . ." he shrugged one shoulder, now appearing confused, "you know?"

"Certainly not!"

Chelsea let out a quick laugh. "Well, it's nice to see there's one man here with a sense of fidelity."

"Chelsea!" Mrs. Clinton stated firmly. "We are in public."

The president appeared unfazed by his daughter's outburst. He had recognized the awkwardness of the situation and now hoped to bring some sense of comfort to our hero's sudden awareness that the first family knew about his sexual inclinations.

"And so this Paul, I'm sure he is very special to you," the president spoke as an affirmation, rather than as a question. "And what line of work is Paul in?"

All enthusiasm that our hero had felt, first in his conversation with Thomas Gulick and then in his introduction to the first family, had disappeared. He had resigned himself to the fact that everyone present at the wedding preception knew the truth of why he and Amy had ended their relationship. He now believed that they all had been looking at him this weekend with a sense of pity, as though a defect in his nature had ended his chances of marrying a congressman's daughter, had depleted his chances of becoming a measurable success.

He answered the president very flatly.

"He's an actor."

"Oh, is he?" Mr. Clinton continued. "Have I seen him in anything?"

"Probably not."

"Is he cute?" Chelsea asked, displaying a flirtatious smile. "Do you have any pictures of him?"

He gazed at the first daughter. Now he could answer with an affirmation. Yes. Paul was very cute. Our hero envisioned with disgust how, when people came to his funeral and asked about his accomplishments, one would say that at one point he was able to muster up a boyfriend who was, indeed, very cute.

"No, I'm sorry," he responded. "I don't have a picture."

"Well, Tom," the president returned his comments to the cattleman. "I told you I would introduce you to the ambassador and his wife. I'm sorry to take ol' Tom away from you, Mitch, but you know how it is. Even during our time to enjoy ourselves, there's always business at hand."

They took their leave after pleasant good-byes, leaving our hero alone. Mr. Gulick had not even mentioned that he would return to hear the ending of Mitch's proposal. In fact, the cattleman had seemed disappointed to hear that Randy had not been Mitch's lover, that their relationship was merely business, which, of course, was not the actual truth. Yet Mitch did not care to tell him more.

For this brief moment, Mitch felt completely lost. He feared that everything to which he aspired—all the goals he had set to accomplish, every path he had attempted to follow—was lost.

He looked around the room, seeing that everyone in the party was merry and speaking to others—everyone but himself. He was alone. Completely, utterly alone.

He now saw the bride and groom, standing side by side near the entrance to the banquet room, as they greeted various guests, clanking champagne glasses with them and speaking of their future aspirations. Matt always appeared the more jovial, using the full swing of his arms and shoulders to greet the guests, while Amy stood more at attention, providing a polite nod to each person. For a brief moment there was a lapse between her conversation with one guest and her greeting of another, and at that instant she turned her head and looked across the room. Her dark eyes caught those of our hero's. Always the master disguiser, the poker-faced charmer, she now softened her eyes and tilted her head slightly toward one shoulder as a sign to Mitch. She sensed the brief loss of direction within him, and now she tried to comfort him from across the room. But this comfort could not last. The next guest approached her, and once again she was providing a pleasant exchange of greetings with the polite nod and the thin smile, speaking of her future aspirations with her new husband.

As Mitch looked at Amy, he thought of what he had lost and how he had replaced her with Paul, a no-name actor whom he didn't even respect enough to keep a photo of in his wallet.

He then recalled his conversation with Tom Gulick and the Clintons and considered how the evening would have ended if he had indeed affirmed to the cattleman that Randy Clayburg was his lover and how they were partners in life as well as in business—and to say it proudly, to get over the mere triviality that they were gay, to assert that they were a powerful, intelligent, creative pairing. A perfect couple. What respect he would have brought to the cattleman, to this potential benefactor.

One of the waiters walked up to him with a tray of champagne glasses. His presence allowed our hero to return to the reality of the moment. He now felt a certain confidence again as he picked up a glass of champagne and walked across the room, ready to greet and converse with the other wedding guests, feeling somewhat satisfied that at this moment he had just accomplished the third goal for which he had come to Washington in the first place.

7

The San Gabrielites

The LA Quake were rocking, up 22-0 at halftime against the San Gabrielites, the same team that got trounced 84-0 by the Santa Monica Seahawks last weekend. The Quake was now considered a force in the league, especially after trouncing the Hollywood Hopefuls by six touchdowns last weekend. Marcus had told the team before the game that the Quake had to keep on winning big to show that they are a powerhouse. Marcus's words had an inspiring effect. Everyone, except Jerry and Dave, had caught every pass that came their way.

Best of all, Curt was back to his old self. Curt had dominated his defender—a frustrated guy with a black beard and a tattoo on his arm that bore the name "Marsha." Curt caught the first two touchdown passes of the half, but he was more proud to see his own man—Al—raise the score to a three-touchdown lead.

Mitch, who had missed last weekend's game to attend Amy's wedding, and Curt now were the two undisputed starters at wide receiver. They won by default because Sam had left the team.

Sam was currently staying in New York for two weeks finishing up a landscape design project in Westchester County. But he had told Jack of his intentions to move there within the next month, since his business was taking off more on the East Coast (that is, New York) than it was on the West Coast (that is, LA). Jack was resigned to the fact that Sam did have some resolve of his own, although in all previous instances he had appeared to be content as the kept boyfriend.

Despite the turmoil of his personal life, Jack's game was his best in years. He had lost the telescopic eye that always caused him to throw long bombs to his boyfriend, since his boyfriend was no longer on the field. He mixed up his passes, throwing short and long, finding the open man, panicking less when a rusher closed in on him. He had not thrown an interception during the first half. Jack's level of play surprised many on the team, but Marcus had predicted it before the game began. He knew how Jack could play when there was no boyfriend around. Marcus told Mitch that Sam's departure from the team was the best thing that could have happened to the Quake.

Most of the players for both teams had returned to the field, stretching and doing light calisthenics in preparation for the second half, but very few of them were actually thinking about the game. The outcome already seemed apparent.

"Fuck, man! I can't believe you're doing this!" Jerry complained to Dave, who stared blankly at the grass, pulling back from his groin stretch. They were seated on the field together, loosening their limbs. "I mean, if you pull out of this, what am I going to say to Jake and Stephen, that now we'll each have to pay forty dollars a night cuz our fourth guy decided he's got to go home and see his mom and dad? Not that the extra amount's going to affect me, but the other guys might be upset."

"I just . . . you know," Dave shrugged his shoulders. "I told my Mom I'd come home when we don't have a weekend game, and it being Easter and all."

"C'mon, Dave! Why don't you just go on another weekend? You can skip a game. We'll still win it without you."

"It's just . . . well, I told you about my dad . . . I really should go see him."

"And then when you get home, what are you going to do for him anyway?"

Jerry jumped up from the ground and began jogging in place and boxing the air. "Look," Jerry continued, "you haven't told your parents yet that you're not playing that week. Just lie. Just go home next weekend instead."

"But we play Vince's team next week."

"Yeah. So go then. That's a big game. You know Jack and Marcus won't play you." Dave looked up at Jerry, who was now taking more prominent jabs as his fists swung through the air.

"I just wouldn't feel right missing that game," Dave replied.

"Then go home the week after Palm Springs. Look, you ought to be relaxed and all before you go see your parents. And the White Party'll do that for you. A week under the desert sun. Getting laid once or twice. That'll get you ready to see them."

Jerry threw a quick right uppercut into the sky.

"Besides, you know how much you want to check it out. I got some X and all."

Their conversation was broken up by a deep, resonant holler from Marcus, who was calling from the sidelines.

"All right now, Quake! Get together, team! We got another half to play!"

The team gathered at the bench.

"All right, Quake!" Marcus began. "Now just because we got a three-touchdown lead don't mean we can give this game away. You all gotta stay psyched! Don't let no cockiness in here 'cause they ain't been playing too good."

The Quake broke their huddle and walked onto the field. Curt and Al took a detour over to a water faucet near the San Gabrielites bench. As they passed the other team, Curt's opponent, the guy with the black beard and the "Marsha" tattoo, was staring him down.

"That your boyfriend you're fuckin' there?" the guy asked.

Curt turned his head slowly, his face in a half smile/half sneer. He looked at his opponent, whose upturned nose and wobbling upper lip were half-hidden by his wild, untrimmed mustache.

"Sounds like you got some trouble with us whipping your fat ass," Curt responded.

The Marsha man spit a wad down on the field, then lifted his head once again to stare at Curt.

"Faggot."

"Fucking asshole," Curt spoke, his voice forceful but not loud. He drew his finger at his opponent. "I guess you want to get whipped off the field as well."

Al quickly grabbed Curt by the waist.

"Curt! Don't you know that's just what he wants you to do? He's trying to psych you out."

Curt stopped, letting Al hold him back, but still staring at his opponent. Marsha man looked back at him; then he spit another black wad onto the field.

"You're right. It's just . . . the fuckin' asshole. If he puts out anymore shit like that, I'm tellin' ya!"

The second half began. The San Gabrielite kicker never got the ball past half field, giving the Quake excellent position to score once again. Jack now kept his eye on Bill and on Curt. Curt and Bill lined up as the right wide-receiver/flanker team, the Marsha man playing a zone deep on their side. Bill, having seen Curt's perturbation from Marsha man's name-calling, had decided they could have a bit of fun. Bill told Curt that on every play one of them should run directly at the guy, and at that point they would cross patterns to "mess him up." On the first play, Curt ran ten yards out toward Marsha man, dug in his right heel and began an inside slant while Bill followed, kicked in his left heel and ran an out pattern five yards past the line of scrimmage. The play fooled Marsha man, who ran out of his zone to follow Curt, while Bill was open for an easy catch, picking up another ten yards to bring them to the twenty-five-yard line.

On the second play, Bill headed out first, and the Marsha man picked him up. Curt then followed behind for an inside deep buttonhook at the five-yard line, caught the ball, and ran it in for the easy touchdown.

Bill laughed as he trotted over to Curt, leaving Marsha man sulking in the end zone. They raised their arms for a high five.

"He's boiling!" Bill exclaimed.

Marsha man redeemed himself by knocking down a short buttonhook pass to Ed, thereby denying the two-point conversion.

"Yea-uhh!" Marsha man grunted, snapping his elbows back, his hands in fists in celebration. His teammates high-fived him as he stared down Curt and Bill.

Mitch miskicked the football and it rolled along the ground for thirty yards before one of the San Gabrielites grabbed it, but the retriever had no room to run as three Quake surrounded him, and Mitch himself pulled the flag. Still, they had the ball on the fifty, and two minutes later, they were on the ten-yard line and ready to score.

Marsha man ran up to the line of scrimmage, his eyes shifting momentarily at Curt, who was playing deep on his side. The San Gabrielite refocused his eyes on the ground at the end zone, and he took in a deep breath that sucked in the hairs of his beard and mustache.

Curt shuffled up, playing just five yards out, hearing the whistle of Marsha man's breath. Al crouched in his defensive pose in front of Curt.

"Hit Marsha man when he goes out," Curt told Al.

"Why don't you just have him slap me, faggot?" replied Marsha man.

The ball was hiked. Marsha man ran out in a huff. Al hit him once, slowing his forward progress, but Marsha man wrapped his arm around Al's neck and pushed him back.

"Fuck you!" Curt yelled, his feet in a quick shuffle, backing up a couple steps to the goal line, preparing for a jab, a slant, an out, or anything Marsha man was ready to give.

It turned out to be a spit. Not just a little goo, but a thick tarlike combination of tobacco and saliva, striking directly on Curt's sock.

Marsha man's tactic worked as the spit distracted Curt, and so he jabbed his right foot and slanted inside toward the open pocket behind Bill. There now was no defender deep, and so, momentarily, Marsha man was wide open.

Bill heard the spat of tobacco and the thumping of Marsha man's cleats behind him. He faded back, and then turned sideways, running toward the San Gabrielite as the ball was thrown.

Bill and Marsha man leapt at the same time, their shoulders striking against each other. But Bill, despite the extra pounds he had gained over the past year, was still thinner than Marsha man and had more spring in his step. He jumped higher.

Interception.

Now it was Curt's turn to raise a fist in celebration. "Heyyyy!" Curt yelled. "Oooh, yeahhh! Fuckin' great, Bill! Oooh!"

Curt was not through rubbing it in. He walked over to Bill, gave him a leaping high ten, and then came back down on the ground and stared the Marsha man right in his face.

"That's the way us faggots play ball," Curt said.

Marsha man's spit another wad at Curt's feet.

"At least we don't get fucked like cunts."

No one could stop Curt now. He sprang at Marsha man, tackling him to the ground. Marsha man spit the rest of his wad onto Curt's face, but this time, it didn't distract Curt from landing a right fist across the man's face.

Curt cocked his fist back, ready to land another punch, but suddenly an arm locked around his neck. Curt was pulled off the ground by the referee's chokehold. He tried to gulp, tried to breathe. He looked up at the sky, the clouds looking hazy white blue, dripping down to the ground. His eyes rolled back.

"What the hell are you doing?" Curt heard Al scream. And with those words, his neck was freed.

Al had locked his arms under the ref's armpits.

"You can kill him that way!"

Curt had fallen on all fours. He was coughing, fighting for breath, when suddenly he was struck in the back. His chin and stomach dropped to the ground.

Marcus flew over to Marsha man, who was posed to stomp his cleat on Curt's back again. But before Marcus could grab him, the San Gabrielite quarterback pulled his teammate back.

"Cool off, Jim! Dammit!" the teammate yelled to Marsha man. "Back off! You're off the team next time. Got it?"

The San Gabrielite quarterback raised one hand, motioning Marcus to stop his advance.

"It's OK," he spoke. "I'll handle it, OK?"

Marcus nodded and turned his eyes to Al, who had let go of the referee now that Curt had been freed.

The whistle blew.

"You . . ." the referee pointed directly at Al. "You're out of here! And so is your friend . . . or whatever he may be!"

"What!?"

Bill ran up to the ref.

"And what about this asshole here?" Bill pointed at Marsha man. "He started it all, calling us fags and all! You heard him!"

"That doesn't give your teammate the right to throw a punch," the referee declared. "I'm about ready to give them the win by default. So don't push me, got it? I could disqualify your team for the season for what he did to an official."

"What!" Bill exclaimed. "You're taking this poor excuse for an individual with his white-trash Marsha tattoo's side? You some fuckin' homophobe as well?"

Now it was Bill who was grabbed from behind. Jack was pulling Bill back.

"Bill, cool off, OK?" Jack demanded. "You heard what the ref said. We're not losing by default, got it? So just cool off."

Bill stared at his captain. For a moment he looked dumbfounded, taking in what had just happened, wondering how everything had gotten so out of hand. Quickly, the muscles in his face relaxed, and a smile came to his face. Then he laughed.

"Oh, Jack, you're so right," Bill said. "How did I get so carried away?" He then placed his arms around Jack's waist and looked over at the referee and Marsha man, who had just been released by his quarterback. "See, ref? Everything's OK now. We'll be good. We love everyone. Sorry for the misstep. Right, Jack?"

With those words, Bill turned his face to Jack and gave him a loud, humming kiss on the lips.

In the end, the Quake did not forfeit the game. Al and Curt were kicked out of the game, and so Al, knowing the outcome was already decided, persuaded Curt to come home for another kind of workout. Meanwhile, the San Gabrielite quarterback benched Marsha man, causing him to storm off the field soon after Al and Curt's departure. Both teams, therefore, were paying more attention to the parking lot, wondering whether Curt and Marsha man might meet up again, and this disruption caused Jack to throw an interception, leading to the San Gabrielites' first touchdown of the game. So in some respect, it was Marsha man's doing that his team did get on the scoreboard. Bill laughed again when he thought about that.

Near the end of the game, Jack called for both Jerry and Dave to be in the offensive lineup. Mitch, who always told Jack that these two second-stringers were so bad they should never be on the field at the same time, did not complain this time as the Quake was up 52-6.

On the last play of the game, Dave ran a bomb up the sideline, beating his man by a few yards. As the ball came down, a perfect spiral ready to land in his arms, Dave dropped the pass just as time expired. The touchdown did not matter anyway. The Quake had won. But it did matter to Dave. So he left the field silently, unable to speak to or look at his teammates. As he walked alone to his car, Dave wondered when he would have the confidence to catch such a pass and dreamed that once he did, once he won the big game on his amazing maneuver and catch, he would dedicate that game to his father. But as he opened his car door and returned to reality, he believed in his heart that he would never have such an experience.

8

Who Do You Love?

Marcus flipped through his self-designed catalog of compact disc package covers, numbered 1 to 200, indicating which slot each CD was located in in his jukebox-style player. Right now Missy Elliott was playing, but due to a mild protest from Mitch, who indicated that his white boy guests might prefer something more soul than rap, Marcus was seeking his Me'Shell Ndegéocello CD at Bill's request.

Mitch was fixing another vodka and cranberry juice cocktail in the kitchen. Meanwhile, Bill stood with his drink in hand, swaying his hips to Missy Elliott while staring down south at the city lights from Marcus's fourth-floor Hollywood Boulevard balcony. Ed sat next to Marcus on the half-circle purple couch, which Marcus had reupholstered with a forest green trim. Ed thumbed the *Sports Illustrated, Architectural Digest,* and *Edge* magazines that were placed on top of the big, round, oak coffee table trimmed with metal reliefs of fleur de lis—an antique Marcus found near the garment district during his twice-weekly trips downtown to find the perfect fabrics for his *design* business.

Marcus's business was a mystery to Mitch and Bill. They never could determine how he actually made money, especially as they looked around his apartment and saw that each piece of furniture jarred with the next. Bill always told Mitch that perhaps the two of them just weren't funky enough.

"So, you happy now with some Me'Shell?" Marcus asked Mitch once he had found Ndegéocello on slot 141 and Mitch had reentered the living room with his filled tumbler. "I don't see no one else finding problems with Missy but you. Look at Bill here, shakin' his wide booty. Man, what you doin' dancin' away there over the city, Bill? I'm thinkin' someone's excited 'bout getting some booty tonight, dressed up in your sexy shirt and all."

Bill was wearing his black, short-sleeved, button-down cotton shirt that revealed his best qualities—tight against his big shoulders and arms—and hid his worst qualities—worn untucked and draped loose around his stomach. He wore it with the first three buttons unbuttoned, just exposing enough of his chest. Of course, no matter how he tried, Bill could never outdo Marcus in the "I'm-gonna-get-me-some-booty" clothes-dressing category. Marcus wore an unzipped black velvet vest that matched the black in his tight orange-and-black tiger-striped jeans with the two-percent spandex.

Bill turned around and walked through the opening of the balcony's sliding door, returning to the living room. He grinned happily as he stared at his three friends, with his tumbler now empty except for the ice. It was the second vodka and cranberry juice he had finished, putting him one drink ahead of the others.

"I broke up with Larry today."

Bill's eyes locked onto the jaguar-motif rug mounted on the wall above Marcus's purple couch. He did not yet want to see how his three friends were reacting to his announcement. He felt a bit in a daze, and his silly smile grew as his lips pursed and his cheeks tightened into little red balls.

"Dude!" Mitch was the first to exclaim. "You really did? I thought you were just talking on the field a few weeks back." Mitch walked up to Bill and patted him on the back. "That's great, man. You feel OK?"

Bill nodded slowly as he felt his friend's hand on his shoulder, but his focus now was on Ed, who leaned forward on the couch, staring at him in disbelief.

"Bill . . . you're kidding?" Ed responded. "You can't really be breaking up with Larry. There's no way. Are you joking?"

"No. I told him right after the game today."

"But you haven't left him yet?" Ed asked. "I just can't believe this. I mean, you guys are so great together. Five years together! And what about the dogs? You're playing with us, aren't you?"

"Oh, so that's why you got your sexy shirt on tonight," Marcus said. "You won't really know if you're broken up until sometime down the road. I mean, you still in the same house?"

"Yeah, you're right, Marcus," Ed nodded. "Two weeks and they'll be back together. I mean, what about the dogs?"

Bill gazed back and forth at Ed and Marcus bantering on the couch. He lost his smile, and his eyes looked dull and sad.

"Well, I am looking for a place now, if any of you know of one. Or a roommate," Bill said. "Like West Hollywood or Hollywood. I tell you, I'm sick of the Valley."

Ed looked pleadingly at Bill.

"But what about the dogs?"

Bill turned away and walked over to the dining room table.

"I don't know. We haven't figured that out yet. I mean, Larry was crying and all, and he kept repeating the same question, what about the dogs, and it's the question on my mind; but . . . I love Larry and all, but I know . . . he's not the right guy for me."

Ed stood up and walked over to Bill.

"But then . . . who is?"

Bill turned around and stared at Ed, feeling anxious that Ed was looking so concerned and wondering what he had meant when he asked that question. But then he looked past Ed, over at Mitch and Marcus, who were waiting for his answer.

"I don't know," Bill shrugged his shoulders. "I mean . . . do you know who's the right guy for you?"

"Man, you is asking the wrong guy there," Marcus responded instead. "Ed falls in love with everyone he sees."

Marcus started hootin' and hollerin' his own joke.

"Very funny, Marcus," Ed replied.

But in the end, Ed himself was laughing with Mitch and Marcus. They all laughed except Bill, who stood next to the dining room, looking sadly at his friends. He then stared down at his empty glass and heaved another sigh before once again returning his eyes to his friends.

"One more drink for the road?" he asked them all.

🏈 🏈 🏈

You pick up the *Men's Exercise* magazine one more time after you get out of the shower, wearing nothing but a towel around your loins.

You look again at the cover model posing for the "Perfect Pecs" article. The guy is young. Real young. You wonder how he developed a great chest at such an early age. You then look at yourself in the mirror behind your couch, staring intently at your own shaved chest. Your frame is smaller than the cover model's, but your chest is just as well developed. In fact, it's more sinewy than his. His is round and robust. Yours is tense and firm. You figure nine out of ten guys would pick your chest over his. It just so happened that the tenth guy was the fitness editor who chose this guy as the cover model.

You look at yourself again, this time noticing how your chest complements your abs. Such a perfect arc, the pectorals curving toward the sculpted two sections on each side of the abs. You have a great body. Everyone notices you when your shirt is off. It's just that . . . you're afraid you're being typecast. The last four times you've modeled for the fitness magazines, it's been for a section on working the abs. Your abs are just too good. The fitness editors aren't looking at your great chest, at your defined deltoids and trapezius, at the marked vein running down each of your well-toned arms. You've become an abs man. They want you only for your abs.

You drop the magazine back down on your glass coffee table, next to the most recent issues of *Muscle & Fitness, GQ,* and *Details.* You walk into the kitchen, checking the time on the stove. 10:04. Dave's going to be here soon. You think how you haven't picked out what you're going to wear to the party. Something tough. Jack Perry, the set designer who works with director Garry Marshall, is attracted to your New York street-smart toughness. You know you'll be wearing your 501s and black boots, but you haven't yet picked out the right shirt. Something tight but tough. Something that shows your muscles but isn't too queer.

You walk into your bedroom and strip off your towel, looking at yourself one more time in the mirror, raising your arms, thinking perhaps shaving your armpits would give you a better chance of getting the spread for the "Awesome Arms" or "Chest of Choice" covers. But you got to keep the hair there. It shows you're tough. Same reason you keep the line of hair that runs down from your navel. It looks tough, like a man should.

You look over at the many pictures of yourself on the side table of your bed and on your chest of drawers. Almost all of them are photographs of you either wearing a tank top or no shirt at all. You think how you don't need to worry about your thirtieth birthday coming up because you look better now than you did in any of those pictures when you were younger. It's when you're thirty that you're really developed. You think back at that cover model for "Perfect Pecs." He did have a nice chest for someone his age. But you think your chest was pretty nice too when you were twenty-four. Only now it's better.

You spot something you had forgotten about. Right behind the eight-by-ten photo of yourself of three years ago when you had dyed your hair blond and wore a goatee. You walk over to your chest of drawers. Behind that photograph you find another picture frame, a very small one, only two inches tall. You pick it up.

It's a picture of Dean, that guy you dated for nearly two months back in 1996. You stare at his happy face, those golden bangs swept to one side of his forehead. The one guy you really fell for hard. The only guy you ever let fuck you. Things weren't the same with you and Dean after that. You got really pissed that he wanted to fuck you again, like you'd really let someone do that to you on a regular basis. Didn't he get it that you're a tough guy from Brooklyn who only gets on top? Well, he had problems. A lot of baggage. Said all the wrong things in public when you were with him. You couldn't deal with that. It was best you guys broke up. And he's gone back to Ohio. What a loser, going back to Ohio. There's something about guys from the Midwest. They're kind of wimpy. How'd you stay in a relationship with him for a whole two months? But you definitely did fall for him, hard, for a while. Made you kind of wimpy yourself, huh?

"Fuck," you say to yourself. You take the small frame with Dean's picture and you go back into the kitchen and throw it into your junk drawer.

You look at the time again. 10:15. Still haven't picked out a shirt and Dave will be here soon. But that's good. Dave would rather see you at first with no shirt on, with your fabulous abs and perfect pecs and awesome arms all exposed. He's just so into your body.

⚙   ⚙   ⚙

Holly sat fidgeting on her couch, a small overnight travel bag at her feet and the casing of a rented videocassette of *What Ever Happened to Baby Jane?* on the cushion next to her. She sat there watching only the blue screen of the TV, ready to start the movie with a press of the play button. She heard the beep of the microwave, then its door opening and smelled the whiff of steamed popcorn as her girlfriend took out the bag, ripped open the top, and poured the popped kernels in a bowl.

She then heard a buzz, and this one was the doorbell. Holly jumped up from the couch, grabbed her overnight bag, and hurried toward the front door of her apartment.

She opened the door to reveal Al staring back at her with a happy grin. His eyes dropped to the bag in her hand.

"What's that? Beauty products for the evening?" he laughed.

"Oh, Al," she said sadly. "My cousin's in the hospital down in Anaheim. She was at Disneyland and . . . something fell on her."

Holly felt comforted by the concern she saw in Al's wide eyes. He then looked over her shoulder as Brenda, who stood several inches taller than her, appeared at the doorway. Soon, however, his eyes returned to Holly.

"Is she all right?"

Holly took a step forward and hugged him.

"Her husband says she's going to be fine, but she was knocked unconscious for a moment. I just can't believe it. I mean, the happiest place on earth and this happens. Poor Julie."

Brenda placed her hand on her girlfriend's shoulder.

"Holly, are you sure you don't want me to go with you? I really don't mind. You should have me drive, you being upset like this."

Holly looked over her shoulder at Brenda and shook her head.

"No. You know Julie doesn't know."

"Holly! I've met her! She won't care if you're gay or not!"

"But she knows people who would care, namely Mom and Dad. I just want to keep this whole issue away from my family."

Brenda threw up her hands and walked away.

"All right. I won't bring up this issue. It's just, your mom and dad live right over in Fullerton. They see you all the time, Holly."

"Right. They live in Fullerton, remember? The center of the Republican Orange Belt."

Holly turned back to Al and smiled. She placed her hand in his and led him into the living room.

"Just because I have to leave doesn't mean you and Brenda can't enjoy some Bette and Joan," she said. "Brenda made popcorn, and there's beer in the fridge."

Al glanced nervously at Brenda, then returned his attention to his best friend.

"Oh. No. Holly, I . . . wouldn't feel right watching the movie without you," he said. "I mean, it was your idea and all for this movie night."

"Actually, it was Brenda's idea," she said.

"But . . . I mean, it's in your apartment and all. Maybe we can watch it another night."

"The movie's got to go back tomorrow," Brenda said from the kitchen.

"Oh, c'mon now," Holly said, grabbing Al's forearm and leading him over to the couch, her travel bag still next to the front door. "You made plans to come here. I don't want you to have nothing to do on a Saturday night."

"Oh, that's OK," he quickly interjected. "I can always hit the bars in West Hollywood. I'm sure I'll bump into somebody."

"And leave me all alone?" Brenda asked, a sly smile on her face as she walked into the living room with a big bowl of popcorn. "I didn't butter it. Do you want it buttered?"

Holly pulled him down on the couch with her. Brenda then sat down on the other side of him, grabbing a few kernels and popping them into her mouth.

"Now tell me," Holly said, tugging at his elbow with both arms, "before I go, I want to know what happened a couple weeks ago after that game and you and Curt went out with that blond straight boy. I'd love to pass the story on to Julie."

"Oh, so you can tell her your best friends are gay, just not you?" Brenda said. "I think perhaps we should put you in some 'Don't Panic' T-shirt, like 'My best friend is gay and I'm not a fag hag.'"

Holly laughed, then tugged Al again. "So, what happened?"

"It was his first time . . . with guys, that is," Al replied. He then faced Brenda. "Wouldn't you know if anyone could seduce a good-looking straight guy, it would be Curt? That's just how Curt is. He's got such sex appeal."

Al looked forward toward the blue screen, then patted both women on the knees.

"I tell you, we all don't realize how lucky we are. I'm so glad to be with Curt. I'd never want to ruin that. So it's good he and I have these three-ways together. And you two—you two are so lucky to have each other. You two have the perfect girl union. I always tell my friends that."

Holly smiled sweetly at Al. She then planted a quick kiss on his cheek and rose from the couch.

"Well, I've got to go. Honestly, Al, you're so sappy sometimes."

She walked around Al's feet and planted a kiss on her girlfriend's lips. Brenda remained seated, staring at the blue screen.

"Don't worry, Holly," Brenda said. "I'm sure after watching the movie, Bette and Joan will knock that sappiness right out of Al."

Why in the world didn't I just say it? It would have been over with. Ed would understand then. Ed, you're the right guy for me. I've known that for years now. And you're unattached now. We're both unattached now. This makes the moment right. Finally, we can be together.

Now how corny does that sound? There's no way I could have said that in front of Mitch and Marcus, especially if Ed ends up just standing there, completely speechless, not knowing what to say; knowing that anything he said would utterly rip me apart because he doesn't share the same feelings for me. That has to be the case. I mean, why did he have to keep asking "What about the dogs?" and saying that Larry and I were such a great couple? Was he trying to tell me he's not interested? Has he known all along that I have this secret crush on him and he's trying to steer me away from going any further with it?

Now here's Marcus passing me a joint. Like that's all I need, to heighten my paranoia.

"No thanks, Marcus. I'm a terrible driver high."

Marcus offers the joint to Ed, who just shakes his head and goes back to reading *Sports Illustrated*. Mitch then takes the joint, but I can see he's taking only a small toke. That means Marcus is going to have the whole joint to himself. Well, at least I'm beating them all in the consumption of alcohol. Look at the four glasses on the table. Mine's the only one that's empty. But three's enough. I needed some. Enough to finally tell Ed my feelings. I have just the right buzz now. So I'll drive Ed over to Akbar, and I'll tell him then. It will be just me and him then. So I get shot down hard. At least Marcus and Mitch won't be around to see it.

"So Ed, you want to ride with me to Akbar?"

He doesn't look up right away. He just says "Hmmm?" and keeps looking down. Probably just finishing an article in the *Sports Illustrated*. But if he asked me the same question, I would have popped my head up with anticipation. Clearly we're on different wavelengths here.

But then he looks up and stares at me, and he's got that sweet smile that complements his sweet eyes, such a light blue. "Sure," he says, but his eyes say more. They say, "I would love to ride to the bar with a good friend such as you." Actions speak louder than words. And his eyes speak louder than action. Now I'm feeling energized. This Me'Shell is a little too down for me, but it's all that's on, and I start snapping my fingers and moving my shoulders. Always dance with my neck and shoulders, but now I got to feel my whole body. So I get off the couch.

"I think it's time we be moving along," I tell my friends, trying to get their butts off the couch. But Marcus still has half a joint to finish.

"You going to finish a whole joint yourself, Marcus?" I ask, trying to get this party moving. "I guess you've got to be pretty stoned to go to Rage, or should I say, under age?"

"Man, you know Jack ain't going to go to Silverlake," Marcus says. "Vine Street is like the Mason-Dixon Line for that child. I already told him I'd see his ass at Rage. You know how he be down with that old Sam shit and all. I tell you, there must be somethin' in the air tonight. Or maybe it was the game. First him and Sam and then you and Larry. Four new eligible bachelors on our hands."

"And one other bachelor going to Rage to move in on the kill," Mitch says.

Marcus does his jerk-his-head-back-and-stare-down-Mitch-hard routine.

"Fuck that, if I think I know what you sayin'. I ain't got no interest in some control queen like Jack. We're just good friends, and I feel as good friends it's important somebody be there when shit happens. You know what I'm saying?"

A good friend. Does Ed feel the same way, thinking he needs to be there for me, now that Larry and I have broken up? But I don't want him there to comfort me. I don't want him to even think that way. Yet he does. And if I approach him tonight, he'll think it's just a rebound move, that I'm not understanding my feelings right now. He can't get it that I planned this around him. It's not because of Larry. It's because of him! Have I made a terrible mistake? And what about the dogs?

The door opens i see jerry with no shirt looking like he's flexing for me abs all ripped and my abs the hardest thing to work on and if i had abs like that i'd have the best-looking men going down on me all the time and maybe at this party all actor types and i'll find someone who wants to take me up to a bedroom and if dad saw me with my legs up he'd just shake his head like he knew all along i turned out wrong couldn't live up to him to my brother that i'd fallen the weak cast into hell damned for eternity and when he dies will he be able to look down on me and see me getting fucked by the men he wanted me to be real men only having a different preference but real men all the same and will he think its more masculine for them to fuck something like me or some girl instead and dad was so proud when angie came home and dad *well, you've found a fine boy in david he won't take advantage of you* but really hoping that i do take advantage of her that i want to fuck her to dominate her like a real man and jerry *hey i got nothing against fuckin' a nice pussy once in a while but straight men are the real wimps what does it take to get down on a woman* jerry and dad more alike than anyone would think does jerry think i want to get fucked by him again he's always talking about how he only gets on top but i don't see him as a real man just trying to act like one

"Hey man," Jerry says, "I'll be ready in a minute. Just picking out a shirt. Hey! You want to borrow a shirt or something?"

i look down at my sweater thinking this is a party be more formal but wanting to wear something sexy and slinky show off my muscles but don't want me and jerry coming to the party looking the same want men to know i'm available to get fucked

"This is too formal?"

"Remember, we're going to Rage afterward." rage queens dance like girls all shaved all bottoms can't find a man. "And this party, it might be Trousdale Estates-adjacent, but it's still a guy party."

getting hard-on thinking of what slinky outfit jerry will put me in maybe some tight cotton and spandex t-shirt letting everyone know i'm a pussyboy i follow him into his bedroom perhaps should stop at the door don't want to look like i want it from him shuddering i pass through that door jerry looking into his closet good we're the same size

"Here you go," he says, "I always get lucky with this one."

he tosses me a gray t-shirt with contrasting white sleeves feels like cotton i look at him wanting it to be just the thing that lets me get fucked tonight he looks back staring at the shirt instead of me

"Try it on."

shuddering i pull off my sweater exposing my upper body to him will he take advantage of me now as soon as i stand half naked in front of him he'll push me on his bed and start fucking me can't look at him

now get on to the business at hand the shirt i roll it up and put my
head through the hole slowly lowering the shirt tucking it tight into
my jeans and i want this to last not to look right away thinking how
perfect this shirt is on me making me a total gym queen so tight and
then slowly i look up into his mirror and i see my body so tense against
this perfect shirt and i feel like a true pussyboy now and ready to find
my man

"Looks good on you," jerry says with his eyes down on my chest and
then he goes back into his closet and finds himself another tight shirt
and puts it on and if only he liked to get fucked we'd be two queens
out for the night

●　●　●

"So . . . should we start the movie?"

Al asked the question with hesitation. Holly had left, and now he
and Brenda were seated side by side, cushion to cushion. Al slipped
himself over to the other side and put his knee up on the middle cushion.

Brenda dropped a few more kernels into her mouth as she studied
Al's body language.

"Do you want to start the movie now?" she repeated his question,
again revealing her sly smile.

"But I asked it first."

"But I want you to answer it."

He looked at her, studying her. Then he nodded his head.

"Let's start it then." He reached his hand for the popcorn bowl to
stress that he had made an important decision.

"I'm ovulating," she said.

Al snapped his hand back from the popcorn bowl.

"What!?"

"Now where did I put the remote?"

She stuffed her hand under the middle couch cushion, then crept it
invisibly toward him. Al watched the cushion rise toward him like the
dirt above a burrowing mole.

"It's on the TV," he said. He rose quickly to retrieve it. Having grabbed the remote, he turned around and stood in one place, looking at Brenda as she exposed her hand once again and placed it on the side of the popcorn bowl. An upturned lip on only one side, she sought popcorn with her other hand.

"Brenda, I . . . well, I have to ask . . . is Holly's cousin really in the hospital? Or is this a ploy . . . to get us alone?"

Brenda placed her head on her hand, studying him.

"Al, I'm not ovulating. I just wanted to see how you would react."

"So . . . this isn't a ploy."

"No Al, this isn't a ploy. Julie really was injured at the happiest place on earth."

Al nodded, his eyes lowered, thinking to himself. He began to walk back to the couch, but then stopped and looked at her.

"Brenda . . . does Holly . . . know about this?"

"That I want you to impregnate me?"

"Well . . . yeah!"

Brenda smiled. "Come here," she said, patting her hand on the cushion next to her.

Al hesitated before moving back to the sofa. He then sat on the cushion on the far end, not on the one she had patted.

"Al, I've decided I really don't want to have your child."

Al stared with an open mouth at first, allowing her to take his hand. He then laughed and squeezed her hand softly. He laughed harder and took a deep breath.

"Oh . . . well. OK. I tell you I don't think I was ready to be a dad anyway. But . . . whew! OK. So should we watch the movie?"

She inched her hand up, now caressing his forearm.

"I just want to have you . . . for one night."

🏈   🏈   🏈

"Thanks for driving," Ed says. I look at him staring out the windshield with his sweet smile. He notices me glance at him, and he turns my way and raises his smile a tad.

I wave him off with one hand, caught smiling myself. "I don't see why we all need to take our cars over to Silverlake anyway, unless . . . of course . . . you wanted to pick someone up . . . or whatever."

There I go stuttering, like it's so obvious what my intentions are. But then, this is the right time. Just Ed and me in the car, following Mitch to Akbar. I've got to tell him now.

Ed snorts, his eyes glassy as he stares out the windshield.

"No, I don't think that's going to happen. I don't have any intention of falling in too deep only to land smack on my face again."

I glance at him, his shining eyes still looking straight ahead, his nose and mouth curving up to ·one side, as if to hold back a cry. I watch his face move, trying to figure how to respond to his words, how to move it forward to what I really want to tell him. But would he think me crazy if I did? I mean, we're too good of friends to be boyfriends.

He shakes his head from one side to the other, blinking several times then widening his eyes.

"Sorry about that," he says to me. "The last thing I want to do is say something like that, wallowing in self-pity. I guess I was thinking that the last time I went to Akbar was with Trent."

"Ed, Trent's an asshole. I mean, that joke back at Marcus's place, about you falling in love with everyone you see. You ought to be just a bit more discriminating, take a step back, think about the kind of person you really want in your life, and then maybe . . ." I pause. Was that an actual gulp going down my throat? "Well, maybe then you'll notice the guy you always wanted was right in front of you in the first place."

I'm so nervous that I said that and so I just keep looking straight out the windshield, too afraid to look over, too afraid of how he's reacting right now. I actually said it. What is he thinking now? Oh God! If I don't look at him now he'll just think I was saying something out of the blue, as though there's no significance to it. But I can't look at him.

"Look!"

He points his finger toward the windshield.

"A parking space . . . right in front of Akbar!"

I brake suddenly, not even knowing where he's pointing. That's his response? Oh man, he has no idea what I'm talking about. Or worse, he does and he just wants to avoid it.

"No, no!" Ed exclaims. "Just past Akbar there. Ah, never mind. Someone just took it. Now where did Mitch park?"

I press my foot on the gas again. "Oh, there are always spaces farther up Sunset," I say.

"I think my problem is," Ed continues, "that I always want the person too much. I get attached too fast. Then the guy realizes that I want him more than he wants me. And then that's it. The game's over. He won. He's got the control. He's got the power. I've become the weakling, and by seeing me like this, he can't really be attracted to me anymore."

Ed swings his left arm behind the back of the seat and stares at me straight on.

"I mean, wanting someone so much is just too much of a turn-off."

I turn my head to look at him, afraid now that he's talking about me, not about himself. Of course he's talking about me. I jerk my head back. I'm sure I'm swerving, ready to sideswipe a car. I shouldn't be driving when I'm emotionally fucked up. Or maybe it's the alcohol. I shouldn't have had three drinks at Marcus's place. Now why can't I find a parking space? I really want to get to Akbar and have a drink.

You arrive at the party, and first you see Tim, another model, one you worked with almost two years ago. He has lost some of his muscle tone. You tell him he looks great. He says he has tried to lose some of his bulk because his main occupation now is as a commercial actor and he has to look more like a regular person on the street. You nod in agreement, even though you realize he's just making an excuse for being lazy and not going to the gym. You have Dave right behind your shoulder and you know he wants to be introduced to this guy, so you introduce him nonchalantly, making Tim recognize that Dave's just a friend from football. Dave shakes his hand, says hello, and then stands silently again. You think Dave probably likes this guy, but he knows he's not in the same league as Tim. You think Tim might be thinking Dave's with you, but if Dave's not in the same league as Tim, he's certainly not in the same league as you. You feel good about yourself knowing you made friends with someone like Dave, someone who's a bit shy and eager to follow the kind of life you lead.

Then you see Klay, the casting director who got you that small role in the playground fight scene of *Good Will Hunting* where you're watching Matt Damon beat up your friend. Klay has three other guys around him when you walk up and shake his hand, and he continues his story about his new BMW Z3, the midnight blue one parked right in front of the house. He's telling the group that it's a special edition with seat warmers. You think how it's prissy for someone to special order seat warmers for driving around in LA. When you lived in Brooklyn you drove your old Jeep around in the winter without any heat and with the top down. You tell that tale to the crowd, getting them to laugh at your anecdotes about how you would be driving around with muffs on your ears to keep them from freezing off. Someone tells you that sounds just like what some tough guy from Brooklyn would do, and Klay states that's exactly why he cast you for the tough South Boston guy in *Good Will Hunting.*

"You were in *Good Will Hunting?*" Dave then asks enviously, and you nod, feeling good that the whole group here knows this now without you ever having to mention it yourself, but you nod without a crack of a smile, showing everyone that it's nothing special.

You move on toward the kitchen, Dave still following you, and there's Jack Perry standing in the doorway speaking to a good-looking guy, but as soon as he sees you, he directs his attention off this guy and onto you, because he's always looking for something better. He's been kind of stuck up since his Oscar nomination. You saw him at an after-Oscars party, and he said he would have won that Oscar if Cameron hadn't spent billions of dollars on the set design for *Titanic,* while his own budget was a mere $10 million. He walks over to you with a martini glass lifted, and he plants a kiss on your lips. You shift your eyes to the good-looking guy he was talking to, hoping he doesn't think that prissy kiss was too queer. But that guy's like you, here to kiss ass in the hopes of getting a part. You hate this part of your business. It's not about your acting talent, like it is in New York. It's about kissing ass. If it wasn't for the work here you'd be back in New York in a second.

"Jerry, you've arrived fashionably late as always," Jack says to you after returning his lips to his martini glass. "And you've brought a friend, I see."

You turn around and see Dave is still right behind your shoulder. You feel like you're baby-sitting this guy now. Why does he keep following you? Doesn't he know anyone here? But you do feel pretty good that Dave admires you. So you introduce Dave to Jack, and again Dave offers his hand and says a quiet hello, and then he stands back again, and his eyes keep rolling over to the good-looking guy next to Jack, and you think how Dave isn't going to earn any brownie points not focusing his attention on Jack, a somebody who knows even bigger somebodies, but then Dave isn't in the business, and so he doesn't have to kiss ass, and now you're envying Dave because he can focus his attention on the good-looking guys. It's just Dave is so obvious with his eyes glancing over at that guy, and he's so quiet about it. What a funny guy this Dave is, you think.

Jack notices Dave's eyes, and he apologizes and turns his shoulder to place his empty hand on the good-looking guy's shoulder.

"Oh, how rude of me," he says. "Jerry and Dave, let me introduce you to Tony Caravahlo. He's just arrived from New York. Another Brooklyn Italian transplant like yourself, Jerry."

Tony reaches out his hand to Dave first and says, "How ya doin'," and you kind of wonder why he didn't reach his hand out to you first, but you figure he's saving the best for last, and when he shakes your hand, he says, "You look familiar. Where have I seen you before?"

So you start mentioning your neighborhood in Brooklyn, but you don't know each other from Brooklyn because he actually grew up in the Bronx, and it's just like Jack, someone born and raised in Los Angeles, to not be able to figure out one borough from the next, and so you figure he's probably seen you on the cover of *Exercise & Health* magazine, and he says no because he never reads those magazines, although you don't really believe him. And so you figure he has mistaken you for some other actor, like Matt Dillon. You always get mistaken for Matt Dillon, but a younger Matt Dillon.

Then Jack puts his arm around your shoulder, and you got to talk the movie schmooze, and you look over his shoulder once or twice and you see that this Tony guy and Dave seem to be having some sort of lively conversation, even though Tony is doing most of the talking, of course, because he's from the Bronx. You're kind of stunned that Tony might be interested in Dave because you and Tony really have more in common and, well, Dave isn't really in Tony's league.

But now you've got away from Jack and his whole talk about how it's long overdue for Garry Marshall to reunite Richard Gere and Julia Roberts, and that when it's finally done, he'll be the set designer and this time he'll come away with the Oscar because you know it's going to be big budget. Now you're back in the kitchen getting a beer from the ice chest. Only three other guys are in the kitchen, and you don't know them and they're all together as a group gabbing away and laughing. You think it's nice to take a break from the party, so you lean up against the kitchen counter, and you drink the cold beer, concentrating on its refreshing taste, and you look over at the other three guys, waiting for them to start looking at you, since none of them are really hot and you know they think you're really hot. But they're too involved in some meaningless conversation, so you start wondering about Dave and that Tony guy and whether they actually could still be talking together. Then suddenly Dave appears, which causes you to take a bigger gulp of beer than you think, and you raise your head up, not wanting to spill any of the beer out of your mouth, realizing that would be so uncool and you would be caught looking kind of stupid, all because Dave appeared in the room. Fuck! Like he means anything to you. But he's not with Tony anymore, and you're kind of relieved about that, although you figure Tony isn't really that cool. He's just come from the Bronx, and he seemed strange, a little distant and all.

"That Jack really seems to like you," Dave begins as he grabs a beer. "You think he might recommend you to Garry Marshall for a role or something?"

You return to leaning your back against the counter, and you take another sip of your beer before you answer.

"Maybe. You never can figure out this business. They don't really know how to pick out acting talent here. That's what really sucks about LA."

You drink your beer again, and Dave does the same. He just nods to your remark and doesn't say anything, so you figure you can change the subject.

"So, you like that Tony guy or something?"

"Yeah, he's a nice guy. He's pretty good-looking, too. Don't you think?"

"Yeah, he's OK. I wonder where he's seen me. Or maybe he just mistook me for some other actor. I get that a lot. But that's the problem being on magazine covers and in the movies. I can't figure out if he asked that and was looking at me that way because he thinks I'm some star or just because I'm good-looking."

Dave again nods and doesn't say anything and returns to his beer. He seems content just being with you now, although you see he's staring out the kitchen doorway back into the party. You look at him for a second and see that tight gray-and-white shirt of yours is fitting him pretty good. He's been working out. Good shoulders now. But he still needs to work on his abs. You figure you ought to say something nice to him.

"It's good I picked out that shirt for you," you say. "It looks good on you, too."

⬤ ⬤ ⬤

"But you told me Curt and you have an open relationship."

Brenda was speaking to a very nervous Al, who had once again arisen from the couch and was pacing behind it.

"Well . . . yeah! We do. But that still doesn't make me not feel guilty. It's like I'm cheating on Curt, having this all arranged, and him thinking you're just a friend of mine."

"But you're not really cheating if you're sleeping with a woman, are you, since I'm not your sexual preference?"

Her question only caused Al to pace faster.

"I don't know! Maybe it's worse. Yes, it's worse! What about Holly? She's one of my best friends. Does she know about this?"

Brenda placed the bowl of popcorn on the coffee table and swung her arm over the back of the couch, now looking directly at Al.

"No. She doesn't."

Al stopped and stared at her open-mouthed.

"Well then, don't you feel guilty? Don't you love her? And what if she came back to her apartment to find us . . . you know . . . doing it in her bed? Oh gosh, I couldn't handle that."

Brenda smiled slyly once again.

"Doesn't that make it all the more exciting?"

He stared at her, then swung his head back in laughter.

"Oh, you are baaad."

Her smile grew.

"I thought you liked that in a person. Isn't that why you're with Curt? You like someone a little more daring than yourself?"

"I'm . . . daring," he defended himself.

"That's why you and Holly are such good friends. You both have that desire to do something bad, but since you can't quench that desire on your own, you find someone who doesn't think twice about doing it."

"Yeah. Right. You don't have any qualms about doing this?"

"If I didn't it wouldn't be so exciting."

Al paced nervously once again, which made Brenda smile, knowing he was actually considering her offer.

"But I didn't even bring a condom. I mean, why would I, coming to see a movie with two girls? Of course, I realized you might want to have sex with me, if Holly wasn't here, but only for the reason of getting pregnant, and so why would I bring a condom even then?"

"I'm on the pill."

Her comment stopped Al dead on his tracks. He stared at her again.

"Wow. You are such a good lesbian. But you don't even know if I'm positive or not, which I'm not. I was just tested three months ago. But still."

His body shook, unable to stay motionless. He was ready to pace again, but Brenda stopped him by swinging out her arm and grabbing him by the forearm. He looked down at her hand, then moved his eyes up to view her face, wide-eyed and determined.

"Al. I've got rubbers, too."

Ed caught himself staring at the man's shoulders, just filled out his flannel shirt so well. His eyes had met Drew Bannister's upon his way to the rest room, and upon returning to the bar at Akbar, he was stopped by this handsome, six-foot-four-inch blond with the blue eyes and the square jaw. The first thing Drew had done to stop Ed in his tracks was to hold out his hand, provide a firm handshake, and say in a deep voice, "Hey there. My name's Drew." Ed was instantly attracted by Drew's forwardness and by the strength of his handshake. And when Drew spoke, since he was so tall, his eyes looked down slightly at an angle at Ed's own eyes. Ed found everything about Drew very masculine, as though he was some straight pro football player lost in a gay bar.

As he stared at Drew's shoulders, which was difficult not to do since they were level with Ed's chin, Ed listened to the man's story about how he prefers being in a club with a straight or mixed clientele because he has concerns that in places such as West Hollywood, the Castro, and Greenwich Village/Chelsea, gays tend to immerse themselves entirely into their own subculture, which he doesn't find very healthy or consensus building. As he listened, Ed also daydreamed, thinking of how nice it would be for him and Drew to live in a big house with a rolling lawn on a lake, and how they would play games of "fetch the stick" with their two black labs.

At the same time, he thought of Mitch and Bill back at the counter and how they were waiting for him to return. Ed did not dare look at the bar, which was now behind his back, for it would be rude to turn away while Drew was telling his story. He thought that perhaps Mitch and Bill were watching him right now. Mitch was probably nodding in approval of Drew, but Ed could not think how Bill might be reacting.

Bill's comments in the car had confused him. Ed thought back to the words Bill had spoken: "Well, maybe then you'll notice the guy you always wanted was right in front of you in the first place." When Bill had said that, Ed had sat in a state of shock, looking straight out the window, too afraid to turn to look at Bill, afraid that if he did so, Bill would see what feelings Ed actually had for him. But the words Bill had spoken were so dead-on. Yes, he was right in front of him or, at least, right by his side. But Ed hated himself for thinking this way. Bill and he were great friends. They couldn't be boyfriends. Besides, Bill had said that only as a figure of speech. He didn't actually mean himself, did he? Then again, Bill had just broken up with Larry. If he had spoken, Ed would be acting as though he was desperate to catch Bill on the rebound. It was good that his announcement of the open parking space had changed the subject. It had all been so awkward at that moment.

"So . . . are you here by yourself?" Drew asked after he finished his comments. "Could I buy you another beer?" As he asked the second question, Drew took his great big hand and squeezed Ed's bicep.

Ed looked down at his squeezed bicep and then looked up into Drew's eyes with a smile of pleasure. He shook his head. "No, my friends Mitch and Bill are over there at the bar. We were planning on going to the Garage tonight."

"Oh?"

Drew looked over at the bar. Ed caught the puzzled tone in Drew's word.

"But . . . I mean, I'm real flexible tonight. That is . . . except I don't have a car."

"Well, if you need a ride . . ."

Drew's words came out instantaneously, even before the raising of his smile or the tightening of his grasp on Ed's bicep. Ed looked into Drew's eyes, struck dumb for a moment.

"Yeah. Maybe I will."

But as soon as he spoke, he looked toward the bar. Mitch was finishing the last sip of his drink, his head back and chin up, not watching the flirting between Ed and Drew. But Bill was looking right at him. Once Bill and Ed made eye contact, Bill lifted his glass toward Ed in support, then drained the rest of his drink.

Ed turned back to Drew.

"Could I maybe catch up with you in about five minutes? My friend over there, Bill, he just broke up with his boyfriend of five years. I should maybe catch up with him for a while."

"Hey. I understand. But don't leave, OK?"

"I won't. In fact, I'm going to the bar. I'll buy you a beer. Or I mean . . . whatever you're drinking. What's that?"

"A cosmopolitan."

Ed had noticed the empty martini glass on the cocktail table next to Drew. It had remnants of red inside. Ed looked up at Drew. As hard as he tried, Ed could not picture Drew holding a martini glass filled with a red drink.

"A cosmopolitan then. See you in a bit."

Ed returned to the bar.

"Can you believe this guy?" Ed spoke as soon as he approached Bill and Mitch. "I mean, he's like an all-pro linebacker!"

Mitch raised his new drink to clank Ed's empty bottle. Bill, seated on a stool so that he was a head lower than Mitch and Ed, slowly raised his glass as well.

"Hey man, he's a real find. What's his name?" Mitch asked.

"Drew Bannister."

"Drew?" Bill asked. "What's with you finding guys with strange first names? First Trent. Now Drew."

"I kind of like it," Ed said. "It seems really original. I tell you guys, it's weird. I'm not like this usually, but I find myself attracted to him because he's so . . . masculine, like a tough guy, you know, like, how in the world can he be gay?"

"Oh, not another one of these too-masculine-to-be-gay beliefs," Bill remarked. "Ed, I didn't think you could be fooled with such a stereotype. Go home and read yourself some Nietzsche, look at the transvaluation of ethics, the Judaeo-Christian-inspired concept that straight men are masculine and gay men are feminine, the whole turn-around concept from the early Greek-conceived thoughts that men who slept with men were actually more masculine. It's all cultural preconceptions. Don't get caught up in your own culture. Transcend it."

"No, I know it's wrong. I don't feel great being attracted to him that way."

Bill nodded, his eyes looking down at his feet.

"Right. Just get to know who this guy really is, rather than as a stereotype."

"Rather than as a piece of meat, you mean?" Mitch interjected.

Bill looked up at Mitch and then laughed.

"Oh, that's right. What am I thinking? If it is only a one-night stand, that is, then he should just be a manly piece of meat. My apologies, Ed."

"Well," Ed smiled at Mitch, "he did offer me a ride."

Ed looked quickly at Bill. "But you know, I'm just going to get his number. I mean, you know, I'm with you guys tonight."

"Ed, if you're worried about me because I broke up with Larry, don't be," Bill responded with a wave of his hand. "Mitch and I will have a great time at the Garage. You're not so much into that kind of music anyway." Bill took a big sip of his drink before continuing. "Besides . . . now, if I pick someone up at the Garage, I won't have to worry about driving you home first before going over to his place."

Ed stared at Bill, unable to read him. What he said certainly was logical, although he felt he had just received a put-down when Bill said he was not as much into alternative music. But the way Bill had explained this logic seemed too abrupt, as if telling him that Ed was abandoning him during this difficult time.

"Are you sure?"

"Yeah, yeah. Go ahead."

"Well, maybe we should just see what happens. I'm supposed to buy him a drink, and we'll see what goes from there."

Ed pushed himself up to the bar and caught the bartender's eye.

"An Amstel Light and a cosmopolitan, please."

Bill furled his eyebrows.

"Who's drinking the cosmopolitan?"

"He is."

A big smile spread over Bill's face.

"Well, it just goes to show," Bill said. "There's a little bit of girl in all of us."

🏈   🏈   🏈

so handsome as though he doesnt know it his eyes so alive as he speaks to me the strong muscles in his neck teasing as he hides his big chest in a white buttondown dress shirt so in contrast with the way others dressed at this party and the shirt tucked into his black jeans so unaware of his sex appeal just so excited when talking and to me talking to me does he want me as a friend as a lover as a fuck buddy is he thinking how it would be to fuck me just the man to fuck me i'd be his totally he stops talking and flips his eyes over to jack and jerry

"You're friend Jerry there. He's kind of a strange guy, don't you think?" strange what does he mean he wants jerry of course talking to me to get jerry

"What do you mean strange?"

he turns back to me and laughs his eyes so expressive under his black wide eyebrows i could melt right now into his arms would he like me to serve him

"Well . . . you know. I have seen him before . . . at auditions. He's just, well, kind of into himself, don't you think?"

a put down he's wanting me not jerry what do i say defend my friend advocate myself

"Well . . . yeah. But he's a nice guy when you get to know him. We play football together." bring up football new respect for me i'm a man he's nodding in approval likes that wants a man to fuck

"No kidding? I use to play college ball, but I quit at Pitt when my dad died my junior year. You know, I wanted to be there for my mom and all." dad died and my dad last week of chemo moms voice shaking *your fathers fine he's in bed sleeping* and i *but its nine in the morning he never gets up past six* and she *well i've got your brother out here watching the ammonds* and i the prodigal son abandoned them all because i'm different and dad would laugh seeing me toil in the field

"Hey, you OK?" places his hand on my shoulder i look up at him his dark eyes looking at me so concerned i could love him

"I'm sorry. It's just . . . what you said. You see, my Dad's undergoing chemo right now. He has lung cancer. And I'm not feeling very good not being there for him." why did i bring that up never a subject to raise i never raise but feel i can with him not sexual do i want him other than that a man just for me he puts his hand on my shoulder

"Hey, I'm real sorry. I know . . ." he stops as though choked up such a real person, "how hard it is going through it."

two other guys run up to tony one slapping him on the back theyre lively like him but not handsome as he he has regular friends a real person

"Hey Tony! We were lookin' for ya," says the curly-haired blond slapping his back. "It's Orbit time, guy! Jason's out by the car already." tony will leave me now

"Yeah, yeah. All right," he turns to me and fumbles in his pockets and takes out a card like a business card but just a picture of him and phone number some type of actors business card. "Call me, OK? If you need someone to talk to."

i take his card cant believe it i have his card and then he gives me a hug and leaves with his friends and i stand there so dizzy such a beautiful man inside and out and before he goes through the door he turns and smiles at me and he likes me and why i'm so quiet and he's such a personality with feelings almost scary a beautiful man to know inside didnt expect at this party everything changes what i dreamed of this night and what actually happens one turn in the road one chance meeting and all is different i will call him but when tomorrow two days from now three days from now dont do that swingers movie thing and jerry what will he think this shirt is working wonders

⬤   ⬤   ⬤

Brenda laid under Al with her legs up and tucked around his back. She had just reversed positions. Al had been so aroused with her on top of him moving her hips as she did the in-and-out motion. Every time she had moved her hips up, his cock would jump, he was so turned on by her motions. But now she chose to be under him, to allow him to move in and out of her. She no longer wanted to be in control. She wanted him to do his thing.

When Holly had announced that she had to see her cousin in the hospital, Brenda had planned out every aspect of the evening. She had everything down, even to the point where she would emphasize she was on the pill, even the number of popcorn kernels she would place in her mouth as a nonchalant exclamation to each major revelation she made to him during the night. He had fallen for it—hook, line, and sinker.

She also had expected that Al had never slept with a woman before, and as he got in bed with her naked body for the first time, he revealed that this was actually the case, primarily to tell her why he was so nervous. But she kissed him softly and soon had her arm sliding up the inside of his leg until she was cradling his balls. When she had done that, his shaking dissolved, and he looked deeply into her eyes with a feeling of tenderness and love that she had seen so few times before.

That look had enraptured her. It had affected all the plans. That look had taken her out of control. And now, as she lay back, her head propped against two pillows, her eyes shut as she felt the intensity, the rhythm in which he moved himself inside her, she desired so much to open her eyes, to look into his own again, to be lost in his soul. So she opened them and, as though he knew, Al opened his as well, and her whole being was covered by his wide brown orbs as he brought his head down and kissed her tenderly on the lips without disturbing the flow of his motion.

The often-repeated phrase that "all the good ones are either married or gay" popped into her mind. But she quickly dispelled that notion, changing it to her new belief that all the good ones are gay. She had slept with many married men before. It satiated her sexual needs for men without disturbing her own lifestyle. But it had only been sex. No true intimacy. She had never found intimacy with a man before, and she expected never to find it with a man. But now she had found it, with a gay man—but not only a gay man, with Al, who was in a relationship and whose best friend was her own girlfriend.

She tried to get back into control. She tried to focus on how their sex was dirty, how it was bad, so wrong, that both of them were breaking Holly's trust. She tried to get excited about how bad they were being. But she couldn't focus on that for long. Every time she did think this way, it was overwhelmed by the desire to open her eyes again and view the most beautiful man, the most endearing male soul she had ever come across.

Did he know, she wondered, that it was he that now was in control? But she knew he did not think this way. He was free from conceiving such notions because as he continued making love to her, with such complete abandon, it was not control that he felt. It was surrender. Or more so, the thought of both of them surrendering to a timeless moment of intimacy.

❧   ❧   ❧

Why does he do it? Why does Ed always come to me seeking my approval of the guy he's just met? Is he completely blind? Doesn't he know how it hurts me? Look at him over there, talking to this . . . Drew. Now he looks like a Drew with that nellie cosmopolitan in his hand. The problem is that person is such a find. Ed certainly does have a weakness for a pretty face. That's what gets him in trouble, the first attraction, when what he really wants is someone to love and to be loved by so tenderly. Why can't I be that guy?

I think I should get off this bar stool. I never can tell how drunk I am when I'm sitting down.

❧   ❧   ❧

You're leaning against a column at the edge of the dance floor at Rage, watching the guys dance. You've just left Marcus and Jack and Dave. This time Dave doesn't follow you. He stays to talk to the football captains. You're tired of talking football. Besides, you're still pissed off that Jack didn't throw to you more often during the game. He threw the ball to you only once, and it was short. Yeah, there was a chance that you could have caught it if you had stopped your forward motion and had come back to the ball. But he had called a ten-yard out-and-slant, not some fuckin' buttonhook, and you're a deep man. If you had caught it, it would have just made him look good for throwing a bad pass. Besides, it's not like that play had any effect on the game anyhow.

You think there's more important things in life to talk about than football, and besides, you want to spend some time alone for a few minutes thinking about how good of an impression you made on Jack and on Klay at the party, and how that's going to help you get cast in another movie. So now you're watching the young crowd at Rage dance so recklessly, as though they think this is a happening place, when it's not. It's just they're too young to know better, and your mind is on that audition you had Thursday for the deodorant commercial, the one where you're in a locker room, your hair all sweaty and tangled, and you're lifting up the deodorant stick while you have one knee down on the locker room bench and your abs flexed and sweaty. Usually callbacks don't come until the next week, but you thought they would have considered you so good in that role that they would have called you back on Friday. But then, some casting directors are sticklers for the rules, and now you think how this is going to disrupt your schedule in the weight room because you're going to have to stick by the phone, and while you got a pager and all, it's time to get a cell phone. It's embarrassing when the subject comes up and you can't say you have a cell.

It's a real young crowd at Rage tonight. All the best guys are over at Orbit, but there was no reason for you to go there tonight, because the real reason for the night was that party anyway. Besides, you don't want to go through the hassle of parking over in that part of town, even though you wouldn't have to wait in line, since you are a priority member and the doorman thinks you're hot. Then you'd have to score some drugs, and you do have that callback coming probably on Monday.

This Rage crowd is so young. Some of the guys look like they haven't even graduated from high school. You wonder if here you might see that "Perfect Pecs" model, since he was so young and all. Then you two could match your pecs side by side. That will show him how many eyes really turn your way instead of his.

This cute blond who can't be any older than twenty-three walks off the dance floor, and his eyes lock right onto you, his long bangs sweaty as he stares at you kind of funny like, like he's seen you before. Then he walks by to one side, but he turns a couple times to look at you. He sees you've got it. That star quality. What they're looking for here in Hollywood. When they look at you, they can't tell whether you can act at first, but they can see star quality. You just got to get your star quality seen by the right people. This guy's too young. He isn't the right person. This isn't the right place to be seen. So you figure you might as well then just concentrate on taking someone home.

You find that blond again, getting a drink at the bar. Perhaps this guy won't get you discovered, but at least he sees that star quality in you. He looks up and sees you staring at him. He smiles as he stirs his drink with his little straw and then shyly lowers his eyes again. You think how this guy's pretty good-looking, and he could be a good lay tonight. Besides that, he'll help you understand how much star quality you really have. It's always best to see your star quality from another guy's perspective. It shows how much you really have it.

You jerk your neck while pulling down at the bottom of your shirt, making sure it's fitting nice and tight against your body. Then you approach this guy you know is so into you.

◐   ◐   ◐

Brenda leaned up on one elbow, looking over at Al as he lay on the mattress, his body covered in sweat, his eyes on the ceiling. He had put his briefs back on, but the rest of his body lay naked before her. He had just returned from the bathroom, where he had flushed the condom down the toilet. He had carried it with one hand under it in case any evidence might spill on Holly's floor. Brenda watched his eyes, so distant, as she wondered what was going through his mind. Was he pondering the beauty of their shared moment together? She hoped that to be the case. Or was he thinking of his deceit of Holly and Curt?

He turned his face toward her and smiled sadly, causing her to hope the former was the case. But his eyes turned once more toward the ceiling, and his face went vacant again.

"I should be going . . . in case Holly returns," he said.

"That probably is best," Brenda replied. As she spoke, she did actually believe that decision to be the best, that his comment was the proper one to make at this moment. But after her words were spoken, she felt both his sentence and her reply were betrayals of their recent experience. Then, after that thought, she realized both of them were conflicted, unsure how to react to this moment. Neither of them had expected to experience what they actually had. Neither of them had control over that.

Al propped himself on an elbow and slid his legs over the side of the bed, placing his feet on the floor. He scanned the floor to find his clothes before moving again. He leaned forward, ready to grab his T-shirt, but he was stopped by Brenda's hand holding him back. He turned around.

"I just wanted to say . . ." she found herself stuttering, "you did a great job . . . for a first time." She let go of him and placed both of her hands on her head, disheveling her hair, as she laughed to her comment. "I mean, really great . . . for any time."

He smiled, gazing at the sheet folded over her lap.

"Thanks. I guess you really got me going . . . you on top like that. It was . . . pretty cool."

He looked into her eyes. Their giddiness ceased as she looked deeply into his wide brown eyes. Embarrassed by her stare, he looked away and reached out for his T-shirt.

"What time is it? Oh gosh, if Holly comes back. I mean . . ."

He sat on the bed, his hands clutching his shirt, now draped on his lap.

"Brenda, please don't get me wrong. What we did tonight was . . . one of the greatest experiences of my life. It's just that . . . Holly is one of my best friends. I mean . . . and she's your girlfriend! And what about Curt? This has got to be a one-nighter. That's just the way it's got to be! I mean, I love Curt!"

Brenda nodded to herself. Al was right. They had to think of Holly. She meant for Al to be only a sexual experiment. She had no intention originally of having him come between her and Holly. Holly was the best thing that ever happened to her. She had always thought that way . . . until tonight.

Brenda lay back in the bed, her head propped up by the two pillows as she watched Al dress. As he finished tying the second of his tennis shoes, he turned to her and gave her a light kiss on the cheek.

"Good night. By the way, how does that *Baby Jane* movie end?"

"I've never seen it."

He laughed. "Well, then, I guess we'd better both watch it in our spare time, just in case the subject comes up."

He began to leave the bedroom.

"Al?"

He turned around.

"I was just thinking . . . if you hadn't met Curt, and I hadn't met Holly . . . do you think . . . there ever could have been something . . . you know . . . between us?"

Al slumped his shoulders in thought.

"I don't know. I mean, Brenda, I'm gay. And you're gay!"

She looked away from him, gazing to the side, contemplating his response.

"Al, will you do me a favor?"

"What's that?"

"The next time you jerk off by yourself, will you tell me who you think about at that moment?"

He stood there, motionless, his mouth open in response. Then composing himself, he nodded his head and walked out the door.

⬤ ⬤ ⬤

Our hero entered the Garage with Bill, his one close friend who also had a great appreciation for the alternative scene that was the antithesis of West Hollywood. The Garage had just begun an alternative music night on Saturdays. Since Trade had closed on Sunset so many years ago, Mitch and Bill had lamented the lack of alternative gay nightclubs. There was Cherry, of course, but it was hampered by the fact that it was located in the heart of West Hollywood. And there was Dragstrip in Silverlake every second Saturday of the month, but for Mitch the fact that it was also a drag bar dampened the alternative concept.

As soon as they entered the dark bar with the black walls, they noticed to their left a rise where a dozen men and a few women were dancing to the music of Nine Inch Nails. The rise was separated from the rest of the dance floor by the club's entry hall and the bar itself. Mitch looked up at the men. He nodded in approval to see their shabby chic thrift-store dress style, as opposed to the tank-tops-and-baseball-hats crowd in West Hollywood.

"Hey, this seems pretty cool," Bill said. "Nine Inch Nails." He bent his shoulders over and began singing, "I want to fuck you like an animal. I want to feel you from the inside."

"Sounds like one of us has had too much to drink . . . again," Mitch replied.

Bill brought up his shoulders. "Then let me buy you a drink . . . so you can catch up."

"I can't catch up if you buy yourself one as well."

"Then I'll switch to beer." Bill walked toward the bar without waiting for a response. Mitch followed, but at a slower pace.

Our hero found his friend quite an enigma tonight. Bill's announcement of his separation from his partner of five years had caught Mitch less by surprise than he would have imagined. Mitch had seen Bill's confidence and ambitions grow during the past few weeks. Then came the catalyst: when Randy Clayburg announced to Bill two days ago that he was able to recommend him for a job as a writer for a new series on the Lifetime channel. Mitch prided himself in playing a major role in helping Bill return from his descent. Mitch had done this by first recommending to Bill that he write an *Ally McBeal* spec script and introducing him and his script to such a major player as Randy—his new partner.

Bill had announced to Mitch several weeks ago, in fact during the halftime of the game against the Centurions, that he was going to break up with Larry, but at that point Mitch was unaware of the extent of Bill's recovery. Besides, he had no time to ponder Bill's unhealthy relationship with Larry. There was a game to be played at that moment.

And then came the second half of the game, when Bill played on a higher level, unmatched by anyone else. Mitch took some responsibility for Bill's playmaking as well. He had seen Bill play that great before, but it had been several years ago, when Bill was twenty pounds lighter and more optimistic about life. Mitch had contributed to Bill feeling that confidence once again.

When Bill made his announcement at Marcus's apartment, Mitch felt a sense of accomplishment. He had told Bill so many times that Larry was holding him back, but he had to speak gingerly on this topic. Although it was hard for him to recognize why, Mitch knew that Bill loved Larry; but he felt it was a love that was binding and detrimental to Bill's growth. "Behind every great man there's a great woman," was a saying Mitch firmly believed, even though he realized that the great person didn't have to actually be a woman. Larry was not a great man so Bill could not be a great man himself.

In fact, he found Bill and Larry's relationship the complete opposite of his own relationship with Randy. Because, with Randy by his side, there was a great man to support him. The only concern, however, was that Mitch, though he tried, did not love Randy. In fact, Randy's lack of sensuality irritated Mitch, and when they made love, his teeth would grind whenever Randy spoke in his nasally high voice. Now their sex was voiceless. In fact, silent. Ever since his breakup with Paul and ever since he had officially become Randy's partner six days ago, Mitch had begun to resent the fact that he now had to have sex with Randy on a regular basis.

Mitch watched as Bill kicked his shoe against the heel of a guy at the bar, then stumbled and caught his balance by placing his hand on the guy's shoulder, only to apologize before ordering the drinks. Mitch could not understand why his friend would drink so much tonight, during one of the most accomplished days of his life. And why did Bill seem so disinterested in the subject of his potential success through his connection with Randy? At Akbar, Mitch had asked Bill what his plans were, now that he was leaving Larry. He asked whether

Bill would seek the writing position at Lifetime. Bill responded only by saying, "I guess so," and then changing the subject to talk about how Ed's trick looked like a boorish and self-involved Nazi. He spoke about Ed's inability to discriminate character, which was a quality both charming and infuriating, since it placed everyone he knew at the same level, allowing many friends and lovers but no one of greater or lesser stature in his eyes.

Bill's inability this night to focus on the important matters of his life led Mitch to believe that his friend was at the moment envious of Ed and that his only true concern at the moment was getting laid himself. Yet Bill did not appear to be seeking sex. He had rarely looked around at Akbar. Instead, he seemed too concentrated on Ed and the man he had met.

Once again, the thought came into Mitch's mind that there was something going on between Bill and Ed.

Bill turned from the bar and, seeing Mitch, lifted his chin in acknowledgment and walked over to him with the drinks. On his way, he slid his beer bottle between the faux breasts of a Miss Kentucky Fried Chicken and licked the glass where it had touched the drag queen. The rest of his walk then became a chicken dance, causing him to spill a portion of Mitch's Absolut and cranberry.

"I love that drag queen. I've seen her at Dragstrip!" Bill exclaimed, handing Mitch his drink. "So antiglamorous."

Mitch removed his right hand from his pants pocket to grab his drink. Bill had put him into a playful mood, and now Mitch was swaying his shoulders back and forth, allowing himself to half-dance but not completely commit to this activity. This was one attribute that Mitch greatly admired in his friend—his ability to play for the joy of it, without considering the consequences. It was an attribute that he longed for but seldom attained. Those moments when he did attain it did not last long, for he soon began to analyze all the possibilities of every action he took.

"There are some nice-looking men around here, don't you think?" Mitch asked. "Real guylike guys, rather than those West Hollywood types."

"Oh, I don't know," Bill replied. "I think they were better looking back at Akbar."

"You weren't even looking back at Akbar! You were just watching that guy Ed was picking up on the whole time."

"No I wasn't. Believe me, that Drew—what a name!—didn't interest me at all. That Ed keeps on picking out pretty faces. I'm looking for a real guy."

Bill chuckled, a laughter that was affected and extended by his drunkenness. He slapped Mitch across the back.

"Looks like you're the only married guy now, huh? Me and Larry broken up. Sam and Jack no longer an item. Marcus always out there hunting some booty. You're the set-in-his-ways, domesticated husband now, it looks like."

Mitch had been perusing the dance floor as Bill spoke. He then turned toward his friend, whose eyes and nose were directed at him and only twelve inches from his face. But before our hero could respond to his friend's comment, Bill spoke once more.

"But really. I want to thank you . . . for everything. Don't think I don't appreciate what you've done . . . always having so much faith in me. You're the one guy who sees it."

Mitch perked up a smile as he looked into his friend's eyes. He placed his arm around Bill's shoulders.

"Hey, that's what friends are for."

Bill placed his arm around Mitch's shoulders as well, then took a drink from his other hand.

"That Randy seems like a great guy. You seem pretty happy with him, huh?"

"Hey, he's a fantastic guy. Very caring and extremely intelligent."

Mitch nodded to himself. The two of them grew quiet for a moment as they stared at the dancers. With the end of their exchange, they dropped their arms back to their sides.

"It's just that," our hero felt inclined to add, "I just wish Randy was a little more experienced with guys. I always feel I'm the one—if I can be excused for making such a pun—who is always 'directing' him in bed."

Bill laughed.

"What is it they say, how a person is often sexually the opposite of what he is in life?"

"I think you're right with Randy. There's so many qualities about the guy that I wouldn't have expected. For example, have you noticed how he always uses the adverb *really*? He *really* likes your script. He *really* loves the way I kiss him. It's such a lazy adverb. He doesn't know how to use a strong verb that *really* packs a jolt on what he is trying to say. Would you expect *really* to always be coming out of an Emmy-winning director?"

Bill laughed again.

"Mitch, this is Hollywood, not *The New Yorker*."

"Well, it does annoy me."

Bill grabbed Mitch by the forearm. His drunkenness always caused him to place his face too close to his friend when he spoke. Mitch could smell the alcohol on his breath.

"Well, that all goes with the territory. There's always things you like and things you don't like about somebody. But if you're going to make it work, you just have to say to yourself how all those things you don't like about the guy are insignificant when it comes down to it, because you love the guy, and all his qualities—good and bad—are a part of him. You accept them. I mean, you've got to if you care about him."

"And that's where you and I disagree," Mitch spoke out. "I don't accept them. If you care about the person, you help him overcome them."

"Oh . . . OK. So have you told Randy that you *really* don't like the way he always says *really* and offered to help him overcome this nasty habit?"

Mitch smirked and snorted. "I believe my friend is not so sober tonight."

Bill placed his arm around our hero once again, then lifted his beer bottle to his lips and surveyed the dance crowd. Mitch also gazed at the dancers.

"That's what I love about us, Mitch," Bill said as he lowered his bottle. "We can have such a stimulating intellectual conversation in a crowd that is thinking only about getting laid and how their hips are moving to the song. But as Marilyn Manson blares over the loud-speakers, we discuss the disintegration of the English language through the prevalence of lazy adverbs."

Mitch nodded. He was very aware of his friend's sarcasm, but he found Bill's words witty and true. He again placed his arm around Bill's shoulder, now realizing that he was not completely sober himself, and as he watched the crowd he thought of Randy, of his nasty little habit. But as was often the case, when thinking of Randy, his mind would wander over to Paul Harris and how perhaps he had not tried hard enough to help his old boyfriend overcome his own nasty little habits. If he had just tried harder, if he had just been able to instill more drive and ambition into Paul, then instead of standing idly by the dance floor watching the crowd, he would be in bed tonight in the arms of the one man he had truly loved.

◉ ◉ ◉

had to bump into jack and marcus dropped so many passes right in my hands and i drop them dad laughing *when the going gets tough the tough get going* cliché how can you fix nerves michael jordan always gets the ball in clutch situations i avoid them will drop the catch give it to me when it doesnt matter i'll catch it then dad knows it i embarrass him to be this way never a man cant handle pressure

"Miss David thing. I like that shirt on you," Marcus says. miss david why does he call me that 'cause i'm a girl. "You been growing those muscles, ain't you been?"

jack looking away with his sea breeze ashamed of me all these muscles and i cant catch a pass muscles have nothing to do with it

"I guess. I've been going to the gym." if dad dies he'll look down on me see me dropping all those passes *i told you so* he says to someone up in heaven *howd you like a son like that not worth a dime* but then if he does i have to catch them he'll be watching me and i'll catch them miss marcus grunts looking at my shoulders he turns to jack

"I shoulda figured you'd be lookin' for a child at Rage once you and Sam was through. Any boy you like?"

"Ha! Pretty!" jack bellows eyes squinting lines on his face wants to fuck a boy. "Miss thing, you always say that, but you can see with Sam it shows that's not always the case."

"Usually the case," Marcus flips his hand. "And Sam is just a big ol' girl at heart who just happens to know how to catch a pass or two."

jack looks at me lines on his face was it disgust he shows the way his eyes look at me cant catch a pass even worse than a big old girl

"Well, at least some of us can catch the ball," jack says lower my eyes ashamed cant move what can i say wish i had followed jerry

"Oh, now you changin' the subject cuz you embarrassed how much you like young things," marcus defends me punches me friendly on the shoulder looking at me

"You know, Dave, you got good hands. It's just game jitters. That's all. You're important to this team, you know."

i nod marcus is a friend so outgoing like to be more like him tony would like that be more talkative like him want to be his the girlfriend of a former pitt gridiron star both of us playing ball

"You should just stop thinkin' so much on the field," Marcus says. "Just let it happen. I see you out there, runnin' a perfect pattern, whippin' your man down the field, ball fallin' right to you, and then you drop it. Just don't think 'bout it, man. Let it happen. And if you do, you'd be one of the best players on the team. I swear to you. It just takes some confidence. You know what I'm saying?"

i nod confidence is all i need i can have it that tony liked me what a man and likes me because of who i am i can catch a pass any pass that comes my way all it takes is knowing i can do it i can do it with tony by my side

"Say, I met this guy tonight. He used to play football for Pitt. It's too bad we already started the league. He might have been a good player to have on the team." why do i say that would tony like others on the team but he likes me those dark eyes so concerned when i spoke of dad his own father having died he understands a connection between us mom would love him

"The Pitt Panthers?" Marcus asks. "What position did he play?" first thing marcus would ask and i didnt even ask him couldnt under the situation quarterback receiver or something i expect

"I didn't ask him. He's not big enough for the line. So I expect a quarterback or receiver or something."

"A quarterback!" Marcus exclaims. "Ooh child, cover Jack's ears when you say that. Another quarterback. Jack'd be out of a job!"

when should i call him why do i act like this met him for ten minutes at the most and now i want him so why bring up expectations he couldnt really care for me but his eyes were so beautiful gazing down on mine i cant recall any part of him below his head just those eyes and that friendly smile and i'm wearing this shirt like some gym queen how could he care about me and i see him taking off his shirt and out appears a dark hairy italian chest so manly and he approaches me and kisses me gently his eyes looking into mine and tumbles over me onto the bed and i embrace him wrap my arms and legs around him and we kiss for eternity and he'll love me and i'll catch every pass that comes my way i'll be the star of every game and he'll be so proud of me and i'll dedicate every game to him my man the one i love except on the day my dad if he dies i'll win the game for him i'll catch the touchdown pass that wins the game i have everything going for me so why cant i catch the pass

"Ha!" Jack utters. "Pretty!"

Curt opened the bedroom door, having just finished his bartending shift at Apache, still dressed in his flannel shirt, jeans, and boots. Driving home, he was eager to catch a glimpse of Al sleeping peacefully in their bed, waiting for the man he loved to return. When Al actually was there, the folded-back sheets exposing his bare upper body on this warm April evening, he breathed deeply, happy that his vision could be realized. He had known that Al had gone to Holly's to watch videos that night, but he had concerns that afterward his boyfriend would hit the bars looking for a trick. He couldn't blame Al if he did. Curt realized how much of an asshole he had been to his man these last few months—Never trusting, always jealous.

As he drove home that night, having rebuked the advances of several of his patrons, even the cute ones he had fooled around with before, he felt a warm glow on his cheeks, thinking that his petty mistrust was unfounded, nothing more than a figment of his imagination. He loved Al, more than anyone he had ever loved before. This love had frightened him, thinking that no one could return such love. So there had been mistrust. There had been jealousy. But at this moment he could only think to himself, "Why have I pushed it away? Al loves me, completely. We are in love."

Actual tears began to fall then. He quickly wiped them away with his fingers and then, catching himself doing so involuntarily, he looked at his red eyes in the rearview mirror and laughed to himself joyously all the way to his Hollywood apartment.

Al stirred as Curt began to close the door, causing a high-pitched creak in the hinge.

"Mmmm . . . Curt," Al murmured, turning his right cheek off the pillow. He opened his eyes.

"Sorry to wake you up, baby," Curt whispered. "I'll be in bed soon."

"I wanted you to wake me," Al replied. He let out a yawn. "I wanted to see you."

"Yeah?"

Curt looked down at his boyfriend. He noticed Al's pillow was wet.

"Did you take a shower?" he asked.

"Uh-huh."

Curt smiled softly, approaching the man he loved. He sat on the bed next to him, then brought down his face and kissed Al gently. Al placed his hand against the back of Curt's head and pulled him down, turning the gentle kiss into a deep embrace.

"Ah, baby," Curt said as his lips parted from Al's. "I've been thinking about you."

Al smiled warmly, shaking his head.

"It's OK if you came tonight," he said.

Curt looked at him, puzzled.

"You see, Curt, I've been dreaming about it for the last couple of hours."

Al raised his back to place his arms around Curt's shoulders, pulling him down on the bed with him. He kissed him again, then moved his lips over to his boyfriend's ear, gently nibbling on his lobe before whispering the contents of his dream.

"I've been desiring it so much . . . to be inside you."

Curt's puzzled gaze lasted a moment longer, but soon the hard lines on his face melted, and he again felt that warm glow on his cheeks. He smiled joyously, nuzzling his nose in the nape of Al's neck. Now, more than anything in the world, he desired to surrender to his man's love.

9

The West Hollywood Warriors

Bill walked onto the fields of Fairfax High. He was the first of the Quake to appear, but as he approached the sidelines he saw all of the Warriors—Vince, of course, with his tall, lean frame, appearing nothing of the athletic type, and yet perhaps the best receiver on either team. Tom, the agent, his red head towering above the rest of his team. Bob, the dark, handsome quarterback-slash-leather-bar bartender with the sexy, stoner eyes. Dan, the blond wide receiver who had moments of brilliance on the field but at other times could drop an easy ten-yard pass. Jim, the young, balding flanker devoted to Vince's style of play of constant five- and ten-yard passes up the field. J. R., the fast Latin flanker with a license plate on his Beemer that read "USC Brat." And Julio, their newest weapon—a straight Latin boy just out of high school who had become their star halfback, providing the Warriors with a running game. Unlike the Quake's informal pregame warm-up, the Warriors had adopted a strict regimen before each game—a session of two lines with receivers on one side and defenders on the other, playing one on one as Bob threw them short passes.

Bill could not understand his teammates' late appearance. This was the big game. After today, only one of the gay teams would remain undefeated—both teams had won their first three games.

The game also marked the end of the first half of the season, as everyone had a week off next Saturday due to the Easter weekend.

Bill dropped his bag next to the team's empty bench. He unzipped his bag and pulled out his jersey. As he removed his T-shirt and was placing his head and arms through the holes of his jersey, he heard a thumping against the soft dirt of the field. It grew louder, and so he rushed to poke his head out the other side of the blue mesh.

The rest of the Quake—all dressed in their jerseys and cleats—ran in unison toward the field. Jack and Marcus were in the lead, followed by Al, Curt, Mitch, and Ed all in a row. Jerry and Dave and one other man brought up the rear. Bill wondered who that last player could be. Then, as they approached, he saw it was Sam. Sam had returned for the big game!

"All right now, Quake!" Marcus led them to the bench. "We got this game now! Big game now! We are the Quake! Let's go now!"

They ran up to Bill, their cleats digging into the ground, pulling up the grass behind them.

"Man! Don't you listen to your answering machine?" Marcus scolded him. "We all were meeting in front of the gym so we could make an appearance!"

Bill looked red-faced at his teammates.

"Well . . . I . . . uh . . . wasn't home last night. I'm single now. Remember?"

"Bill, you know what Muhammad Ali always said: no sex the night before a big bout," Ed teased him.

"Fuck that!" Bill exclaimed. "Jack, you just throw me the ball and see what I'm going to do."

Bill walked up to Sam and extended his hand.

"Welcome back, Sam. I thought you moved to New York."

Sam bypassed Bill's hand and gave him a hug instead.

"I'm in transition right now. I thought, since I'm back in LA this week, I couldn't pass up the big game."

"Yeah, yeah, right!" said Jack, who again hid his emotion with his dark sunglasses. "We got a big game now, Quake! Stop all your gossiping, and let's get on the field."

Mitch kicked the ball long to the right side of the field, just as he intended, so that it would stay out of the hands of Julio and go instead into Dan's possession. Although Dan had speed, he never ran straight toward the goal line when he saw one or more defenders running him down. With three defenders in front of him, Dan ran to the side, hoping for some blocking from Tom and Bob, but Curt rushed in fast and pulled his flag at the thirty-yard line.

"All right, Curt!" Bill yelled. "That's the way to start, Quake! That's the way to start!"

The Quake set up on defense.

"Watch for the long pass!" Marcus yelled. "I know that Vince. Watch the pass to him."

The Warriors lined up with Bob back in shotgun formation, five yards behind the center. Julio was crouched to Bob's right.

"Hike!"

Julio flared out to the right behind the line of scrimmage. Tom stayed back to defend Ed, who was rushing the quarterback. Bill stayed at the scrimmage line, waiting for Bob's move, which turned out to be a side lateral to Julio.

"They're running! They're running!" Marcus yelled.

Marcus and Mitch raced up to the line of scrimmage. Then, suddenly, Vince kicked his right foot out and ran up the sideline. Mitch and Marcus could not react in time. Marcus tried to reverse his momentum and run back, but he slid on some mud and fell. Now it was only Curt to break up the play, but Vince was three strides ahead of him.

Julio threw the pass over Curt's head and into Vince's arms.

Touchdown.

The Quake looked away from the end zone, not wanting to watch the Warriors cheering as they ran toward Vince and hugged him. Marcus, his hands on his hips, looked at the individual members of his team, seeing their downcast eyes and their enthusiasm suddenly drained by a single catch.

"All right now, Quake! Set up on defense!" Marcus yelled. "Don't give them the two points. They've showed us what they can do now, and we're gonna adjust. Man, it's stupid of them to show everything they got right away. We got this game now."

The two-point conversion play looked exactly like the last, with Julio flaring out behind the line of scrimmage. Bill and the rest did not run up to the line, staying in their place, not wanting to be fooled again. The pass was then thrown to Julio, who ran it this time for the two-point conversion.

The Warriors were up 8-0.

"That's OK, Quake! That's OK!" Marcus encouraged his team, clapping his hands. "Now it's the Quake's turn. Let's show them what we can do."

Mitch returned the kickoff to the forty-five-yard line, setting up good field position for their first set of downs. The Quake had agreed before the game that Mitch and Curt would remain the wide receivers, while Sam would be rotated into the flanker position. Al had told Sam that he could start over him, since Sam had not played for a few weeks.

The Quake came to the line. Vince saw Mitch and Curt line up close to the flankers.

"Watch the short pass!" Vince called out to his team.

Jack scowled when he heard Vince's words. He stepped back into shotgun formation. He looked at his line on his left. Then he looked at his line on his right.

"Hike!"

Everyone on the team ran perfect patterns. J. R. followed Mitch toward the middle of the field, leaving Ed open on the right sideline. When Mitch and Curt crossed in the middle, the Warrior defenders were confused, and both receivers became open in the middle field fifteen yards out. Jack now had three open men for an easy first down.

Instead, Jack's eyes were on Sam.

Vince and Julio—the two deep defenders—had both picked up on Sam as he ran toward the end zone. Sam had caught up with Vince and picked up a stride or two on him. But then Julio came over and effortlessly matched Sam's steps.

The ball was thrown with Julio and Sam side by side. They both jumped . . .

Julio came down with the ball.

Sam could not turn around in time, as Julio squared himself with the goal line on the far side of the field and began running with the ball. He had as his first blocker Vince, who dove down on Curt's waist, knocking him to the ground. Julio now ran up the right sideline directly at Ed, who had no one blocking him. Ed squared up, ready to pull the flag, but Julio twisted his hips and cut into the middle, leaving Ed standing.

With Bill out of the picture on the left sideline, only Jack and Marcus were between Julio and the end zone. Bob placed a block on Jack, so now it was only Marcus, who fought off Tom's powerful heave and ran toward Julio. They now were neck and neck, Marcus needing only a hand's length to pull the flag. Marcus dove, trying to pull the flag. But Julio was too quick, and he shot past him.

Touchdown.

"Damn!" Curt yelled. He ran up to Jack. "What the fuck was that!"

"Dammit, Jack!" Mitch added. "Why should we follow what you call in the huddle if you don't follow it yourself?"

"I'm sorry," Jack tried to defend himself. "It's just when Vince said we were throwing the short pass . . . well, that got me flustered."

"Jack!" Mitch exclaimed. "You're telling me Vince is psyching you out!?"

"It ain't Vince who's psyching him out," Marcus argued as he walked up to Jack, his hands on his hips.

Marcus placed his lips to Jack's ear, whispering, "You ain't gonna win him back, you know. So play the game right. Don't fuck it up for the rest of us."

Bob connected on an inside slant pass to Dan for the two-point conversion. It was now the Warriors 16, the Quake nothing.

The kickoff return brought the Quake to their own thirty-yard line. Heeding the warnings of his teammates, Jack followed the original strategy the Quake had come up with for this game, connecting on short passes to Al, Marcus, and Ed on the inside and Mitch and Curt in the middle pocket, while Sam sat out the first five plays. They now had a first down at the Warriors' twenty-yard line and were threatening to score.

But trouble came again when Sam substituted in for Ed.

On first down, Sam stayed back to give Tom a hit, slowing his progress to the quarterback. At the last moment Sam ran out five yards. Jack passed the ball to him, but Bob was right there to knock it down. On second down, Sam ran a post pattern across the field, while

Mitch ran long up the right sideline and Curt and Al crossed in the middle. Again, Jack threw it to Sam, but the ball went high over his head.

Third down. Marcus told Jack to keep Sam back to block while Marcus himself would flare out and up the left sideline, the rest of the team slanting right to clear one side of the field for him. Jack bobbled the hike, however, and seeing Tom get clear of Sam, Jack rolled to the right, trying to stay away from the rusher. J. R. then came in as a second rusher, so Jack threw a desperate short pass to Sam that hit the ground before Sam could run up to retrieve it.

Fourth and ten.

There was total silence in the huddle. No one could believe what was happening. All they could do was stare at the ground, reliving the past few minutes when everything that could go wrong did go wrong.

Marcus pulled Jack out of the huddle, away from the others, to talk to him captain to captain.

"Man, ain't you just winning Sam back with all those passes to him? Don't matter if the throws suck, just as long as you throw it to him."

"Dammit, Mother! You see he missed the block on Tom. I had to roll out."

Marcus nodded, his lips pursed, hands on his hips.

"Uh-huh. I think maybe we should get out Mitch's throwing arm."

"Fuck that, Mother! You'll see. We're going to get this first down."

This time, Jack didn't even get a chance to throw it to Sam. Al's hike was low, hitting Jack on his shins. The ball was down, and now the Warriors had possession.

"Dammit, Al! What was that?" Jack argued.

"Hey, you don't have the right to argue about Al's hike!" Curt yelled. "Fuck that! He's not the one losing the game for us."

During the Warriors' series of downs, Bob played his usual style of game, throwing the short passes. They called no huddles but came straight to the line. No pass was thrown longer than ten yards, but they all were caught. And the Warriors' possession ended the same as each possession had before, on a touchdown, this time a twenty-yard run by Julio. They followed that with another run by Julio for the two-point conversion.

The Warriors were whipping the Quake 24-0.

"Why am I even playing this game?" Bill argued. "We're down by three touchdowns, and I haven't touched the ball yet."

Bill said this to no one in particular, but it was Ed who overheard him. Ed walked up to him and put his hand on Bill's shoulder.

"Fuck!" Bill yelled again, this time to Ed. "You know what we've got to do."

But Marcus had overhead Bill, and he walked over to them, nodding.

"Yeah, Bill. I know what we got to do."

Marcus called a time-out. The entire team huddled on the field.

"We got to do something," Marcus said. "And I think we all know what that is."

Marcus looked directly at Jack.

"OK, Mitch." Marcus grabbed his wide receiver by the forearm. "You're quarterbacking this series. Dave, you come in. Jack and Sam are out."

Jack looked back at the huddle.

"Mother, what are you talking about? You know Mitch doesn't have a strong enough throwing arm."

"He knows how to connect on the short passes, and that's what we need. Besides, we need to start thinking more of the run, man. They don't have the speed up close. We'll get a first down every time on a run."

"If I recall, I'm the captain on offense," Jack argued.

"Oh?" Marcus gave him a long look. Then he turned to the other teammates. "How many of you want Jack captaining us on offense right now?"

Jack looked from player to player, his face reddening, embarrassed that this had to be taken to a vote. No one raised a hand.

"Sorry, Jack," Bill said. "I just think we need to try something different."

Marcus nodded.

"So you and Sam go sit over there on the sidelines, work out whatever is going on between you two, and we'll play ball," Marcus said.

"Fuck, Marcus!" Sam interrupted, "Don't put the blame on me!"

"You're right, Sam. I can't put no blame on you. It's just you are an unfortunate player in whatever game is going on in Jack's mind."

They all watched Jack as he marched toward the bench. The referee walked up to the Quake.

"One minute, guys!" the referee yelled. "Let's get this game going."

Al turned to Marcus.

"Let Sam go in for me. Now that Jack is out, there's no problem with him in."

Sam shook his head.

"Nah. That's OK, Al."

Sam then turned to each teammate and shook their hands.

"It was a pleasure to be a Quake. But, you know, I'm tired of being butch."

Sam left the huddle and walked toward the sidelines.

"OK now. OK. Sam made his choice," Marcus said. "Huddle up now, Quake."

But Mitch called no play, as his teammates' eyes were watching Sam as he stopped next to Jack, who had put his dark sunglasses on and was holding his hands on his hips as though they were a necessary support to keep standing. Sam then leaned over and wrapped his long arms around Jack's back.

"Remember, Quake?" Mitch brought them back into reality. "We got a huddle here?"

On the first play of this series, Mitch kept the ball and ran up the sideline for a first down. The rules of the league allow one run per first down, and so the Quake had the opportunity to run again. This time, Mitch threw a lateral to Marcus, who ran behind Ed's and Curt's blocks for a touchdown.

"That's it, Quake! That's it!" Bill yelled as he ran up to the running back and the blockers. "Now we're rolling!"

Mitch handed the ball off to Marcus again, but the Warriors had expected another run, and Bob pulled Marcus's flag two yards before he could reach the end zone.

24-6, Warriors.

The Quake were able to play out the last two minutes of the half without allowing the Warriors to score again. When the whistle blew, the Quake returned to their silent bench, but Jack was not there.

The second half was almost ready to begin, and Jack had not returned. Marcus and Bill had spent most of halftime searching for him, and when they returned to their teammates saying they could not find their quarterback, Jerry lashed out.

"What the fuck does it matter anyway?" Jerry spoke to Marcus directly. "I don't get it why you allowed Sam to start the game. If I had been put in more, it would be a different game, especially with Jack so fucked up throwing to his old boyfriend."

"Don't put the blame on Sam. He had nothing to do with it."

The Quake turned their heads when they heard this voice from behind. Jack had returned.

"You're right, Jerry. I'm the one who fucked up," Jack said. "Put the blame on me, OK?"

Marcus walked up to his quarterback.

"No more distractions now?"

Jack shook his head.

"No more distractions. I know now. Sam's gone."

"'Cause you know we can't win this game without you."

Jack took off his sunglasses and stood face to face with the other captain. Marcus could see the redness in his eyes.

"All right then, Quake!" Marcus yelled. "Let's show them motherfuckers what we're made of!"

The Warriors kicked off. The ball landed firmly in the arms of Mitch, who got behind a wedge formation of Ed, Bill, and Jerry, all three of them making perfect blocks to get Mitch just past the fifty-yard line.

Then Jack took over. He started with a ten-yard buttonhook to Al for a first down. Then he threw a seven-yard pass out to Curt and a fifteen-yard pass out to Mitch for a first down. On his signature play, Bill picked up another fifteen yards when all the other receivers slanted right, and he ran under them to the left, catching the ball five yards out and picking up ten more yards on the run. On the next play, Marcus rolled out to the right, received a lateral from Jack, and ran it uncontested into the end zone.

Touchdown.

Cross blocking from Curt and Bill then allowed Marcus to run up the left side of the center for the two-point conversion.

24-14, the Warriors.

The Warriors came to the line. The ball was hiked. Vince ran a fifteen-yard buttonhook. At the same time, Julio rolled out to the left and raced up the sideline. Curt and Bill went with Julio, while Mitch covered the possible pass to Vince up the middle.

Suddenly, Vince kicked his foot in and began running a flag up the right side of the field. Mitch, caught off guard for a moment, dug in and began chasing him.

The ball was thrown, a long, high arching pass to Vince.

Mitch caught up a step, but he was still a stride behind Vince. The ball hung long in the air, and then came down.

Mitch leapt, and as he did his leadoff foot caught the back of Vince's shoe. Mitch rose up in the air and caught the ball, while Vince tripped to the ground.

"That's it, Mitch!" Bill yelled, pounding his fists on his chest plate like King Kong. "Oooh yeah!"

As soon as he was back up on his feet, Vince walked up to the referee. He twisted his foot around to show the official how his shoe had been pulled off his heel.

The referee blew his whistle. The Quake, unaware of Vince's protests, suddenly turned to where the whistle had been blown.

"Pass interference!" the ref yelled. "It's Warriors' possession where the ball was caught!"

"What!" Mitch yelled.

"Fuck that 'what' shit!" Vince yelled back. "You tripped me. Dammit! What is that showing the league, the way you guys play dirty ball? I tell you, I'm damn glad now we picked our own teams."

"Oh, fuck you, Vince!" Mitch said. "I never tripped you! I caught the ball over you, and you have to complain like you always do, trying to show the ref you're the real sport, and so you always get your way with them. Don't give us shit like that!"

Vince stared Mitch down with a scowl, but then his lips rose in a condescending grin before he turned to his teammates.

"Let's huddle, Warriors! We got fifteen yards for a touchdown!"

The referee's call had infuriated the Quake, but it also had blown steam out of their comeback. When Julio ran around Tom's and J. R.'s block for a touchdown, most of Quake began to think that they would have to wait another day for a victory against the Warriors.

The Quake picked up two more touchdowns, including Dave's first score of the season when he sprinted out from the center position and caught the ball over his shoulder, beating both Vince and Julio down the field for the touchdown. It was the play of the day, the catch that Dave had always dreamed he could never make, and yet it went unnoticed as the outcome of the game had already been decided. When the whistle blew two minutes later, the Quake had lost their first game of the season by a score of 38-28, causing Dave to believe he had only made that catch because it meant nothing, and so there was no pressure on him.

Bill walked off the field. When the Quake won, Bill felt like he was part of the team. But when they lost, he felt alone. As he approached his car, Bill turned and saw Marcus walking ten yards behind him. For a moment their eyes connected, and both of them knew they felt the same loneliness, the same shame, the same isolation. Bill, seeing his own expression on Marcus's face, finally realized he was not alone. He was part of a team. The Quake had become one, and as he entered his car and drove away, Bill began believing it would be that oneness through which he and all his teammates would find what they were searching for.

🔷 10 🔷

Here We Go!

Just a two-hour drive from Los Angeles on the eastbound 10
freeway lies the city of Palm Springs in the Coachella Valley at the
edge of the towering, rocky, orange brown San Jacinto Mountains.
Home to 45,000 residents in the summer and 90,000 in the winter,
Palm Springs is renowned for its sculpted designer golf courses, retir-
ees living in manicured trailer parks, the second mansions of TV ce-
lebrities, the late Sonny Bono, Bob Hope, lesbians at the Dinah Shore
Classic, white leather and rhinestone fashions, waterfall oases, palm
trees, lush lawns uprooted twice a year for the summer sod and the
winter rye, gay couples in their fifties finally leaving LA and now living on quiet cul-de-sacs, temperatures in the 110s, shimmering pools
surrounded by chaise longues and misting hoses, and, most of all, the
biggest spring break on the West Coast.

Within this city, among the hundreds of lodgings ranging from the
Motel 6 to the Merv Griffin's Resort, is situated the Marquis Hotel,
complete with 315 rooms, a villa and suite annex across the street,
two restaurants, a salon, and a fitness center. As is the case with every
hotel in Palm Springs, the main attraction of the Marquis is its swim-
ming pool—not so that the hotel guests can swim, but so they can
lounge around this shimmering showcase in their Speedos, arriving
early to snatch the most coveted chaise longues, so they can spread
out on their towels, with their backpacks, their tanning oil, their
magazines, their diet sodas, their water bottles, their sunglasses, their
Walkmans, and their cell phones.

Six weeks ago, the place to be had been New Orleans and Bourbon
Street, but now, during this final weekend of Lent, the circuit boys
were at the Marquis Hotel in Palm Springs.

The ninth annual White Party weekend had begun.

Among the 5,000 revelers at the White Party would be eight members of the Quake. Several months ago Jack had purchased two VIP packages—one for himself and one for Sam—but with Sam's departure to New York, Marcus had bought the $250 package from Jack for $100. The package included two nights at the Marquis (double occupancy), a VIP pass to six parties (Friday's Military Ball and the Afterhours Party, Saturday's White Party and the Climax 6 Afterhours Party, and Sunday's Sunset T-Dance and the Closing Party), a gay welcome packet, a gay guide to Palm Springs, and a White Party T-shirt.

Jerry had successfully persuaded Dave to come to Palm Springs, and now they shared with two other guys a single room containing one double bed. Dave had brought his sleeping bag, knowing that Jerry and Jake had already claimed the bed. The fourth guest—Stephen—had slept on the floor closest to the bathroom on Friday night, but he vowed that tonight—Saturday—he would find a man and sleep in someone else's room.

Curt and Al had taken a ground-floor room in the villa near the pool. Curt hadn't missed a White Party in the past six years. At last year's White Party Curt had picked up two uncut German boys for a ménage à trois. This year, he hoped that he could share a similar experience with Al, believing another three-way might strengthen their love for each other and also assure them they were still two cool guys who weren't stuck in some binding, marriage-style relationship.

Bill and Mitch arrived today but are staying just outside Palm Springs at the country club home of Ted Morkelson, an HBO producer and a friend of Randy Clayburg. Having business back in LA that kept him from enjoying his desert home this Easter weekend, Ted had lent his keys to Mitch for a one-night stay. The home was located in Cathedral City, just down Palm Canyon Drive from Palm Springs. Since they were not staying at the Marquis, Bill and Mitch had arranged to meet Jack and Marcus in their hotel room at 9:30 that night.

Before we begin the events of this evening, let us put into perspective the logistics of the Marquis so the reader can visualize the comings and goings of our friends and the other party revelers. As a point of direction, we will stand in the courtyard just behind and to the east of the hotel lobby. Facing west from this red-tiled courtyard, there is the main building with the restaurant to the left and the lobby in the middle. The White Party will take place in the basement, which spans the entire breadth of this building.

On the south (left) side of the courtyard is a Jacuzzi. On the north (right) side is a three-story building of guest rooms. Jack and Marcus are staying on the second floor of this building in Room 202, located very close to the lobby. Jerry and Dave are staying on the third floor in Room 343.

Turning away from the main building and looking east from the courtyard, there is a two-lane street. We must cross this street to enter the suites and villas of the Marquis. As we cross this street heading east, we come upon another courtyard, and in the back of this courtyard is the pool. To the south of this pool are the large suites. To the north of this pool are the smaller rooms of the villa. Curt and Al are in the villa on the first floor in room V125. Their window looks out onto the pool.

It is 9:45 p.m. The temperature is finally falling below seventy degrees. There is not a cloud to be seen, just thousands of stars in a black desert sky. Music is blaring from at least twenty different rooms. Dozens of guys in white tank tops are walking through the main courtyard as they make their way toward the White Party. Bill and Mitch are now driving to the hotel—Bill wearing a light cream knit shirt and 501s, Mitch in a tight blue V-neck polyester/spandex shirt and black cargo pants. Jack and Marcus are in their room smoking marijuana and drinking sea breezes—Jack wearing a white tank top and black 501s, Marcus in a foam green tank top and black leather pants. Jerry and Dave are in their room alone drinking Budweisers—Jerry in a white tank top and black 501s, Dave wearing an ordinary white T-shirt and blue 501s. Curt and Al have just woken up from their disco nap and are both drinking Samuel Adams beer. They are wearing nothing.

It is now 9:46 p.m. By some coincidence, unbeknownst to any of them, at this very minute each one of our eight friends is chewing up an ecstasy pill at exactly the same time.

All except one, that is.

And so ready—

Here we go!

"It's going to be a while, maybe an hour or so, before it kicks in," Jerry speaks, his breath steaming up the bathroom mirror as he twists a short lock of his hair between two fingers so that it curves up and then out for the proper effect above his forehead. "Jake says it's good shit. So . . . glad you came now?"

Dave sits on one edge of the bed, flipping through a men's magazine that Jerry had brought. He stops at one page displaying a muscular blond guy—completely shaved from ankle to neck—wearing nothing but a red Speedo and a small workout towel draped over a shoulder of glistening skin.

"Yeah. I guess so. This guy in the magazine. I saw him down at the pool today."

"The one in the red swimsuit?"

"Yeah."

"Yeah, I saw him, too. He sure looks bigger in the magazine than in real life. That's for a leg workout article, right? I didn't think his legs were so hot down at the pool. Say, we got any more beers?"

"I thought we should only be drinking water with this."

"Hey, I've got to have my beer. If it doesn't kick in right, I'll just move on over to K."

"Do you think this is OK, this T-shirt? I just don't have much that's white."

Jerry comes out of the room. He walks over to the ice bucket and pulls out the last Budweiser. He shrugs his shoulders, twists off the cap, and takes a big gulp.

"It's all right. You've got a white tank top, don't you? It's hot tonight."

"I've been looking down at the courtyard. Everyone's wearing a white tank top."

"It doesn't matter. You won't be wearing your shirt anyway once you get to the party. Hey! Do you feel it kicking in at all?"

"I thought it took an hour."

Jerry walks over to Dave and cocks his head to look down at the model in the red Speedo. "Yeah, I remember you were gawking at him at the pool. In fact, you were doing a lot of gawking."

Dave flips the magazine closed. "No, I wasn't. It's just . . . I mean . . . I've never seen that many guys with . . . such great bodies."

Jerry shrugs his shoulders again.

"Ah, it wasn't that great. You should see when I'm on one of my photo shoots. Once, in Milan, there were five of us with perfect bodies. And all these women on the streets were gawking at us. And good-looking young Italian girls. I fucked one of them, right after I fucked one of the models."

Jerry takes another big gulp, his eyes widening.

"Fuck, I can't believe Jake and Stephen took off so early. What is it? Not even ten."

"They said there'd be a line by now."

"Ah, I won't have to stand in the line." Jerry looks in the mirror above a chest of drawers. "Yeah, I timed it right. See. Look, I still got the pump. It's been nearly four hours since the gym, and I still got it." He plants his face and one flexed arm closer to the mirror. "Yeah. This is the time to go on down."

Jerry backs up from the mirror.

"You ready?"

Dave stands up from the bed.

"Got your keys?

Dave nods.

Jerry opens the door, and they walk onto the outdoor hallway overlooking the courtyard.

"I gotta walk back to my truck first," Jerry says. "Left the K there."

"Are you supposed to mix K with X?"

"That's the only way to take it."

They enter the courtyard, Jerry strutting his shoulders more than usual as he walks behind three muscular men all in white tank tops. They enter the lobby and then walk out onto the parking lot.

"Hey! There's Bill and Mitch!" Dave points.

Jerry nods as Bill and Mitch approach.

"Hey, fellas," Jerry speaks first. "See you downstairs? Hey Mitch, nice shirt. Been working out, huh? Well, we'll see you down there. I got to get something in my truck."

"Let me guess," Bill says, "drugs?"

Dave smiles sheepishly. "Well . . . it is a circuit party."

Bill slaps Dave on the shoulder, laughing.

"Hey, Dave. It's OK. I'm sure the next time you see me, I'll be totally fucked up."

"Well, we'll see you guys in there," Mitch states, and then he and Bill enter the lobby.

"You think we should have invited them up to Jack's room?" Bill asks.

"No. I mean, can you really consider having a conversation with Jerry?" Mitch slaps his forehead. "Fuck! I said 'really'! I'm picking up Randy's bad habit."

Bill laughs, looking Mitch up and down.

"I just can't believe you're wearing that shirt. It's so gay for you. And what is it with those pockets on the side of your pants?"

"You think the shirt's too much? I asked you before back at the house. You said you liked it."

"I do. If I was as skinny as you, I'd wear something like that, too. It's just, well, I'm proud of you. It shows you're beginning to accept your homosexuality."

"Fuck you. And they're called cargo pants. L.L. Bean. I ordered them over the Internet. They say they're coming into fashion."

"Right. That'll be the day. It reminds me when we were wearing wool Army pants back in college."

"You are dating yourself, my friend."

"Oh, I know. I hate it when I get to this age and I see all these things I wore in college are back in style, and I wonder where in the hell did I keep all those clothes. I could recycle them now. Well, I'm just glad we're going to be around Jack. I'll feel so much younger then. So . . . when is this X supposed to kick in?"

Bill's question never receives an answer as they arrive at Room 202. Mitch knocks on the door. The door opens. Jack is holding the inside doorknob.

"Where the hell have you two been?" Jack yells. "I thought we said nine-thirty. It's close to ten. Mother here has already gone through two bowls."

Jack swings the door open to display Marcus sitting with his legs crossed in the office chair on the far side of the room, a pipe in his hand.

"Hey, Whazzhappening, man?" Marcus says. "Don't you listen to Miss Thing trying to say I'm some drug addict. She's the one already talking about hitting a line or two until the X kicks in."

Bill walks into the room and leaps butt first onto the nearest of the two beds.

"Look at us all here, completely fucked up, and Vince and his team were out practicing today," Bill says, dropping the back of his head down on the mattress. "I tell you, if we get a chance for a rematch with them in the playoffs, we're going to whip their ass."

"Uh-huh," Marcus flips his hand out to express himself, then realizing the pipe is still in his hands, he looks over to see that he hasn't thrown any weed or ashes onto the floor. "Fuck, Jack! Didn't you say you were bringing the papers? What's with this pipe shit, man? It's too harsh."

"So . . . you guys want to hit a line, while we're waiting for the X?" Jack asks. "How long ago did you take it?"

"About fifteen minutes ago," Mitch replies as he walks into the room. He gives Jack a hug and then walks over to Marcus and they clasp hands.

"Oooh, look at Mitch here and his muscle shirt," Marcus says. "Uh-huh. Is someone wanting a piece really bad tonight? Randy at home with the kittens?"

"Nahh. Actually, he flew out to New York. I'm sure he's partying out there as well."

"Uh-huh," Marcus checks Mitch up and down. "Both of you looking for pieces. Tired of the same old piece. Hey man, I like them pants."

Marcus raises the pipe up to his lips, and then he sees he has no lighter and there's no weed in the pipe.

"Anyway, what I was saying," Marcus begins again, "I tell you, what Vince don't know is it can't be all work. If you don't have the right amount of play, you don't do your job right. And Vince and his nasty-ass team are going to be so overworked, once the playoffs come, they just gonna be drained out. While us Quake, getting an Easter break here in Palm Springs, will come back with new freshness for the second half of the season. With new vigor, man. And we'll be smoking, man. Smoking."

Marcus turns to Jack.

"Fuck, man! Whatchoo do with the lighter?"

"Let's do a snort each," Jack tells them. "Get a little high before getting down there. The X won't kick in for another hour or so."

Jack walks to the bathroom and comes back with a little vial with a gold chain and a tiny spoon attached. He walks over to Marcus first, opens the vial, places the spoon down into the powder, and then lowers the spoon under Marcus's left nostril.

"Whatcha doin', spoon-feeding him?" Bill asks.

"Well, since Mother doesn't want to get out of his chair, I've got to spoon it to him, which is fine with me because if she got a hold of this vial, there'd be nothing left for the rest of us."

Marcus snorts up the coke, smiles at Mitch and Bill, his legs still crossed and his hands on his lap. Then he looks up to Jack.

"Oh Miss Thing, you are so hilarious tonight. How'd you get to be so hilarious?"

Jack then takes a snort of his own and passes the vial on to Mitch and Bill.

"You two missed the Speedo competition at the pool," Jack says. "I actually saw a half dozen thongs today."

"And Miss Thing here came out in his baggy old volleyball shorts," Marcus says. "Too sensitive to show off his upper thighs, lifting the shorts over his flab like some old man in Florida."

"Ha! Pretty!"

Mitch takes a snort and passes the vial to Bill, who takes a snort. Bill then hands the vial back to Jack, and he sees the boom box underneath a desk to the right of where Marcus is sitting.

"Marcus, what is this, not playing your music?" Bill asks.

Marcus looks down at the boom box.

"I forgot. We finished the tape. Here. Here's another."

"Not more of your rap!" Jack complains.

"That's how much you know about music, you being stuck in Village People and KC and the Sunshine Band. It ain't rap I been playing. It's hip-hop."

"I don't care what it is. It's noise all the same."

Marcus starts the tape.

"I know it's just unbelievable what guys look like now," Bill says. "And I can just picture what the pool was like. And do you see? Everyone is wearing a white tank top down to the party. Just like yours, Jack. No individuality. No one wants to look different. All want to be the same. Show who they are. Clones, clones, clones. Now what were we talking about? Oh yeah. I bet there were some great bodies. It would be nice to have some sex tonight. So, you guys haven't even asked me about my new job."

"What in the world are you raving about?" Jack asks. "I tell you, Bill, you go off on these wild tangents. No one knows what the hell you're talking about."

"I asked you why haven't you asked me about my new job."

"So how's your new job?"

"Well, I haven't started it yet." Bill smiles and hops up and down, raising his arms in glee. "But I gave notice! Finally, I'm out of this nothing job! Marcus, what is this noise? You got anything electronic? We need to dance!"

"Well then, let's get down to the party," Jack says. "Marcus, you got your pass?"

"Why you ask do I got my pass? Of course I got my pass! What do you think I am? Just 'cause I bought Sam's package off of you, don't think you can treat me like you did Sam. Shee-it!"

"Ha! It wasn't like you bought it off me. You got a deal paying only a hundred bucks. The White Party is sixty dollars alone."

"I can't believe I'm spending sixty dollars for one party where I'm just going to be embarrassed being so much older than everyone," Bill remarks. "I'm glad you came too, Jack."

"Ha! Pretty!"

"So Jack, how much we owe you on the party drug?" Mitch asks. Jack waves him off.

"Forget it. My treat."

Marcus stands up.

"My, aren't we generous this weekend? Hey man, you'd be eating two hundred and fifty bucks instead of one hundred and fifty if I didn't do you this favor."

Marcus looks in mirror, then licks his right middle finger and places it to a curl of his short-cut afro, smoothing it back, then turns to the three and smiles.

"Shall we?" and he leads them out the door. Bill follows Marcus, then Mitch, and then Jack. Mitch falls back with Jack a few steps behind Marcus and Bill.

"It's too bad you and Sam couldn't have had this last weekend together," Mitch says. "Jack, I really feel for you, what you're going through, but, my friend, you knew it was coming. You're just another victim of this societal trend of having two breadwinners in the family."

"I never expected Sam to be a breadwinner. Actually, I was hoping he would, but . . . I wasn't thinking of the consequences."

Mitch nods and says, "I often get tired of the conservatives always depicting gay relationships as short-lived without including the reason why they don't last. They always say that gay men just can't commit to relationships, but they don't explain the reason why they don't commit, and that is because of conflicting careers, not because their love for each other is any less than that of a man and a woman. In the old days, only the man was the breadwinner, and the woman followed him. And they stayed together for life. Well, in our society, whether it is a straight or gay relationship, that just isn't the case anymore."

"Pretty. But I think you're mistaken, Mitch. You forget the main reason gay men don't stay together."

"What's that?"

"We like to fuck too much."

"Jack, what you doing straggling back there?" Marcus interrupts. "You say you know this Winston guy at the door. Get on up here. I don't want to be waiting in no line."

Marcus turns to Bill.

"Look at that fine ass on that man in the black tank top. Ooh child, his hand is approaching his ass, rubbing right above it. I could see my hand right there myself."

"Marcus. That's Curt."

"Oooh." Marcus laughs loud, placing his hand on Bill's shoulder. "You are right. What was I thinking? I couldn't tell at first. I think the X is kickin' in."

They see Al to Curt's side. Al's wearing a white Adidas V-neck jersey with three black racing stripes down the short sleeves. He and Curt are standing at the end of the line going into the White Party. There are about 100 guys in front of them.

"Hey look!" Al exclaims to Curt. "It's Marcus and Jack and Mitch and Bill! Hey guys! Good timing, all of us here at the same time. Now we can all wait in line together."

"Wait in line?" Marcus gasps. "Fuck that shit, man. Jack, you say you can get us up front, man!"

Jack walks up to Curt and Al and shakes their hands.

"My friend Winston promised to let me and my friends in, but I told him four," Jack speaks directly to Curt. "You two can try to get in with us, but I can't promise you anything."

Curt waves him off.

"That's OK. The line's going pretty quick. Besides, we're not ready to be in there anyhow, if you know what I mean."

"Ooh child!" Marcus emotes, extending his long brown arm and circling his index finger on Curt's chest just above his tank top. "I see we all be partyin' tonight."

"Well, we'll see you guys in there then," Bill says. "Say Al, this shirt doesn't make me look too fat, does it?"

Marcus takes his finger off Curt and swats Bill across the chest.

"Why you care 'bout that, man? You look fine. Besides, you won't be wearing no shirt once you inside."

Jack and Marcus and Bill and Mitch continue their way up the line, leaving Curt and Al behind.

"I think I'm coming down from the coke," Bill says. "I wish this X would kick in soon. We're almost in."

They walk to the front of the line and Jack approaches the doorman while the other three stand a few feet back, Marcus watching Jack's conversation closely. Mitch looks over at Bill.

"You think Paul could be in there?" Mitch asks. "It's strange, but here we are staying at Ted's home because he had to be in LA for business. And Randy's not here because he's in New York on business. And I'm thinking, now that Paul got a lead role in a new series, he won't be here either because he's probably somewhere else 'on business,' and here I am, the only one not having any business, partying it up in Palm Springs."

"You say that as though it's a bad thing."

"I just can't believe what happens to Paul right after I break up with him. He gets a new agent, a movie, the lead in a TV series, and he's soon to become America's new Hercules!"

Bill laughs.

"But think on the good side. Now you've got Randy, and he *really* is much more successful than Paul will ever be, don't you *really* think?"

"Very funny, my friend. At least I haven't spent years in a bad relationship all the while jealous about Ed and his going out with six-foot-four linebacker material."

"What are you talking about, me jealous about Ed? Why would I care who Ed is going out with? You know, I think that shirt has done something to your head. You're really sounding like a West Hollywood queen."

Mitch drops his hands deep in his pants pockets and shrugs his shoulders.

"Oh well. Once this X kicks in, Ed and Paul and Randy will be far from our minds."

Mitch looks up at Jack, who is motioning to them with his hand.

"All right. We're in."

They show their tickets and walk through the door, the music blasting in their faces as they enter. It's dark at first, but then they see the lights of the bar and their eyes adjust and it's only 10:30 but already there are hundreds of men making the dance floor about half full, and almost all of them have their shirts off already, and Mitch tugs on Bill's arm, getting his attention, since Bill's eyes had strayed on all the wonderful bodies, and Mitch shows Bill he's taking off his shirt and he stuffs it into one of his cargo pockets, and he nods to Bill, and Bill grimaces, but he takes off his shirt as well and slides it through the inside of his belt so it will stay, and then they turn to see Jack at the bar having just purchased four small bottles of water, and Jack hands one to Marcus, and then he comes over to Bill and Mitch and hands them their water.

"You feel anything kicking in?" Jack asks.

"I don't know," Bill answers. "Maybe. Let's get closer to the dance floor."

"No. Before it gets too crowded, let's go to the bathroom and take another hit," Jack says.

And so the four of them, all of them with their shirts off, walk to the corner of the room and toward the women's rest room, and first Jack and Marcus go into the rest room, leaving Mitch and Bill out drinking their water.

"Look at these guys here," Bill says to Mitch. "It's as though they were born with liposuction. Not an inch of fat! And I spend my entire waking day trying to get rid of these love handles."

Mitch looks Bill over.

"Hey buddy, you're looking great! How much have you lost?"

"About ten pounds, but none of it seems to come off my stomach." Bill peers out over the men on the dance floor. "But you know, despite how perfect these guys' bodies are, look at their faces. I mean, there are some ugly faces out there, and they can't do anything about that. At least we've got pretty faces, don't we?"

"It doesn't matter, my friend. Even if you got an ugly face, you're beautiful if you've got the body. The ugly face actually makes you look more like a man, rather than some gay boy with a body. I know you always talk about how you have to lose weight, but at least you've got that muscular build. My problem is I don't bulk up. See that guy there. The dark-haired guy with the barbed-wire tattoo? That's the physical type I like. Tan skinned. Lots of muscles. Like a pro line-backer. But I can tell you now, I'm not his type. I don't have the bulk."

"You think he'd like me then?"

"Bill, I believe the X is kicking in. You're becoming shallow."

Marcus and Jack come out of the rest room. Jack's right hand is clutched in a fist, and he brings that fist into Mitch's left hand, and then Mitch's left hand is in a fist, and he and Bill enter the rest room, and they walk into a stall and close the door and Mitch exposes the vial and he opens it and he snorts a spoonful, and then he hands it to Bill and he snorts a spoonful and then Bill closes the vial and puts it in his pocket and they lick their fingers and wipe under their nostrils and they come out of the stall.

"It's strange how our concept of beauty continues to change," Mitch says as they walk over to the sinks and wash their hands and sniff some water up their noses. "It's more evident with female beauty. Think of the Twiggy look, how that was so strange to be considered beauty after years of Marilyn Monroe, Elizabeth Taylor, and all those full-figured girls. And now the Twiggy look is probably too full-figured itself as a model of beauty. Well, that might be an exaggeration. But think of Jim Morrison. I thought he was sexy when I was a kid. But today, if someone looked at him now as he was then, he wouldn't have a chance with the men out here, not even with those men with the ugly faces."

Bill nods.

"Yeah. Now you have to have no fat, plenty of muscle, and absolutely no body hair. You think I got too much chest hair? You know, I think I'll use this chest hair to my advantage. It makes me different. There's got to be at least twenty OK-looking men out there who like chest hair, don't you think?"

"I like chest hair. Believe me, I wish I had more than I have."

Bill laughs and nudges Mitch.

"I do think the X is kicking in. You're sounding shallow, too."

They walk out of the bathroom, and they see that Jerry and Dave are standing next to Jack and Marcus, and they all have their shirts off, and they're all drinking their water, except Jerry, who is drinking his Budweiser, and they're not saying much, just staring at all the men walking back and forth in the human corridor in front of them as well as at all the men just beyond on the dance floor, and Jerry turns to Dave at his side.

"See. There's the guy in the red Speedo. I told you he's way too nellie, him with those white leather pants. He's just wanting a good fucking, don't you think? And to think they chose him for the deodorant commercial over me. Actually, it was antiperspirant, not straight deodorant. They probably needed someone a little more faggy for an antiperspirant commercial, 'cause straight guys in lockers probably are more into straight deodorant, 'cause they don't care if they have pit stains at the end of the day. Fuck! Look at him, the way he dances out there. If the casting director saw him like that, no way would he have got that commercial."

"But you have to admit he's . . . really good looking."

Jerry shrugs his shoulders.

"I guess. But there's no sex appeal there." Jerry turns to the others. "Marcus, what do you think about that blond guy in the white leather pants? You think he's got sex appeal?"

"Ooh child. My eyes haven't left him. That leather just folds so sexy over that beautiful butt of his. He must have some fine legs under all that."

"Stop looking and start doing," Bill says. "Let's get on the dance floor."

"Are you all partying?" Jerry asks.

Mitch has begun swaying his shoulders, his forearms out in front of him, rocking them back and forth in tune to the music.

"We is partying," Mitch says. "I think it's kickin' in."

"Yeah!" Bill exclaims. "Let's go!"

He and Mitch flow onto the dance floor, pushing their way through bodies just beginning to sweat. They don't look back and they find an opening close to the small Latin go-go boy on the stand wearing only a gold chain, a thong, black boots, and white socks, and the music changes, seems faster, but really it's just the same beat with a change of lights moving faster around, and Bill raises his eyes and a wide-open smile in excitement to the new music and then closes his eyes and feels the music in him and Mitch gets wild by flaring his arms out a little wider as he dances and he closes his eyes too, but they soon open again to stare at the go-go boy, and suddenly they feel some dry warm skin against them and there are Marcus and Jack, and following them are Jerry and Dave, and soon they're all together again and all of them are closing their eyes and getting into the music, except Jack, who is concentrating on the go-go boy, and Jerry, who is sipping from the beer bottle and moving his head around looking at everybody.

And the music changes once more and they all open their eyes and touch the sweat on their bodies and Marcus looks over at Dave, whose eyes are concentrating on one beautiful dark-haired man with a Cincinnati Reds baseball cap and a big gold chain around his massive hairless chest. Dave's eyes are staring down at the man's thin waist that seems to magically hold up a pair of baggy jeans without actually touching them.

"Ooh my!" Marcus says to Dave. "You've found yourself a re-deekulous piece there. He's just staring you down like a bad-ass motherfucker."

"You think he's looking at me?"

"Are you blind? All of his body is moving, but his eyes stay right on you. Look at him there. He gave you a nod. Why don't you go see him over there?"

"Oh . . . I don't know. I'm really not feeling anything yet, you know . . . high or anything."

"What? You think you gotta wait until the drugs kick in? Man, you're a trip! It's obvious he's into you, and you're into him, but you never make the move. Damn! You can't be so shy. It's just like on the field, man. I just couldn't believe that catch you made last week. It was amazing, man. And yet, you're sittin' second string. Why? 'Cause you won't go for it. You don't call it. You don't say, this is mine. This play's going to me. I've got an opening here that I'm going to capital-ize on. Man, you got to capitalize on this, 'cause you know, there's thousands of men here, and this guy ain't going to be spending all night waiting for you."

Dave nods but says nothing, still staring at the man, seeing a smile rise on the man's lips as he stares back. Dave turns to Marcus, who gives him a "go-and-do-it" look, and then Dave walks across the dance floor and over to the man with the red cap. He stops in front of him and sort of dances slow, looking at the man at first, who smiles bigger, his dark brown eyes upon him. Dave then dances a little faster and drops his eyes on the floor, watching how his black shoes twist on the surface. He looks back up at the man, who now is looking to one side, still wearing that smile, dancing with his elbows planted against his sides so that his biceps are flexed. Dave steps a step closer and mimics the guy's dance style. The guy looks down at Dave's biceps, and then he makes his hands into fists and begins to punch Dave softly in the chest. Dave takes the impact with a nervous shudder. He then pauses and gives the guy a punch back. But Dave feels funny about this little punching game. So he closes his eyes, trying to dance to the music.

"Are you partying?"

Dave opens his eyes when he hears the question, said in a deep voice. He looks strangely at the man in the red cap at first.

"Huh?"

But then Dave understands.

"You mean X? Well . . . yeah, but it hasn't kicked in yet."

The guy smiles and nods and closes his eyes and goes back to dancing, allowing Dave to look down at his amazing, strong abs and the thin waist and how his loose jeans move back and forth on that waist. The guy then opens his eyes and takes a water bottle out of his back pocket and drinks the water. Again, David mimics his move, since he also has a water bottle in his back pocket. As they finish drinking, they put their bottles back in their pockets at the same time and go on dancing.

Again, Dave opens his eyes when he feels the guy's punches on his chest. Dave punches him back, but only once. The guy then closes his eyes and dances, and the song keeps going on but the guy just concentrates on the music as though he's forgotten about Dave.

But Dave can't get into the music as he's trying to figure out whether this guy really likes him. The guy opens his eyes just for a second, stares at Dave, but this time he doesn't smile because he has a kind of glazed-over look as though he doesn't want to change any expression on his face that might alter the feeling he has at the moment. Again he closes his eyes.

"Well, I got to go back to my friends," Dave says. The guy opens his eyes, but he doesn't change his expression.

"I'll . . . see you around."

The guy nods and then closes his eyes and keeps on dancing. Dave walks back to his teammates.

Once Dave is back, Bill stares him down.

"Man! Who was that sexy guy you were dancing with? I just wanted to reach my hand down in those loose jeans of his. Why did you leave him?"

"Oh . . . he's a lot higher than I am."

Then Dave goes back to dancing and Bill looks at him, and he smiles and he puts his hand on Dave's shoulder, which isn't as sweaty as the rest of them.

"You had a great catch last week, Dave," Bill says. "You're really becoming athletic." Then Bill rubs Dave's shoulder and slides his hand down onto Dave's chest. "Look at you now. You got some strong pecs."

"Oooh now!" Marcus says, seeing Bill and laughing. "Look at Bill over here, rubbing up and down Dave. You know he's partying now."

"Oh, you know I am," Bill replies. "I think I'm going to take a little tour. I better leave our little group before I begin feeling you all up and down."

Mitch smiles and says, "Hey, buddy. I'll follow you. See the rest of you later."

Mitch follows Bill across the dance floor, which is now completely packed with guys, and all of them have glistening, perspiring skin and almost all of them with their shirts off, and Bill moves slowly, sliding his sweaty skin against the sweaty skins of other dancers as he passes by them and occasionally reaching his hand out to feel a man's shoulder as though he's pushing the shoulder back in his attempt to get to the other side of the dance floor, but once he gets there, he makes a wide arc and begins pushing through the dance floor on the other side now, and Mitch follows, smiling at Bill's antics and trying to replicate them and then he has to stop because one of the men Bill has touched—a short, hairless Latin boy wearing white Adidas sweat-pants and matching Adidas basketball shoes—is touching Bill back and they have their hands around each other's waists and they're gy-rating their hips together, their dicks touching and now they're kiss-ing and Mitch has to stand and watch and then he looks to one side and he sees Curt and Al on the dance floor, and both of them have their shirts off, and he walks over to them and behind them and he scoots in between them putting his arms around their shoulders.

"Well, it's about time you two got in!" he exclaims. "So are you all partying now?"

"Uh-huh," Al replies. "Hey Mitch! Meet Dirk here!" Mitch looks over at a short blond guy wearing a baby blue NC baseball cap above an oval face, blue eyes, a Roman nose, and a small mouth with big pouty lips. The guy has a tight, compact body that's completely un-tanned, in fact is in a beautiful shade of soft pink. "We met him in line, and we've all been dancing since."

Mitch reaches his arms out and says, "How ya doing?" and Dirk nods in recognition and goes back to dancing.

Al turns to Mitch and places his lips right up to Mitch's ear so that no one else can hear, and he says, "You know, I've met this guy before in LA. Once at Revolver and once at Cherry, and I'd talk to him and all, but he just didn't seem interested in me, and now, all of a sudden, he won't take his eyes off me. And you know why? You know what I think? It's because of the X. I'm more beautiful to him when I'm on X. Because when you're on X you have this look, you know, like bed-room eyes, kind of in a daze. And that's really a sexy look to guys, don't you think? So Curt's getting us water, and Dirk here starts touching me now that we're alone, and you know what I say to him? I say, 'you're one of the most beautiful men I've ever seen in my life, and I've wanted you for so long, and I'd love to share an intimate moment with you, but right now, I'm with my boyfriend, and I am so in love with him, and if you're into a three-way, maybe we can do that, as long as you pay attention to my boyfriend as well.' Well, now he can't stop looking at Curt! I guess he wants this three-way."

"He is a good-looking guy. Is he partying, too?"

"He's on crystal."

"Interesting," Mitch says, "Can you have a ménage à trois with two guys on X and one on crystal."

"He's also on Viagra."

Mitch starts dancing and Al touches Mitch on the shoulder and asks, "So, where are the others?"

"Jack and Marcus and Jerry and Dave are all dancing over in that corner there. Bill and I left them to do a tour of the dance floor, and then Bill met a cute little Latin boy. There he is, see? Their mouths have been locked for the last five minutes."

Curt overhears and looks over at Bill.

"Looks like everybody's getting lucky tonight," Curt says.

Mitch then asks both of them, "Say, either of you guys seen Paul here?"

Curt and Al look at each other and then they both shake their heads.

"I just thought I might bump into him here," Mitch says.

"Where's Randy?"

Mitch shrugs his shoulders.

"Who cares?"

Neither Curt or Al question him, and so they go back to dancing, and Curt steps forward and locks his right leg between Dirk's two legs, and then Al comes up behind Curt and starts doing a danc-ing/humping thing against Curt's butt, and Mitch approaches them and says, "I think I'm going back to Marcus and the guys. You all be good now."

Al laughs at Mitch's last comment, but Curt and Dirk don't pay any attention to him as Curt's right thigh rubs against Dirk's cock, and so Mitch leaves, and Al presses closer to Curt's butt but then he swings to one side and he begins feeling Dirk's chest.

"Let's do it," Curt says, and Dirk looks up from his glassy stare down at Curt's right leg, and his eyes try unsuccessfully to focus on Curt's eyes and those thick, black sexy eyebrows, and Dirk gives a lit-tle nod, and they all walk off the dance floor.

"I wonder what the line looks like, if we'll have to wait long to get back in," Al says as they walk toward the front door.

"We'll take our chances," Curt says, his huge hands now clasped against the napes of both Dirk and Al's necks, pushing them along.

The line has gotten shorter, as almost everyone is inside. The three of them walk up the stairs into the lobby and then out onto the court-yard, and they feel the air, still in the sixties, cool against their wet skin. Dirk crosses his arms together to stay warm, but none of them put their shirts back on.

"We're back by the pool," Al says, and they cross the courtyard, they cross the street, they go into the other courtyard and walk to-ward their first-floor unit, and Al unlocks and opens the door and they all go inside, and Curt releases them.

"Now let's see how big that cock is on Viagra," Curt says to Dirk, and Dirk looks at him, hesitates, and says, "You got anything to drink in your room?" Curt says, "Just Jack Daniels. No ice. No mixer." Dirk says, "I'll go for that. You got one of those plastic cups they keep wrapped in the bathroom?" and Curt nods and walks into the bath-room, and all of a sudden Dirk pulls his cock out, and it's real hard, and he approaches Al and says, "You know, I'm doing this because I really want to be with you," which causes Al to take a step back and Dirk pulls his cock back in before Curt returns, and Curt has come out of the bathroom and is in the short hallway at the table that's built into the wall, and this is where the bottle of whiskey is, and he's using his teeth to tear the wrap off the cup, and he throws the wrap in the wastebasket and now he's pouring the whiskey in the cup three-quar-ters full, and he comes into the bedroom, sips the whiskey, then hands it to Al, who takes a sip and then Al hands the cup to Dirk.

"The rest is yours," Curt says to Dirk. Dirk laughs and he says, "Like you're trying to get me fucked up." Curt says, "That's right. Now show us that cock of yours," and Dirk takes a big drink, and Al says, "I got to go pee," and he walks to the bathroom and closes the door, and Dirk puts the cup down on the stand next to the bed, and he exposes his cock and says to Curt, "I was first really into your boy-friend, but you know, you're the one I really want to be with," and Curt approaches him and drops his hand down and feels Dirk's cock and scoots his fingers toward the base of his scrotum, and Dirk stretches his neck back in pleasure, and the toilet flushes, and Al comes out of the bathroom and he goes behind Dirk and pulls his jeans down from behind and begins caressing Dirk's butt, and Curt looks over Dirk's shoulder to Al.

"Let's both of us fuck him," Curt says to Al.

Dirk laughs at Curt's comment, but Al says, "How about if you fuck him and I'll fuck you, and then you can be in the middle, like a sandwich. Wouldn't that be cool?"

Dirk laughs again, but Curt says, "Why don't we have Dirk in the middle, since he is our guest?"

Dirk laughs again, but Al says, "But you know, I'd like to be with you in this, Curt, either me in you or you in me."

Dirk laughs again, and he says, "I like the idea of me in the middle." Curt asks him, "Then who do you want to fuck and who do you want to have fuck you?" Dirk says, "I'd like to have you fuck me, but hey! Hold on a sec," and then Dirk reaches down in his jeans and pulls a vial out of the side pocket and he opens the vial and sniffs a couple spoonfuls, and he offers it to Curt and Al, but they both shake their heads no, and he says, "We're going to fuck long, 'cause I won't be cumming for hours," and Curt and Al look at each other, and all of a sudden both of them have lost interest in Dirk, and while Dirk is putting his vial back in his pants pocket, Curt and Al step to one side by the window, and Curt pulls the curtains back a bit, and they both look out at the dark, starry sky and the glistening blue pool all lit, and they see a half dozen couples there kissing at poolside, and Curt drops the curtain from his hands, and Al and Curt look at each other, and they put their arms around each other, and they put their lips together, and they open their mouths, and they feel each other's tongues, embracing, feeling the wholeness of each other in their tongues, and their heads get light, spinning, and they forget about Dirk and their thoughts are only of each other and how much love they feel.

"Hey! What about me?" Dirk asks, and the two lovers turn and see him, and Curt says, "You know, I don't think I want to be cooped up in this room for the next several hours," and he turns to Al, "How about you, baby? Want to get back to the party?"

Al nods. "Yeah. Let's go."

So Curt opens the door and Dirk has to pull up his pants, and as he does, he says, "Fuck! I should have taken X instead."

Then they all walk out the door and into the courtyard and across the street and then into the main courtyard, and they're approaching the lobby when Al sees a solitary figure with his pants rolled up and sitting with his feet and ankles in the Jacuzzi, and Al feels sad, seeing this guy all alone, and he walks up to take a closer look.

"Dave?"

Dave looks up and sees Curt and Al with another guy. He shivers.

"Oh . . . Hi, Al. Hi, Curt."

"Hey Dave," Curt says. "What are you doing out here all by yourself?"

Dave shrugs his shoulders.

"Well . . . I just wanted to step outside, see the stars . . . Just have a change of pace for a moment . . . you know."

"Are you partying?" Curt asks.

Dave shivers again.

"Yeah. But you know . . . I don't think I got anything very good."

"You going to be okay?" Al asks. "You coming back in?"

Dave nods.

"Yeah, I'll be in a few minutes. Just catching my breath."

"Good, 'cause I think all of us Quake should get together and dance," Al says. "That's what I'm really looking forward to . . . all of us together."

Dave nods. "I'd like to end the night that way. All our teammates together."

Curt and Al then wave good-bye and the third guy looks a little hungrily at Dave, but he leaves with the other two, and so Dave is all alone again.

Dave sits back on his elbows, staring up at the thousands of stars. He finds the Big Dipper, and then he locates the North Star. He looks northwest, believing that he is now looking in the direction of his family's home. He closes his eyes and takes in a deep breath. He sits up and reopens his eyes, now staring at the whiteness of his feet in the Jacuzzi.

He looks over the rest of his body, looking down at his chest, now closely shaved. He tries to recall his image when he lived in Ripon compared to his image now. Before and after.

"Dave?"

He shivers and turns slowly, again afraid what a friend would say seeing him alone at a party with 5,000 men.

The face is dark at first, silhouetted against the thousand stars. The man approaches, and suddenly he is bathed in a floodlight from the main building.

It is Tony Caravahlo.

Unlike the others strolling through the courtyard, Tony is clothed above with a white V-neck T-shirt. Dave sees a huge smile on Tony, who utters a laughter of surprise.

"Dave! It's great to see you here!"

"Hi, Tony," Dave feels his heart race, but he is afraid to appear too excited.

"That looks good what you're doing," Tony says as he stares down at Dave's feet under the water. "Mind if I join you?"

Dave shivers.

"Uh . . . no! I'd . . . really like that."

Tony takes off his tennis shoes and socks and pulls up the pant legs of his jeans. He sits down next to Dave and plants his feet in the Jacuzzi, actually taking the step too fast as he creates a splash, causing the bottom of his pants to get soaked. Dave laughs.

"What was the use then of pulling up your pants?"

Tony chuckles. After his laughter dissipates, he lets out a long sigh and looks up at the sky.

"Just look at those stars. You never can see this many of them in LA."

"Yes. It's . . . beautiful."

Dave brings his face down, and he turns to look at Tony. Tony looks at him, and they both smile warmly.

"So," Tony pauses, "are you . . . on anything? I mean . . . as far as drugs?"

Dave smiles. "Do you mean am I partying?"

"Yeah! I've been hearing that question a lot tonight."

Dave says nothing. Instead he places his thumb and forefinger into the coin pocket in the front pocket of his jeans. He opens the palm of his hands to expose a little white pill.

"It's ecstasy," Dave says. "Jerry gave it to me. I've been telling everyone I'm on X but that it's no good."

Tony sighs and nods.

"So . . . you're like me. One of the dozen drug-free partiers among a myriad of men so speeded up there's no way you can relate to them."

"Yeah."

Tony looks down at the pill. Dave puts it back in his pocket.

"So . . . why didn't you take it? Isn't that the point of this whole weekend?"

"I didn't feel right about it."

Tony looks at Dave with his dark brown eyes, but Dave has dropped his head down and is staring at the ripples his legs are making in the Jacuzzi.

"Because of your dad?"

Dave nods.

"I got a call from my mom, just minutes before I was going out my front door for the weekend. She told me they found the cancer had spread, into the brain. The chemo hadn't worked. And then she asked if there was any way I could drive up there this weekend, and . . ."

Dave brought his head up, looking at the stars again. He took a big sniff to hide any tears.

"I said no . . . that I couldn't get away this weekend. But I told her I'd come up next Saturday. I mean . . . I was thinking how I had planned this weekend for so long, and I had a commitment since I was paying for a quarter of a room here, and I couldn't let the other guys down. I mean . . . I don't know. I felt like I was lying to her, and . . ."

Dave feels Tony's arm rest across his shoulders. He turns to see this beautiful man, with the dark eyes and the curly black hair, looking at him so sweetly.

"And I can't believe I'm telling you all this. I mean . . . I didn't even call you or anything. I wanted to, but I was scared."

"Hey! That's OK!" Tony says. Dave feels Tony's arms holding him tighter. "I'm just glad I found you tonight."

Dave stares into Tony's eyes, wondering whether he wishes to kiss him, but he looks away.

"It's just, I can't understand why, when all I talk about is my dad dying. Believe me. I've never brought this subject up with anyone else. I don't know why I do with you."

Tony smiles at him. Then, with his left arm around Dave's shoulder, he pulls himself a little closer to Dave.

"Maybe you just felt you could."

A shiver runs through Dave. Tony feels his nervousness, and so he clasps his hand around Dave's shoulder. They both look up at the stars once again.

"I think I understand what it was when I met you, Dave," Tony says. "I come from a very close family, a big family, Grandma living just down the street, and my uncles and aunts all in the same neighborhood. A year ago I left them to become an actor, and . . . you know, my trouble is, I just have a hard time finding anyone who is real out here. I can't find anyone who just wants to be himself." He sighs, patting Dave on the shoulder. "They're all talking about how important they are or talking the industry talk or trying to put someone down as a way of putting themselves up. And then I meet you, and . . . well, you open yourself up to me like this, and I think this is the genuine thing. And so two weeks go by, and I get kind of disappointed that you didn't call me."

"Then . . . why are you here . . . at the White Party?"

Tony shakes his head.

"I don't know. I knew I couldn't get into it in the end. It's just . . . well," he looks at Dave. "Do you ever have fantasies?"

Dave shivers.

"Well . . . I guess. Doesn't . . . everyone?"

Tony looks at him tenderly again and nods. "Yeah. I guess so." He then turns away. "Well, I'm not going to tell them to you." He smiles from one side of his mouth. "At least, not yet. I kind of want to get to know you first."

Dave is looking at Tony, completely enraptured, and Tony sees that and he pulls Dave toward him.

"My one fantasy right now," Tony says, "is to kiss you."

He pulls Dave toward him as Dave sees Tony's face and his lips come toward him. He closes his eyes and opens his mouth, and suddenly sweet lips are upon him. He brings his arm around Tony and they embrace under the stars, and he feels that this kiss is a prayer, a prayer that will go to the heavens and be brought back down by God to his father, to make him well, because the love he feels right now for this man at this moment can only be good, can only be saving grace.

Tony pulls back, his cheeks now all rosy and flushed, and he raises his eyes and looks deeply into Dave's eyes.

"So . . . you want to party?"

Dave looks at him. He's still coming down from the dizziness of the kiss and he's trying to understand what Tony's concept of "party" might actually be.

"What?"

Now it's Tony's turn this time to pull a pill out of his coin pocket. It looks similar to Dave's white pill, only larger, thicker, and yellow.

"You've got X that you never took either."

Tony shakes his head.

"It's No-Doz. Want to split one?"

Dave laughs as Tony bites off one side and hands the other to Dave. They then stand up and wince as they chew the bitter pill.

"Should we go back to the party for a while?" Tony asks. "Or . . . well, I'm staying at a friend's house just a mile or so away."

"Let's go back first," Dave says. "Just for a couple dances. I've got one thing I want us to do before I go."

Tony takes Dave's hand, and they walk toward the lobby, and just before they enter the building, Tony asks, "So . . . have you ever thought about wearing leather?"

Dave laughs and presses Tony's hands.

"Yeah. Yeah, I have."

They walk down the stairs. There's no line. So they show their hand stamps and walk into the White Party. The music, the men, the blaring lights moving back and forth. It's all overwhelming to them at first.

"This way," Dave says. "This is where I left everyone."

He leads Tony onto the dance floor and they walk past dozens of dancers, their hands still clasped, and then Dave spots Marcus and Jack. There's also Mitch and Curt and Al, although Dirk is no longer by their side.

"Dave!" Al exclaims as he sees Dave approach, and Dave leads Tony into their circle.

"Hi, everyone! This here is Tony. Tony . . . this is my team. The Quake!"

And everyone is looking at Tony, and they're looking at Dave, who has the biggest smile on his face, and no one can ever remember Dave wearing such a big smile.

"Mmm hmm! How ya doin', Tony?" Marcus says, sliding his hand down Tony's arm. "Why you got your shirt on?"

"We were just outside," Dave says, and he looks around. "Say, where's Jerry? And Bill?"

"Mmm child. Jerry got that man with the white leather pants over there. He don't want to bring him nowhere near us, as you can see. And Bill . . . Mitch, didn't you say he was off with some Latin boy."

"Yes, I did, and here he comes this very moment," Mitch says.

They all see Bill approach the group with the Latin guy at his side. Bill is beaming a smile nearly as wide as Dave's.

"Everyone's here!" he yells. "Everyone, this here is Enrique."

"So how ya doin', Enrique?" Marcus says, and Enrique just stands there, nodding and smiling.

"He doesn't know much English," Bill says laughing. "Isn't that great!"

"Pretty!" Jack exclaims, and then Bill turns to Jack.

"You and Marcus aren't going to use your room for the next half hour or so, are you, Jack? Could I perhaps borrow your key? I'll be back in thirty minutes. I promise."

"Ha! How can I know you'll really be back so quickly?"

"Then you can knock on the door. Believe me, his dick is so hard right now. And big! I need this, Jack. Believe me, I need this."

Marcus gives a nod to Jack, and Jack hands Bill his keys, and suddenly Bill's arms are around Jack, and he gives him a big kiss and then his arms are around Marcus, and he gives him a big kiss.

"You guys are the best, I tell you," and he turns to Mitch, "and you are the very best, getting me this job and all. I tell you, Mitch, I love you," and he turns to the entire circle. "I love you all!"

They give one another hugs, and Tony and Enrique get hugs from the group as well, and the song changes, and the lights move in another pattern, and they all think the lights are moving faster, and this is a faster song, and a bunch of yelling spreads throughout the room, and everyone raises their arms up, swaying them back and forth, gyrating their hips to the music, to the speed, to the ecstasy, to all the beautiful men, to their friends, to their lovers, to life!

"Fucking Quake!" Bill screams. "We are going to win the league!"

And the rest of the Quake yell their approval, and so they dance and dance until they're lighter than air, and they all huddle together, their arms clasped together, pouring out their sweat, and all of them thinking it's friends like these that make life worth living.

The Real Men of "Ammond" Country

pass the mall just one exit left for modesto and then in ripon back to my family back to my dad old and balding ready to die among the almond fields funny how they say almond down in la not ammond almonds to the left of me black walnuts up ahead remember the sweet smell of onions down in bakersfield of drying grapes in fresno of artichokes in merced squashed red balls of tomatoes everywhere on the 99 but now coming to the almond capital of the world once my home thought never to return and here i am the young leaves growing blossoms on the ground just the startings of the nuts always an exciting time ripon in the springtime now its dull

pass the last exit to modesto another sign water equals food do they understand that down in la hoarders of our water now on their side dad would hate me god guts and guns is what made america great didnt see that sign this time old farmer tilson finally took it down times a-changing i've changed no longer aggie son but a west hollywood queen not a queen what would tony think he's so far away now 350 miles down south in a land he doesnt care for what is it he sees in me if only he knew me i must tell him and tony *wait till you see this see here this is me and my friend tom at this leather store in the village* erect seeing him in leather the hat and all he has that embarrassed smile that keeps him from looking like a leather queen just some real man masquerading and tony *i think i kind of get into leather* i let out a laugh afraid its a giggle and he places his arms around me just wearing our briefs and nothing else and he kisses me we rub against each other so happy but scared he'll know the real me i want to tell him i like jewelry and spandex just a queen wanting him to fuck me but too scared

what would he think some fucking nellie queen passing as a football
player the last time in the valley i drove the 5 up to san francisco and
ready to go out to the castro and buy a bracelet buy it somewhere
where no one would know me and then i'd be a real queen with a
bracelet what if i had worn it when tony had met me or seen me at the
white party would he still be interested in me what would dad think
youre no son of mine and mom *that mrs de hoog going to church in her fur and
jewelry what do they think that god is going to bring her to heaven faster because she dresses well* and dad *now rachel just let people be its only god to judge
in the end* wouldnt dad judge if i came home with a bracelet and ear-
rings and being just the girl and wouldnt tony am i judging myself
who am i maybe i'll know when dad dies

almond orchards on both sides of the 99 the minimart gas station
coming up at my exit hate myself thinking dads dying think of something else—the game! whats the time 12:30 theyre in the second half
versus the beer bellies we're winning or perhaps losing 'cause i'm not
theyre winning 'cause i'm not there they're happy i chose to take the
weekend off but i made that catch last game but there was no pressure
give me pressure and i'll drop it and marcus *youre sitting second string
why 'cause you wont go for it man you dont call it you dont say this is mine the
plays going to me i've got an opening here that i'm going to capitalize on*

pulling off the 99 into ripon feel good now feel i can be somebody
feel i can make that catch theres something in me that i'm holding
back on but now i'm calling it tony likes me someone as good as that
likes me make that winning touchdown and he'll love me dad will
love me i'll love me

ripons so tiny now a two-block town the ripon record to the left and
now the handy market to the right ate two big beef ribs there every
time i came to see mom setting up the classified advertising at the record now she's gone from there and i dont eat red meat and life
changes what will they think of me now have i changed much to them
for better or for worse wearing khaki shorts and polo shirt look just
like i left jack tone road my heart beating highland turning the steering wheel and up a quarter mile my home will they all be in the driveway waiting for me dad leaning on a cane in a wheelchair hunched

over mom holding him just the long dusty driveway through the almond trees my home once but no more

drip lines dripping water onto the dry brown dirt between the mounded trees smell of rotting blossoms and the sweet green leaves the moist dirt its getting hot already and dusty once loved these days spending the warm nights with angie under these trees seeing the stars through the branches and the leaves always turned westward toward san francisco looking at angie thinking if she had a dildo to strap on her the fake thing the real thing in san francisco

stop in front of the house it needs a fresh coat of green the wooden panes are stripped on the bottom dirty dad never would allow it but who can help him

pull my left hand on the lever unlatching the trunk step out of the driver's seat and walk to the back of the car mom emerges through the front door and onto the front porch, stopping at the steps, watching me, her pleasant smile

"You made good time. Brian's not even here yet. I've got your room all cleared for you. What did you do, pack a whole suitcase?"

"Well, I didn't know how cold it would be . . ."

she laughs i've become a queen overpacking

"David, when has it ever been cold in April? I think your blood has thinned down there in Los Angeles."

stupid me gone so long the prodigal son

"Well, I just thought, with El Niño, it could rain and all . . ."

"Oh please, dear, don't mention those two words . . ." mom walks down the steps to greet me "Your father has a fit every time it's mentioned. Haven't you noticed the trees? The almonds are stunted. We've had to raise the mounds so they don't get too much water, but there's talk of root rot, especially out in the south fields, closer to the river. Down on Ruess Avenue, the Bailey and the Doak farms don't expect half the crop they had last year. And then there's the co-op . . . I'm sure Brian will fill you in on all that."

she walks up to me and puts her arms around me kiss on my cheek i look at her straight up for a second i see her hair graying i look down grease on her apron already in the kitchen cooking having the whole family home for a late breakfast

"So, where's Dad?"

"In the office. Why don't you go tell him you're here? Your brother and Jennie and the kids will be here soon. I've got to thicken the gravy."

I follow her, my bag in hand. White Bible with gold lettering displayed behind the glass case of the hutch and tomorrows sunday and we'll all go to church and bag in hand should i drop it off in my room before seeing dad but manners. I drop the bag in the foyer and walk to the hallway and left to the office. The door is slightly ajar dad didnt close knowing i'd be home

Rapping on the door.

"Dad?"

Clearing his throat.

"Yes . . . David."

A creak. His chair scooting back. I push the door open.

Dad turns three quarters toward me, his arm set on the desk, a pencil between his fingers. A bony, gray arm. I look into his eyes. They are gray, his hair is gray what's left of it liver spot on one side of his skull never recognized that before. He looks at me the gray sprouts of his brows a dull look no fight in them he's my father but I see something else now or is it a lacking of what he once was down to the shell. Wearing his faded short-sleeved madras button-down shirt and his old pair of dark brown khakis with the wide, peeling belt, the flapping end longer now, down to the fifth slot lost weight, his worn boots. Scoots his chair further back and drops the pencil.

"So you finally made it home. How long has it been? Three months?"

I walk into the office looking down at his papers. He turns to look at them as well.

"The season hires. See here . . ." He points to figures on the green accounting sheets. "The latest co-op reports. I've got to cut back a third of the hires. It's going to be an off season, David. Many of the families . . . God grant they get through this."

I look over the figures. I see the balance. Jerky writing. Dad's eyes are upon me but as he sees me seeing him seeing me, he drops them down in shame sees i'm seeing his figures and understanding.

"But Dad, the price per pound is going to rise, isn't it? Didn't UC Davis report anything like that? Supply and demand?"

"Ahhh." Dad looks over the figures again. "But it's a bumper crop in Israel." He smiles and looks away. "David, how do you compete with the Holy Land?" flowing with milk and honey dad saw that in the san joaquin valley the new israel his holy land the flatland the dust the fog the water the heat look at the figures again feel dad's eyes looking at me from his chair me towering over him him sizing me up what does he think i'm a man now left a boy returned a man and now he less than a man

"Still pretty good with those figures, I see." Dad stands up now at my level. "You're looking thin."

I look at Dad and look at my stomach its thin no longer the paunch. Look back at Dad him standing next to me still taller but thin just bones and skin and how can he talk? He raises a smile and laughs.

"Well, I'm sure Rachel's going to try to change that while you're here." He laughs back to his hearty laugh but it comes out weak and then it wheezes. He raises his hand to his mouth. Clears his throat. It turns into a cough. He blows out trying to rid himself of the congestion. A cough erupts he can't control. I step back not wanting to look at him not see him in his weakness he wouldnt want that he tries to control it wants control in front of me. He turns away toward the window out toward the west orchard and the almond trees in perfect unison row upon row. I turn to the door the sound of tires rolling over the dirt driveway rescues me.

"I guess that's Brian," I say. Dad's cough weakens. "I'll put my bag away and go say hello."

I walk out before a reply saving dad from the moment he wants me to see him strong not weak like this i was the weak one to him he always stronger than me always the man korean war vet never weak never crying a real man brian a real man and i something else but now i am stronger than him i'm a man and he is less than one but am i west hollywood queen football player fag sissy lover of tony a real man a man and a queen and as long as theres brian theres still one real man in the house brian the man me the queen and dad the once-man dying how can he die who will I be then

I walk back into the foyer. Put my eye close to the beveled glass of the front door. Brian leading his family up the walkway and glass distorts them but Brian looking fatter than ever now the father of an aggie family never changed except his weight eating the farmer breakfasts no longer the athlete now a paunchy man given over to his family a real man all the same

I open the door. Brian looks up and smiles, his fat cheeks raised and rosy.

"Hey, hey! David! Welcome home, little bro!" he turns to Jennie and Tommy and Sandra. "Hey guys! Look! Uncle David!"

Tommy in overalls and Sandra in a long flowered dress release their hands from Jennie and run ahead. Their yellow hair shining and ruffling. Sandra gives me a hug but Tommy stops, tries to look uninterested, and pulls a Gameboy out of his pocket staring at it.

"You play Mortal Kombat?" he asks, never looking up from the game. Brian laughs and places his hand on his son's back.

"Later, Tommy! Uncle David just got here, and Grandma's making a big breakfast." He sniffs. "I can smell it now. You must be missing Mom's cookin', ay, David?" He looks down at my body. "Whoa, man! You been pumpin' the iron?"

"Yeah . . . kind of." Brian impressed never expected such a man in me. I turn away turning red uncomfortable with my brother. I turn to Jennie, her wide rosy cheeks and yellow hair. She's looking at me sweetly. She approaches me.

"It's good to see you, David." We hug, her tighter than me can't hug a brother's wife too tight. "We haven't seen you in months." She looks toward the hallway and to the left toward the living room, then at me. "So, you've seen Clyde?" she says softly almost a whisper. "How's he looking to you?" dying like he's dying

"Skinnier . . . and balder . . . but all right."

Brian swats my chest with the back of his hand playful mood I never could be so carefree he had all the attributes so he can be but now I dont know

"Ah, Dad looks great! You know Dad! Too tough for anything to get him down." Brian laughs. "He wants to go out to the north orchard with me this afternoon to put down new drip lines. He won't stop for nothing, you know."

"Brian!" Jennie looks angry. "Why are you two doing that today? David hasn't been home in months!"

"I'll help."

Brian looks at me stunned at first by my volunteering he smiles and lets out his hearty laugh.

"Now David, you don't expect we had you come all this way from LA just to work in the orchards. Mom would have a fuss if she heard that. Look, your bag's still in the hall and you're talking about helping us with the drip lines? Don't worry. Dad and I can do it. It won't take more than two hours . . . tops."

Brian thinking i'm soft despite the arms that i'm still the weakling the one cut from university of pacific football he and dad the real men dad still the man over me i can do twice the work they can dad small and frail brian big and fat like the three bears i'm just right damn him always will be the fragile one why am i here

to see dad die

"Well, I'm going to see if Rachel needs any help in the kitchen," Jennie says as she walks toward the hallway. Mom comes out. They almost bump into each other. Mom smiles at Jennie and says, "Good! We're all here. Breakfast's ready. Will someone go get your father?"

"Tommy! Sandra! Breakfast, kids!" Brian looks for his kids. I look at Mom.

"I'll go get him," I say i should be the one to get him never see him its my responsibility the prodigal son

"You've got everything done already?" Jennie asks Mom as they walk back to the kitchen. I follow then turn left to the office. The door is wide open why hasnt dad come out yet heart racing left him coughing not waiting for a reply but it was subsiding and what have i done? I race into the room and theres dad back over the figures again

"Dad. Breakfast's ready. Everybody's here."

He doesn't turn around.

"All right, David. I'll be there in just a moment."

He doesn't make a move. I stare at him, seeing his back arched over those papers is he all right is he waiting for a spell to pass what do i do

I walk away abandoning him again the judas

I walk into the kitchen joyous the big yellow kitchen the artichoke green trim the big wooden dining table, Mom pulling the pot of white gravy off the stove and setting it on the wicker mat on the table, Brian coming in with the kids and Tommy and Sandra running up to their chairs. Mom smiles at me.

"Sit! Sit!" she motions. There's my setting where its always been by the window closest to the back door always can get away first from that chair and dad next to me at the head of the table and brian at the far end, the two coveted positions father and firstborn and mom and jennie on the other side closest to the stove as is a womans place here the men away from the stove the women up close i'm farthest from the stove and less the man and if tony was here seeing my family and knowing where i came from he'd see the real me and we could go out into the orchards two friends to mom and dad but actually lovers and copulate among the leaves and dust and water and almonds and why does he like me am i hiding myself from him but its early but of all the men i've known never have i felt this wanting us to be partners to be equal to be man and man is this what manhood really is rather than faux gym butchness theres butchness and theres masculinity one is real and one is false i've lived falseness tony is real

Dad walks into the kitchen.

"Now, Rachel, you know we've got company . . ." he speaks right away wants the attention. "I hope you didn't skimp on the butter in the gravy this time."

"Oh, Clyde!" Mom laughs and turns to us. "Your father gets upset that I've been cutting back on the butter because of his cholesterol."

Brian laughs and looks at me as he sits down at his place.

"David, you remember that time when Mom bought one of those tubs of margarine and how Dad had a fit and all?"

"Rachel is still trying to push that on me," Clyde nods. "It's not natural, having some whipped up corn oil replace real cow's butter. Over the years the scientists are going to find we never were meant to eat margarine in the first place."

"Like father, like son," Jennie says, placing her hand on Brian's forearm. She seats herself down to his right. "Brian always demands butter on everything. But I give the kids margarine. Sandra actually likes it better."

"Well, it's true you can't substitute for the real taste of butter," Mom defends her family as she hurries back and forth between counter and table, putting down the biscuits, the ham, the bacon, the scrambled eggs, the persimmons, the sliced tomatoes, the white bread, the butter, the almond butter, the jelly, the milk, the orange juice. "But what I've been reading, there's not much good in it for you. Now look at you, David. You look so skinny now. You must be eating margarine."

only in ripon am i skinny in la i'm fat where can i be just right

"Actually, I don't eat much of either."

Mom sits down at the table and looks at me.

"Well, I can see that. Your face has gotten thin. I'm afraid you're not eating right down there. I hope you're not living off TV dinners."

"No, Mom. I cook. Vegetables. Pasta. Rice. Stuff that's good for you." She cant understand didnt mention meat *but what about the meat* she'll ask that.

Jennie grabs Tommy's forearm as he reaches for a biscuit.

"Tommy, where're your manners?" she says. "We haven't said grace yet."

Dad clears his throat and looks at me. "I think David should do the honors, seeing he's been away so long." Not me leading grace what do I say dear lord please let tony want to fuck me every moment of the day make him the top and me his pussyboy never can say a decent prayer *dear lord please let me win the baseball game tomorrow and let mom get her dishwasher and help dad with his high cholesterol* and dad *david you should thank the lord for what weve got not for what you want us to have thank him for everything he has blessed upon you* and i wonder what has he blessed upon me he has blessed tony upon me

I bow my head.

"Dear Lord, thank you for this wonderful meal and bringing us all together this weekend. Please see that it is a good crop this year, and . . ." should I ask to have dads cancer cured but why bring up the subject keep it quiet thats what dad wants . . . "bless all of our houses, and help the LA Quake win the West LA Championship, and . . ." should i say . . . say it quickly "see that Dad gets better. Amen."

"Amen" circles the table. Dad chuckles.

"There you go again, David, asking for things we don't have yet." He grabs the plate of tomatoes and slides two slices onto his plate. "But that's just who you are, always looking to the future. Perhaps someday you'll be satisfied with the present."

He laughs, congested and phlegmy, as he puts down the plate and reaches for the plate of bacon.

"But I'll pray, too, that your team wins the championship."

Brian adds a laugh. He passes the plate of ham to Sandra and grabs the plate of biscuits.

"Can you believe that it's David who's had the longest football career of all of us?" saying i'm no athlete and yet look at him and look at me. "Say, didn't you have a game today?"

"Uh-huh. I missed it. It should have just got over. I'll have to make a call to see if we won. But we're playing an easy team."

"So who were you playing today?"

"The Beer Bellies. We need the win if we're going to get a rematch with our rivals."

"Oh?" Mom says. "You have rivals?"

"Yeah. The West Hollywood Warriors."

Brian laughs.

"West Hollywood!? Well, I'm sure your team can beat them. They're probably just a bunch of fags."

"Brian!" Jennie stares angry at him. "That's very rude to say, especially in front of the kids."

shaking staring down at my plate feel a nudge. Sandra passing the ham look up at Mom she looks concerned at me looking down at my plate

"David, aren't you going to eat?" she asks. "You have nothing but tomatoes and persimmons on your plate. What kind of diet is that?"

I take the plate of ham salvation I remove two slices. "Oh. Sorry. I guess I got caught up thinking about my team." I look at Brian homophobe he cant understand never leaving the farm. "Actually, the Warriors already beat us once. Our only loss this season."

"So . . ." Dad puts down his fork and wipes his lips, "Rachel said you made the game-winning catch two weeks ago. Is that right, David?"

I smile mom exaggerates.

"No. That actually was the game we lost. But it was my best catch. I ran up the sideline, beating my man and caught the ball over my shoulder."

"Over your shoulder?" Brian exclaims. "No way! You never could catch a ball over your shoulder."

Dad chuckles again. It's all congested afraid he could start coughing anytime.

"Well, Brian, some people just blossom later in life."

Blossom later in life? my dad said this he is proud of me i've gone away and become what he always wanted me to be i have changed and he approves what was it he didn't like in me before a lack of self-confidence i've gained confidence become a man if only so but why do i always doubt it but i dont doubt it as much and tony why do i doubt he likes me why do i fear he wont like me when he knows who i really am a pussyboy queen but i'm not just like to get fucked that is me i am someone who likes to get fucked he'll know that he knows that now maybe but he still likes me and why does it matter i just need to go for what i want i call it this play is mine i'm going for it i'm going for tony hopefully he likes who i am if he doesnt its just the way it is i am who i am but who am i what does my dad see what does tony see

"It's too bad you couldn't have come up last weekend for Easter," Mom says. I look at her, her eyes are down on her food. "Then you wouldn't have had to miss a game." i already explained this to her she is hurt.

"Well, I know, but a bunch of my friends all had paid for a room in Palm Springs, and if I had backed out, they would have had to pay more. I didn't feel right about that. Anyway . . . if I had come up last weekend, then I wouldn't be here now, would I?" She looks up at me. I smile at her and finally a smile comes to her lips. She looks gray and careworn dads cancer has an effect on her appearance as well she lives with it every day i live with it one weekend every three months must be the strong one for her. She looks down at her plate again.

"Well, I'm glad to hear you're making friends, especially with all those crazy people down there in LA."

"Yeah, I do have a lot of good friends, Mom." Tell them about tony i want to so. "Hey, one of my friends, Tony Caravalho, used to play ball at Pitt. A defensive back."

"How interesting," Jennie remarks. does she know she knows or believes but says nothing thats why she scolded brian does anyone else know am i so obvious? I look up at her. She is smiling at me, then turns her face to Tommy and makes him put his hands above the table.

"David, would you like more gravy?" Mom hands me the ladle. "You have hardly any on your biscuits. You always loved my gravy. I wish you would eat healthier, at least while you're here." No understanding of nutrition. I put up my hand.

"Mom, I love your gravy. It's just . . . I'm not used to so much grease anymore, and if I go help Dad and Brian with the drip lines . . ."

"It's not grease! I drained the fat!"

"Well, butter then."

"Now David, you don't have to help Brian and me with the drip lines," Dad says, "You didn't need to come all the way up here just to work out in the orchards."

"But I thought, you know . . ." his cancer in his brain he's out in the fields and me just relaxing.

"I know what you thought," Dad says he does know. "We can manage."

I look over at Mom. She's staring at Dad, worried, and she looks at me.

"They've got peaches already out on Manley Road, out on the Vermeulen farm," she says. "I've got your old bike in the garage. You could ride out there and pick some from the road. Jack and Alice would love to see you, though I'm sure they'll tell you an earful about Angie. You know she just had another girl."

and dad *that angie would make a fine housewife but you should not even think of marriage until you know you love her so now youre at college make sure you know what you want but always remember god family and team*

Brian laughs.

"Don't expect her and James will have anything but girls."

Jennie gives him another angry look.

"And what do you mean by that?"

"Well, you've seen James. Kind of scrawny. I'm sure he's got some kind of defective Y chromosome or something. And he's been hoping so hard for a boy. Poor guy." james oliphant a little man not a man angie likes boys not men effeminate boys first me then james but now i'm a man and if he has a son james also is verified a man but i will have none and angie *is there something youre not telling me* and i *what do you mean* and angie *you went to san francisco who do you know there* and i *i just wanted to get out of the valley i'm tired of it here* and she *why cant you be happy with what you have* and i *i don't know i just want something more* and she *what is it and why do you think you can find it in the city* and i *i dont know its just something about a big city* and angie *david are you gay*

"I'm sure Angie would love to see you while you're up here, but she's in Stockton now," Mom says. "It gets harder to see old friends when you're raising a family. But you should give her a call."

"You know, James is thinking of leaving the co-op," Brian says. "Nobody's trusting us right now. But I tell them, go up to Davis. Check out the reports!" Brian slams his fist on the table didn't see he was upset talk of James co-op on his mind always

"Brian!" Jennie exclaims.

"I'm sorry, but can't the farmers learn to live the cycles rather than season to season? Next year they're reporting a bumper crop, a dry season but the reservoirs will be full. But they're saying, why can't you charge more a bushel? So they want to start their own independent co-op, saying we're making mistakes. Well, yeah! We make mistakes, but we're trying the hardest we can." He forks his gravy, swirling it around the top of his biscuits and ham. "Don't they understand team-work? Try to make things better from the inside, rather than fighting from the outside."

and dad *all the schooling in the world wont prepare you for the world as much as being on a team dedicated as a cohesive body working together with drive the three most important things in this world your god your family and your team and if it be football all the better*

Brian catches himself swirling his gravy, and he looks over at me and nods his head in frustration.

"I guess this subject doesn't interest you too much, does it, David? You being down in LA now, listening to the bickering of some farmers up in the valley." my brother sees me different he is now irrelevant to me i will change that reassure him

"Sounds much more exciting than what I'm doing. My whole work now is just ensuring hospital towers are being built to meet new seismic regulations. I'm sure none of us wants to talk about that."

Brian looks at me dumbfounded for a moment. He laughs and goes back to eating his gravy and biscuits.

"I guess it doesn't matter where you are or what you do," he says, "just as long as you do it as well as you know how."

Mom looks worried at me and picks up the plate of bacon.

"David, don't tell me you're through. You didn't even have any bacon."

I put my hand up.

"No, Mom. I'm full." I look around the table and everyone has stopped eating. All the plates are empty except Tommy and Sandra's, and they sit fidgeting. Only Brian is still eating, scraping the last remains of the gravy from his plate. Dad drops his napkin on his plate. He scoots his chair back.

"Well, I'm going to get on the old boots and walk on out to the north orchard. Brian, the drip lines are back by the shed. I'll meet you back there."

"I'll get the lines. I'll meet you in row seven."

"How many lines do you have to do?" I ask.

"Twenty-five, but we're only going to get started on five today," Brian says. "At least Dad agreed on that, since you're home and all."

"I don't see why we don't get the hires in earlier this year to do all that," Mom says.

"Rachel, I've told you, the season is nearly a month late. Then what do we do with them after the lines are through?" Dad says, cantankerous and congested losing his patience never loses his patience only when mom points out his weakness is what she's doing i want to point it out too scream it out *why are you doing this dad youre dying let someone else do it enjoy your last days* he wants to live as he's always lived happy with the present moment me always seeking something different something more living in the future never happy with now but now theres tony can i now find peace

Mom turns to me, gives a quick eye to Dad, and then smiles carefully at me.

"David, did you know that James and Angie are doing very well on their farm? One of the most productive fifty acres of almonds in the valley. And do you know why? It's what they taught James up at UC Davis . . ."

Dad snickers as he scoots back his chair. He rises. Then clears his throat.

"There she goes again, trying to make trouble in a room full of University of Pacific alumni, trying to say they teach ag right up there in Davis."

Mom gives Dad a hard stare.

"No, Clyde. You're right. They teach ag right at UOP. Davis just gives their grads a better sense of business."

She turns my way.

"Now James, he's rarely out in his orchards. He's got workers doing that for him, so he can spend more of his time on the business end. And it's working."

"See, there you go, Rachel," Dad says, "trying to teach those State of California secular ways of doing agribusiness. But that's not ag, you see. You're not a farmer if you grow distant from your own fields. You can't just look at the numbers. You've got to be out there, seeing the crops, smelling the dirt, hearing the wind humming through the inside hollows of the hulls, sensing how much the almond has grown inside. You got to see, smell, taste the growth of your crops. Because you are part of that crop, just as much as is the trunk or the leaves or the branches or the water or the dirt or the sun. That's what ag is, Rachel. That's what it always will be—becoming one with the Lord's miraculous handiwork."

dad looking down at the tiles of the floor justifying himself why he goes into the orchards though he's dying one with the universe satisfied with the moment i could never be like him i am not a man only because i cannot be satisfied with who i am at the present but there is no future or past only the present that is what dad knows theres no dying with the present seize the moment live the now

Dad turns away walking out of the kitchen getting his boots.

"Dad."

My voice sounds weak wonders if he heard that squeak.

He stops and turns.

"Why can't I go out in the orchards with you and Brian? I'd really like to."

He looks up at me, his cheeks and eye sockets hollow. He looks me up and down.

"Your clothes are kind of clean," he says. "Got anything to change into?"

I nod will be out there one with the farm one with nature one with god

He walks away.

"Meet us in the north orchard. Row seven."

He disappears into the hallways watching him leave. I turn to Mom. She too is watching him leave. She looks at me, a smile rising into her dry brown cheeks. She puts her arms around me and gives me a hug.

"I'm glad you're going out there," she says. "Just make it look like he's doing most of the work."

12

The Crenshaw Cool

All of the Quake's fortunes would come down to this second half. They were up by only two points, 24-22, playing the Crenshaw Cool in the final game of the regular season. Last weekend they had demolished the Beer Bellies 78-6, but it was this game that counted. It was this Cool/Quake game that would determine the third and fourth seeds in the playoffs.

The West Hollywood Warriors already were assured the second seed, having defeated the Cool by two touchdowns the week before. The Warriors had not lost a game during the regular season until this morning, when they were soundly defeated by the Santa Monica Seahawks 42-20. Almost everyone had resigned themselves to the fact that the Seahawks could not be beat. That is why this afternoon's game was so important to the Quake. Lose and next week they would face the Seahawks, the number-one seed, in the semifinals. Win today and they would get what they craved—the chance for a rematch against Vince and the West Hollywood Warriors.

"Come on now, Quake!" Marcus rallied the team at halftime. "This is our game now! We lose this and then we lose to the Seahawks in the semifinals, you know what that says, you know? It says that Vince's team had a better season than us. We got to beat the Cool so we can kick some ass against the Warriors next week!"

"Yeah. We can't drop those passes now!" Jack added. "If Ed had caught that pass thrown right to him, we'd be up by eight or ten points. Any more mistakes like that and we lose the game!"

Ed looked down at his feet. He had dropped two easy passes, one right in the end zone. Jack's words stung, and he was ashamed to look at his teammates. But he brought his eyes back up after feeling Bill reassuring him with a tug on his shoulder.

They broke to prepare for the second half, Ed and Bill walking onto the field together.

"Hey, don't sweat it, Ed," Bill said. "We've all got games like this. Fuck Jack anyway. You've been one of the most reliable receivers this whole season. I mean, look at Curt. He was completely off his game at the beginning of the season. And look at him now. He's scored two touchdowns. You can shake it, too."

"I guess," Ed shrugged his shoulders. "It's just . . ."

He stopped suddenly.

"Bill . . . I . . ."

Ed looked down at the ground, unable to finish his sentence.

"Hey, c'mon, Ed," Bill tugged on his shoulder again. "What is it?"

Ed swung his leg in an arc, kicking away a stone with his cleat.

"I think Drew might be fooling around. But, um . . . I think he's fooling around with a woman."

Bill stared at him, his eyes opened wide.

"Whoa. You're kidding. What gay man fools around with a woman on the side? It's always the other way around, I thought."

"I found a pair of pantyhose under his bed."

Bill let out a chuckle, but he quickly covered his mouth.

"Sorry. It's just that . . . well . . . have you said anything to him?"

"No. I mean, I don't know what to say. It's like . . . well, it's hard for me to believe."

Again Ed stopped and looked at Bill.

"Remember when I first met Drew? I thought he was so masculine and all. Well . . . when you get to know him, he's not really what you first imagine."

Ed started walking again, faster this time.

"But then maybe he is. You see, when we're in bed, you know . . . he's kind of passive. I mean, he's been on top before, but . . . you know . . . he kind of . . . likes swinging the other way. But now, finding the pantyhose, I'm thinking perhaps he's, you know, bi-something. He likes to be a dominant top with a woman but a passive bottom with a man. Does that sound possible?"

"Ed, I don't know. The guys I'm around never seem that complicated, though I'm not sure if that's good or bad."

"But no! I mean . . . well . . . I don't know. It's just . . . he's always . . . well, he's so secretive about things. I say let's do something, and he says he has a previous engagement. I mean, just like that. He calls it a previous engagement. He never actually describes what that engagement is. And maybe that's because he's going out with some woman!" Ed shakes his head. "I can't believe I'm jealous about the part of him she's getting. I mean, I guess my part's okay. It's just, well . . . I want all of him."

The second half began with the Cool returning the kickoff to the Quake forty-yard line. The Cool relied primarily on their big three—Walter the scrambling quarterback, Terrence the big and explosive running back, and Thomas the fastest receiver in the league. But the biggest trouble opposing teams had with the Cool was Perry, their 250-pound center, who always stayed back to keep the rushers away from his quarterback. That allowed Walter to throw the deep pass again and again to Thomas, who had made all three of the Cool's first-half touchdowns.

Marcus played deep, fifteen yards back. From his position he could survey both the defense and the offense. Mitch stood near him to his left, and Curt to his right.

"Come on now, Quake! Don't let Thomas fake you out! They can't throw the same shit at us time after time!"

"Oh, just watch us!" Thomas yelled as he approached the line. "Your ass will try to be catchin' me from behind. I see you got no confidence, giving me all those yards up close. Won't do you no good anyhow."

"Pfff!" Marcus reacted, taking his hands off his hips and tensing his shoulders for the play to come.

The ball was hiked. Thomas ran out like a bullet.

"Stay back, Curt!" Marcus yelled. "Stay back!"

Both Curt and Marcus stayed at least five yards in front of Thomas. Al, meanwhile, backpedaled fifteen yards back to help out in case

Thomas suddenly stopped in the middle pocket. But Thomas had faked them all, for Walter the quarterback had called the run. Walter ran to his left and then pitched off to Terrence the running back. From the short middle, Bill could not get over in time, and so the Cool picked up fifteen yards before Al pulled Terrence's flag.

"Damn!" Marcus yelled. Thomas responded by displaying a wide-toothed grin.

"Fooled your ass!" Thomas said as he returned to the Cool huddle.

"Fuck, man!" Marcus yelled. "We can't keep givin' them that shit. They only got three guys to worry about. So how come the Cool's in this game?"

The Quake, however, were able to hold the Cool this series as they began to learn how to play their opponents. But the Cool had learned the Quake's weaknesses as well, and now they began sending Terrence in as the rusher, knowing that Jack did not pass well under pressure. At the center position, Ed was unable to hold Terrence away from the quarterback, and so now Marcus had to stay back to block, but Terrence was able to get by him nearly every other play. So the Quake ended their first series of the second half with an incomplete pass on fourth down in midfield.

"Damn it, man!" Marcus yelled as Jack threw another long pass up the middle when threatened by the rusher. "Jack, you know you can't throw long under these circumstances. I can only hold him so long. Their short defenders are slow and can't handle crosses. Start crossing the flankers short in the middle, man!"

The Cool picked up a first down by throwing five-yard passes to their flankers. And then Walter, getting plenty of time in the pocket, threw a pass over the outstretched hands of Curt and Marcus and into the arms of Thomas for a touchdown.

The Cool were up 28-24. They then stretched their lead by making the two-point conversion.

The Quake again were unable to connect on a fourth-down play, giving the ball over to the Cool with only three minutes to play. Suddenly, a feeling of dread spread over the team. What if they lost this game and were almost assured a loss to the Seahawks next weekend? What if, at the same time, the Warriors again defeated the Cool to end up in the finals? None of them would be able to face Vince ever again. They all would have to retire from football in complete humiliation. The rematch they had longed for with the Warriors would never take place. They'd have to move away from LA. They could never, ever be seen in public again. Their lives would be lost.

Walter started the series of downs by connecting on a couple short passes and by handing off the ball to Terrence for a ten-yard pickup. The Cool were playing it smart, knowing to stay conservative with the lead late in the game. Mitch, Curt, and Marcus were afraid they wouldn't see any action unless they tried something different. So when the Cool went into their huddle, the Quake's defensive backs did the same.

Both huddles broke. When the Cool ran to their positions, they saw a new defense. Mitch, Marcus, and Curt were playing only five yards off the scrimmage line.

"Damn!" Thomas remarked with his hands on his hips. "I don't know what all you Quake are thinking, but I do know your asses are going to be sorrier than they ever was."

"You'll be the sorry ass, talking trash like that," Marcus fired back.

Thomas turned toward his quarterback and gave him a nod. Marcus caught their sign, and he looked at Curt and Mitch and gave them a nod as well.

The ball was hiked. Mitch, Curt, and Marcus quickly faded back. Thomas ran straight out fifteen yards, then slanted right, cutting a post pattern to the right. Meanwhile, Ed ran toward the quarterback. Perry was there, centered in Ed's way. Ed brought out his right forearm, ready for contact with the massive center. He struck his forearm, feeling the impact. And then he brought his arm over Perry's head.

The old forearm shiver worked. Perry had centered on Ed's right shoulder and forearm, but Ed had slipped them over Perry and now was heading straight for the quarterback.

Walter saw Ed's approach. He moved to the right, but Ed shifted with him. And then Walter saw Thomas down the field slanting to the right end zone. He cocked his arm back and threw a deep, high ball toward his main receiver.

Dan Boyle 217

Thomas had passed by Mitch and was now a step ahead of Marcus. The ball was soaring up toward them. It looked like another touchdown pass.

But Curt had sprinted back forty yards off the line of scrimmage as soon as the ball was hiked. He now ran across the field toward Thomas, and as the ball came down, they both ended up in the same location.

Until Curt ran in front of Thomas and picked off the pass.

Unable to slow down his motion across the field, Curt ran out of bounds. The Quake now had the ball, but they would have to bring the ball sixty yards down the field with less than a minute to go to win the game.

On the first play, the two wide receivers—Mitch and Curt—crossed fifteen yards out. In a zone defense, the Cool's two fastest defensive backs—Thomas and Walter—stuck on Curt, since he was the one making all the plays for the Quake. That left Jess, the slower defensive back, on Mitch, but Jess had been confused momentarily when the two receivers crossed, giving Mitch a couple steps on him. Jack then threw a perfect pass to Mitch, who ran the ball another ten yards before Walter pulled his flag. Now the Quake was threatening on the Cool's thirty-five-yard line.

The Quake went to their huddle.

"OK, Marcus, what do you think?" Jack asked. "The Bill play?"

Marcus nodded firmly.

"Let's do it, man. I never saw the Cool scouting us. We'll bury their ass."

They broke the huddle and everyone lined up right of the center. Everyone but Bill, that is, who lined up just to the left of Ed.

Ed hiked the ball.

Everyone on the line slanted to the left side of the field. Bill appeared to stay back to give Perry one good block. But then suddenly, Bill slanted out toward the right sidelines.

The Cool were fooled, running with the Quake to the left sidelines, while Bill ended up all alone for a ten-yard pass. He ran undefended up the right sideline.

Touchdown.

The score was tied thirty-all and the Quake going for the two-point conversion.

The ball was hiked. Curt and Bill veered to the left sideline as Mitch, Al, and Ed formed a wedge, running down the right side. Jack handed the ball to Marcus, who followed his three blockers down the right.

As the rusher, Terrence barreled through the middle and toward the quarterback. But seeing Marcus running to the right, Terrence pulled his foot in and now ran after the Quake running back from behind. Marcus felt Terrence's heavy breath come closer and closer. His blockers were not running fast enough. Terrence would grab his flag before he crossed the goal line.

So Marcus planted his left foot and leapt. He soared over the blockers and landed with a thud.

"Ughh!" Marcus groaned as he hit the ground on one shoulder.

All the players looked down at Marcus.

The line of white chalk marking the end zone was behind him.

The Quake had gone ahead.

"Bring on the Warriors!" the Quake exclaimed.

They were ready to taste the sweet flavor of revenge. The Quake would get their rematch.

☙ 13 ❧

Another Night Together

FADE IN

INT. HOLLYWOOD HILLS HOME—NIGHT

A small hallway with glass block walls, marble floors, and a marble side table with a large crystal vase holding calla lilies. The hallway opens up to a spacious living/dining room center done in white, with a jade marble gas fireplace ablaze. Cher is playing over the speakers.

The doorbell rings. The door opens into the hallway, and Marcus enters. He is wearing a black mesh see-through muscle shirt, brown leather pants, and a wide black belt with a huge round buckle. He stares at the lilies for a moment, then hears the music and rolls his eyes as he walks into the living/dining room.

MARCUS: Child, this Cher thing is so tired, if you know what I mean. Every time I enter your pad, it's either Cher or Madonna on your stereo.

JACK (O.S.): Pretty! And don't be going changing the receiver to your rap while I'm finishing up.

MARCUS: Finishing up? You were the one saying I had to be here ten-thirty sharp. I already gave myself an extra half hour knowing you're never ready, and you're still finishing up?

Jack enters the dining room from a back hallway. He is wearing only a towel wrapped around his waist. Marcus is conspicuously looking down at his loins.

JACK: Ahh, quit your yapping. Make yourself a drink, and I'll be ready in five minutes.

MARCUS: Oh, bashful are we? Wrapping a towel around yourself to be presentable. Like I ain't seen that before.

Marcus walks into the kitchen in the back of the dining room and opens the freezer door. He takes out a bottle of vodka.

JACK: Always trying, aren't you, Marcus? Well, you're not getting any.

MARCUS: Ooh, child, don't even go there. You wouldn't know what to do with a black man if you ever had one, you being the whitest mother around, playing that Cher and shit.

JACK: Ha! And Mother can talk, the whitest black man if ever there was one. You wouldn't last five minutes in South Central.

Marcus finishes fixing his drink, then grabs the glass and saunters past Jack into the living room, where he sits down on the white couch in front of the fireplace.

MARCUS: I know one thing about you, Miss Thing. You are too afraid. You know how we get down, and you'd look like some sorry ass trying to keep up. Afraid we're just too experienced. And so you settle on those young white boys at Rage who think you're all experienced, talking about you being such a dominant top and all. You're just afraid of being with anyone who finds you out for what you really are.

JACK: Pretty! Why don't you smoke some weed? Calm yourself down, 'cause somehow you've gotten too aroused. Looks like I better get into some clothes quick.

MARCUS: Five minutes, hmmm? You haven't even fixed your hair yet. You know that takes fifteen minutes itself, with all the hairspray and shit you put all in it.

Marcus looks around the room.

MARCUS: Where's that killer herb you keep talking about?

JACK: On the other table, by the TV.

Jack exits into the back hallway. Marcus stands up and moves over to the other couch, where he sees three joints in an ashtray on the coffee table. He picks one up. Cher finishes up on the speakers, and now he hears Madonna's "Ray of Light."

MARCUS: Damn, he's white.

EXT. POOLSIDE—NIGHT

Marcus is sitting in a chaise longue next to Jack's lighted, azure blue pool. The Jacuzzi is raised on the far side of the pool, and a small waterfall cascades from the Jacuzzi into the pool. Marcus is finishing the joint and looking into the glass picture windows of Jack's living room.

Jack emerges from the back hallway, wearing a white tank top, blue 501s, and black boots. Jack spots Marcus out by the pool. Jack slides the glass door back and walks toward the pool.

MARCUS: You call that five minutes? Someone ain't got no sense of time.

JACK: Believe me, I rushed as quick as I could, knowing you were here alone with my liquor and my weed, wondering if I got any of either left.

MARCUS: You need to be a better host, talking that shit and all. So where is it we're going tonight? And I ain't going to no Rage, having you pretend you don't know me as you stare down some boy half your age.

JACK: Marcus, don't go giving me shit either. I'm not ready to be getting involved with anyone for a while, especially some young boy looking for a daddy.

MARCUS: That's right, 'cause that seems to be the only ones you keep looking for, and then look what happens when they don't need you no more.

JACK: Ah, fuck you, Mother!

MARCUS: Hey, I know that hurt, Jack, and I'm sorry it does, but you know, I'm just saying the truth. If you want something, you got to start it with someone you respect from the start, someone who's already a success in his own mind, not someone who wants you 'cause you're a success and all. You know what I mean?

JACK: Can we change the subject? Not that I'm trying to hide from this, but I don't think I want to get advice on this from someone who's out sluttin' every night.

MARCUS: What do you mean, out sluttin'? My relationships have been more meaningful than yours ever will, Miss Thing. You got no right saying I'm sluttin'. You know the circumstances. You know if Andy hadn't gotten sick and all, I might be with him today.

Marcus hands the joint to Jack.

MARCUS: So, where we goin'?

JACK: I guess Axis then. Where else?

MARCUS: We're always goin' to Axis. It's tired, too.

JACK: Then what do you propose, Mother?

MARCUS: [sighs] I guess it's Axis. You got anything to party on? 'Cause if I'm going out with you again to Axis, doing the same shit over and over, I might as well have fun.

Jack stands up and pulls out his keys and a vial of coke and displays it to Marcus.

JACK: Take a bump now.

Jack puts a key into the vial, and the groove of the key emerges with the coke. Jack sniffs it into his nostril and hands both the key and the vial to Marcus, who begins to do the same.

JACK: Yeah, another night together at the Axis. Are we two sorry motherfuckers or what?

FADE OUT

14

The Rematch

Dave was not there for the biggest game of the season, the rematch against the West Hollywood Warriors. Tony Caravahlo had come to the game five minutes before kickoff, and he broke the news to the Quake that Dave's father had passed away two days ago. So when the Quake huddled right before the opening whistle, they all agreed that this game would be dedicated to Dave's father.

Although Dave was unable to be with his team, the Quake did find themselves with a new booster club. They arrived in short red skirts and matching tops, big hairdos, blue eye shadow, shaved legs, and pom-poms.

No one knew how the West Hollywood Cheerleaders had heard about the game. No one on either team would admit that they had told the cheerleaders about the rematch. So, for better or for worse, the teams found the cheerleaders splitting into two teams—four rooting for the Warriors and four rooting for the Quake.

"We've got spirit. Yes, we do. We've got spirit. How about you?" the cheerleaders on the Warriors side began to chant.

"We've got spirit. Yes, we do," the cheerleaders on the Quake side repeated. "We've got spirit. We're tired of you."

"Fuckin' drag queens," Jerry responded. "You know it was some sissy on the Warriors who fuckin' asked them to come."

But the cheerleaders were just what the Quake needed, lifting their spirits after hearing the news of Dave's father. Bill laughed at their antics and nudged Ed.

"Look at that big girl on our side, the one with the blue beehive," he said. "She keeps looking at you, Ed. I think she's got a crush on somebody."

"Very funny," Ed responded.

The Quake set up in three rows—short, middle, and deep—as they all nervously waited for the kickoff. This was it. They had to get off to a good start. They did not want to get behind and play catch-up as they had in the previous game against the Warriors. They wanted this game from the start.

Vince kicked the ball deep, back to the twenty-yard line. Curt, who played deep with Mitch, ran back and caught it over his shoulder. As he squared himself toward the goal again, Julio was rushing toward him.

Curt jabbed right. Julio took the fake as Curt quickly changed directions and began running up the left side of the field.

Marcus, his shoulder still sore from his diving two-point conversion last week, suddenly was inspired by Curt's fake. He brought his shoulders down and made a firm block on J. R., knocking him to the ground.

"Let's go, Curt! Let's go!" Al yelled, now running in front of his boyfriend. Tom, the Warriors' burly redhead, was barreling down on him. Al picked up speed, brought his head down, and hit Tom squarely in the stomach.

"Oomph!" Tom reeled back, trying to catch his breath. Curt ran by him.

Now it was only Vince between Curt and the goal line. Curt tried to shake him, but Vince squared on him and deftly pulled his flag. Curt had picked up fifty yards, and the Quake were threatening on the twenty-yard line.

"Dammit!" Vince exclaimed as Tom approached him. "Tom, how the fuck did you let Al bring you down?"

"All right now, Quake! Huddle!" Jack yelled as he ran onto the field. All the players ran into the circle pumping their fists.

"All right! We got Vince frazzled," Jack said. "Let's keep him frazzled all the way to the end."

On first down, Jack threw a pass into the arms of Al, who ran it to the five-yard line before Bob pulled his flag. On the next play, Jack handed the ball to Marcus, who slipped by Tom and ran it up the middle for the touchdown.

"Fuck!" Vince yelled. He ran up and put his face an inch from Tom's own. "Are you in this game or what!"

Marcus raised his fists. He felt it. The Quake were in a zone.

But Vince wasn't ready to concede. As Bill and Al crossed deep in the back of the end zone and Jack threw it Al's way, Vince dove and slapped the ball away, denying the two-point conversion.

The Quake led 6-0, their first lead of the season against the Warriors.

The game was far from over. On their first series of plays, the Warriors also scored after Bob connected on a number of short passes, and then Julio ran it in for a touchdown. The Warriors also ran in the points after, and the Warriors led 8-6.

Leads changed hands as the first half went as such:

Mitch returned the kickoff to the fifty-yard line. Jack connected on a ten-yard and out to Al. Marcus came out of the backfield and caught a fifteen-yard pass in the pocket. Ed dropped an open pass seven yards up the middle. Ed caught a ten-yard and in. Curt ran a deep inside to catch it past Julio's outstretched arms for a touchdown. The Quake connected on the two-pointer with a five-yard pass to Jerry. The Quake were up 14-8.

The Warriors returned the kickoff back to their own thirty-five-yard line. Bob faked a pass and ran it himself behind Jim's and Vince's blocks for a seven-yard pickup. Jim picked up five yards, capitalizing on the Quake's one weakness—Jerry at the right linebacker position. Vince ran past Mitch and picked up a twenty-five-yard pass, only to have his flag pulled by Marcus the instant he brought the ball into his arms. Julio followed Dan's, J. R.'s, and Bob's blocks and ran twenty-eight yards for a touchdown. Again the Warriors connected on the two-point, and they were up 16-14.

The Quake came back with a deep outside flag pattern to Mitch, who caught it three strides in front of Dan. Julio pulled Mitch's flag as he came down with the catch at the ten-yard line. Jack faked a handoff to Marcus, only to run the other way for his first touchdown run of the season. The Quake scored the extra points as Bill scooped up a short pass at his knees and ran it in. The Quake were up 22-16.

The Warriors brought the kickoff back to midfield. But a series of dropped passes—one by Tom, one by J. R., and one by Jim, left them at fourth and ten. With only twenty seconds to play in the half, Bob had his wide receivers run straight and deep, and he threw a desperation pass to Vince, only to have Mitch knock the ball down.

Halftime.

Marcus and Jack left the field agreeing that holding the Warriors on the last series of plays had changed the tide of the game in their favor. Vince, meanwhile, was yelling at Tom and his two flankers to get into the game. The Warriors had lost their cool. Marcus was sure of it.

"That's it, Quake. Just play the way we're playing. Bring it up a notch in the second half, and we got it," Marcus yelled, clapping to his team.

Ed walked over to the Quake bench and sat down. The four cheerleaders now towered over him from behind the bench. He looked over his shoulder at the tall cheerleader, the one with the blue beehive and the silver glitter eyelashes. Again, the cheerleader was smiling at him and fluttering his lashes.

Now that most of the players had come over to their respective benches, the cheerleaders on the Warriors side suddenly ran over to their rivals on the Quake side. It was the halftime entertainment.

"Our team's going to beat yours, you sluts!" one of them screamed as they raised their hands and began slapping the Quake cheerleaders. The Quake cheerleaders slapped back until there were sixteen hands, all in white gloves, flapping up and down.

The players all stood and watched the exchange, laughing. One cheerleader, enjoying the attention, then extended his arm all the way out and knocked off the wig of the tall Quake cheerleader. The blue beehive flew more than ten yards over the field, only to land point down, exposing all the bobby pins needed to keep it on the cheerleader's hair.

Ed laughed hard, watching the cheerleader who had been flirting with him chasing his wig and exposing his pink bumblebee-patterned panties as he bent over to retrieve it.

Suddenly, Ed's eyes widened in dismay.

He had seen those panties before.

The cheerleader kept his face away from Ed, desperately trying to place the beehive back on his head, his short blond hair now exposed. Ed stared at the cheerleader's wide, muscular back, wondering whether he should dare approach him.

Ed walked over to the cheerleader and placed his arm on his shoulder, turning him around. The cheerleader's eyes looked panicked under his silvery lashes, his one hand holding his beehive as he stared at Ed.

"Drew?"

"Surprise?" Drew asked nervously.

Ed did not know what to say. He stood there staring, his mouth open. But when it finally sunk in that his boyfriend was a West Hollywood Cheerleader, he became numb in the recognition that his team also became aware of this fact. He now was frozen, too scared to look to his left or to his right, wondering whether his teammates were laughing at him.

"Um," Ed stuttered. "Could we . . . maybe . . . go somewhere . . . for a moment?"

Drew stood up, clasping his hairdo in one hand. The two of them then silently walked off the field.

Ed returned alone to the field only two minutes before the start of the second half. Bill, stretching on the field, saw his friend sitting with his head down between his knees on the Quake bench. Bill ran over to him.

"You OK?"

Ed, his eyes staring at the grass, nodded slowly.

"He told me he had been trying to give me clues all along. The pantyhose. And yeah, I saw the women's panties, too, and once some lipstick on the kitchen counter. And I did think he was giving me clues, but I thought he was trying to tell me he had a girlfriend. Now I find out *he's* the girlfriend."

Bill sat next to him.

"All right! That's great!" Bill exclaimed. "You don't have to worry anymore about him cheating on you. That'll get you out of your funk, won't it . . . for the second half?"

Ed looked up at Bill with a look of desperation.

"Bill, don't you see? My boyfriend's a drag queen!"

Having lost one of their members, the other seven West Hollywood Cheerleaders decided to root together for whoever was on offense at the time. They would first cheer for the Warriors, who returned the kickoff to their own forty-two-yard line. After the Warriors picked up two first downs on a series of five plays, Marcus began to see that Vince and Bob had lost confidence in their nonstar players—J. R., Tom, and Jim. All the passes were being thrown to Vince and Dan, and Julio had carried the ball twice. The Quake defense huddled.

"OK, we're going to a half zone, half man on man," Marcus said. "That'll shake them up. Curt, you stay on Julio's ass. Mitch, you got Dan. I've got Vince. The rest of you, play your regular zones, but play loose, about five yards off the line. We'll give them the short ones. I don't think the flankers are going to be getting many passes their way anyhow."

Curt and Marcus were on fire. No matter how they tried, Julio and Vince could not shake their defenders. Dan did catch a fifteen-yard pass on Mitch, who had played him too loosely, but it was the last first down the Warriors had in that series. Then, at fourth down and eighteen yards from the goal, Bob had to resort to a pass up the middle to Jim, who bobbled the ball before it landed on the ground.

"That's it, Quake!" Curt yelled. "That's it! We got the game!"

With the Quake now on offense, Jack connected on seven passes in a row. Then Marcus was handed the ball for a short, three-yard touchdown run. Again, Vince picked off the pass for the extra points, but still the Quake had the biggest lead of the game, 28-16.

The Warriors quickly scored again on a running play by Julio, after Tom made a square hit on Curt to get him out of the way. The Warriors connected on an inside slant pass to Vince for the two extra points. It was now 28-24.

Not to be outdone, Marcus caught the ball on the kickoff and ran back fifty yards to the twenty-yard line. Then Jack executed a series of short inside crosses and outside slants to Al, Bill, and Mitch, who ran it in for the touchdown. This time, Jack connected on Curt for the two-point conversion. The Quake were up 36-24.

The Warriors had not yet held the Quake on offense, and when J. R. again bobbled a pass and the ball fell into Bill's hands for an interception, Vince and his team were beginning to realize that the Quake would have their revenge.

The Quake played out the game with a run and a series of short, uncontested passes. When the whistle blew, the Quake piled on top of one another at midfield in celebration.

They were going to the finals against the Santa Monica Seahawks.

The Warriors waited for the pile to dissipate before walking over to their opponents and shaking their hands. Vince, who had felt anger at his flankers and at Tom for not playing the game they should, now began to blame himself for the loss, realizing the anger he had felt had actually affected his own abilities on the field. Trying to manage these emotions, he waited for the rest of the Warriors to congratulate the Quake before he walked up to Marcus and Jack.

"Well, it looks as though we finished this league in a dead heat, us winning one and you winning one," Vince said as he extended his hand. "I guess our teams were pretty evenly matched in the end."

Marcus looked at Jack, wondering what they should do now that Vince was trying to play down this moment. Both of them wanted to make a quick retort, to rub it in Vince's face, but as they looked at each other, they understood that neither of them would do this. Yes, the Warriors had been their rivals. But now, they were through being enemies. That moment in time was over.

Marcus shook Vince's outstretched hand.

"You're right, man. Even teams. No hard feelings. The Warriors are a great team."

"Yeah. I'm kind of missing our games at Hollywood High," Jack added. "The way our teams played, it's just going to make the fall league all the more exciting."

Vince nodded.

"And I'm sorry I'm not going to see you guys in the championship," he said. "But then, what's the point? You know you all don't got a chance against the Seahawks. They crushed the Cool by forty-eight points today."

Again, Marcus and Jack looked at each other, wondering how to respond.

"Well, that's too bad you won't be there," Marcus said. "'Cause you are going to miss one helluva game."

◆ 15 ◆

Makeup to Breakup

Sunday, 1 p.m.

"Hello."

"Hi, Drew."

"Ed! Well, hi. Hey . . . I'm glad you called. Look, I'm sorry. I'm thinking . . . I was wrong. I just thought . . . well the best way to break the news to you was just show it all at one time. But . . . it's just for fun. I'm not a serious drag queen."

"Yeah. I know. I mean, you can't be. You look so much better as a guy."

"So, you're not upset?"

"No. I mean, at first I was kind of embarrassed with my friends around and all, and me mentioning to Bill that I thought you were fooling around with a woman, which I guess wasn't really that untrue."

"Ed . . . I don't consider myself a woman at all."

"Oh. I know. And you know, I really don't consider myself all that macho either. I mean, people think I am because I play football. But, you know, like a friend said to me, I think there's a little bit of both in us. Yin yang, or something like that."

"Well . . ."

"But, you know, Drew, and it has nothing to do with you being a cheerleader or anything, but . . . well, it's funny, when I found out it was you in that outfit, after the initial shock, that is, I was kind of thinking something else."

"What's that?"

"I was thinking how we met at Akbar, and it was you who approached me. And then I thought, you know, every single relationship I've been in, it's been the other guy who initially approached me. I've never approached them. Not to say I wasn't glad you approached me. Believe me, I was."

"Well, I do tend to go for what I like."

"And that's one thing I like about you. It's a quality I wish I had."

"Oh, I see it in you."

"And then I was also thinking, every time I've had a relationship break up, it was the other guy who broke up with me. I never initiated that either."

"Well, Ed . . . what are you saying? Ed?"

"Like I said, Drew, it has nothing to do with you wearing a skirt. Well, it's not that I haven't enjoyed us being together and, really, I haven't found someone new. Believe me. I wouldn't do that to you."

"Ed! Dammit! Just tell me. Do you want to break up?"

"How can I just tell you? Believe me, I've had guys break up with me without ever telling me the real reason. I couldn't do that to you, Drew. It's just . . . well, I haven't been honest with myself. Even before I met you. But now I know, and I haven't done anything because I never took the initiative, but . . ."

"Ed, I don't know what you're saying."

"There is someone else. Someone I've known for a long time now. You see . . . I understand it now. I think I might be in love with him. I'm sorry, but . . . well, the guy I always wanted was right in front of me in the first place."

● 16 ●

The Santa Monica Seahawks

All their friends were there to root the Quake to victory. Tony was there, rooting for Dave, who had returned Wednesday from his father's funeral. So far, only one pass had come Dave's way, and he had dropped it. Then there were Holly and Brenda, and Tom Jacobs, the only West Hollywood Warrior to watch the league championship game. Randy Clayburg had come as well.

The first half ended with the Quake trailing 22 to nothing. Vince had been right. The Seahawks were unstoppable. They would have led the league even if their only weapon was their six-foot-four quarterback Rick, who had run for sixty yards the first half and passed for an additional 180 yards—half of those coming from two long bombs in which he barely had to cock the ball behind his head to let it fly like a bullet out of the backfield, its perfect spiral landing like a heat-seeking missile into the arms of his primary receiver.

But the Seahawks also had Ken, the best receiver in the league. Then there was Tom, their running back, who had picked up fifty yards of his own. The dual running team of Rick and Tom had kept the Quake's short defense double guessing who would carry the ball. And then there was Steve, their 235-pound center, who not only blocked for the quarterback but also was a deceptively quick rusher on defense. The other receivers—Dale, Jack, and Chris—although not as skilled as their four teammates, had sure hands and picked up those crucial five- and six-yard passes for first downs when they were needed.

With the first half a blowout, Marcus and Jack were not as concerned about winning as they were about not losing by too much. The

Warriors had lost to the Seahawks by twenty-two points, and the Quake wanted to make sure their point differential was less than that.

Dave and Mitch did not play well during the first half, but they could not match the rut that Ed was in. As the rusher, Ed never once got around the center to threaten the Seahawk quarterback. As center on offense, he was continually battered by Steve, who got past Ed's block almost every time. Three times in the game Ed ran out for a pass while Marcus stayed back to block, but every time Ed dropped the ball. Ed again feared that Jack would say something in the huddle, but Jack appeared resigned to the fact that the Quake could do nothing to stop the Seahawks.

"You got to get a break next half," Bill said to Ed. "Tell Jack to put you at flanker. Let Al or Dave take over as center and block that big guy. Hey, you need some ibuprofen or something?"

"Oh, boy," Ed said in an exasperated wheeze. "It's just one more half, and then I'm taking a long break from the game. I mean, what am I doing out here at thirty-four? We're not healing as fast as we used to."

Bill nodded.

"Yeah, I know. Marcus won't say it, but I can see his shoulder is still sore from the game against the Cool."

They sat down on the bench. Bill fumbled in his bag to take out a bottle of ibuprofen. He lifted the cap and shook out three of the pills, then handed the bottle over to Ed.

"This is it for me," Bill said, "my last game. I would have liked to go out on top, but I had planned this would be it since the beginning of the league. Just one more season of glory, you know. And then . . . on to middle age."

Ed also swallowed three pills. After taking a long drink from his water bottle, he looked over at Bill. Bill's words brought on a feeling of melancholy within Ed as he thought of times past. A sad smile raised on his lips.

"Yeah. It's going to be hard leaving all of this. You and I've been playing together for more than four years now. It's the end of an era."

Bill nodded.

"Well," he said, "out with the old and in with the new. Next fall there will be a whole new slew of gay boys on the field at Hollywood High and playing for the LA team at the next Gay Games. And we'll be off somewhere else, doing . . . whatever. I don't know. Maybe I'll be in New York accepting the Pulitzer, and you . . . you'll be taking Drew in his shimmering new evening gown to the Oscar Ball."

"Bill."

Ed nudged him on the shoulder.

"I . . . broke up with Drew."

"You did?"

"I know. I mean . . . is that shallow of me, finding out he's a drag queen and then breaking up with him?"

"Oh, I don't know," Bill said. "Look at me. I broke up with Larry because he's fat."

Ed nudged Bill harder. They both laughed. Now that they were down by so many points, they felt lighthearted, as though they did not have to concentrate on winning a game.

"Oh, you did not," Ed replied. "But . . . that's not why I broke up with Drew either. Not because he was a cross-dresser. I guess, I just knew I wouldn't fall in love with him."

Bill dropped his eyes and nodded, but in reality, he was unsure what was going on in Ed's mind. He thought of looking at him, but he was afraid his eyes would give away too much. Still, it was just too much not to look.

He raised his eyes.

Those azure rays of light were upon him. He felt it again, that moment four years before, when they had danced at Studio One. Bill drew a breath and blinked his eyes, a tear sinking into his lower lashes.

Again Bill shook it off.

"Well, that's it then," Bill said. He lowered his head, ready to retie his shoes, and though he saw his laces were tight enough as is, still he untied the laces and tied them up again.

"The second half will be starting up soon," Bill said as he tied. "We'd better get on the field."

Ed remained gazing at Bill. He had felt it, too. He felt a possibility that something could happen. A sense of peace fell over him. He no longer felt the pain. He felt stronger than ever, lighter than air. Back to his team, to his comrades.

The second half opened with the Seahawks kicking off. The kick-off had been the Seahawks's one weakness, as Chris could sail it only past midfield. This time, the ball soared right into Ed's waiting hands near the right sideline.

Bill saw the ball come down. He ran in front of Ed. The first Seahawk running down that right-hand side was Steve, the same man who had given Ed a beating the entire first half. Bill was ready to change that. He ran, faster than ever, directly at Steve. It was like two rams attacking. Steve had the strength, but Bill had the resolve. They butted, and Steve was the one who ended up on the ground.

Seeing Bill's accomplishment, Ed felt a burst of energy. There was no ground beneath him. He was flying. He worked off Dave's block to get around Rick. Now there was only Tom. They ran side by side, Tom trying to make up the three feet between him and the runner, but it was no use. Ed ran in for a touchdown.

"I don't believe! I don't believe it!" Jack yelled. "Ed! Ed!"

The Quake ran to Ed, cheering. Then they approached Bill and congratulated him on the best block of the season.

"Now we got it, Quake," Marcus said to them. "We'll give these Seahawks a show at least."

"At least?" Bill repeated. "Marcus, we're winning this!"

Bill turned his head and caught Ed's eyes. Again, he felt it, the connection. It was true now. He was sure of it. How could they not win?

On the two-point conversion, Bill took a jab, faking out the short zone defense, then cut out. Jack threw it to him to make it 22-8.

What Bill and Ed felt made its way to other teammates. Mitch, feeling Bill's energy, kicked the ball all the way back into the end zone, and so the Seahawks started out on their own twenty-yard line.

Ed lined up at the rusher position. He now saw a very small center and a very slow quarterback.

The ball was hiked. Ed rushed in, Steve grew taller and taller as he came closer and closer. But not tall enough. Ed felt his momentum, feeling nothing could stop him. He landed his right shoulder into

Steve's chest. He gave Steve the forearm shiver, striking, then rolling his forearm over Steve's crouched head. Ed passed on through.

It was the first time Rick the quarterback had seen a defender coming down on him. He scrambled to his right. Ed followed. Running to the sideline, he flipped a short pass out to Steve. But Steve was still feeling Ed's blow, and he bobbled the ball until it fell on the ground.

It was a tediously slow series as the Seahawks kept converting on the third and fourth downs, causing them to get one first down after another. Ten plays later they were again in the end zone, despite Ed's inspirational play. But then Curt knocked down a pass to Ken to foil the two-point conversion, and the score was 28-8.

"Damn!" Marcus yelled to his Quake. "Next time we're on D, we can't give them that much time. They took five minutes off the clock with that series of plays. We gotta be jammin' now."

Marcus returned the kickoff to midfield. Jack began mixing up the plays—a run for Marcus, some inside slants caught each time by either Bill or Al, and some deep post patterns to Curt and Mitch. The series ended with Mitch catching the ball over his shoulder and running past Rick for a touchdown.

The next play was Marcus's turn, as he followed his blockers right, then kicked left and ran it up the middle past Steve and Dale.

The Quake trailed 28-16.

Mitch flubbed up on the kickoff, sending the ball sideways and out of bounds at midfield. The Seahawks now had excellent field position. Ed felt himself tiring. His burst of energy could last only so long. This time Steve held him back as Rick sailed the ball down the middle and toward the waiting hands of Tom, who had come out of the backfield.

Bill had seen Tom and was running back from his middle linebacker position. The ball was flying fast and low, with barely an arc on it. Bill leapt. His fingers barely tapped the pigskin, but that was enough. Tom could not stop fast enough to follow the ball's new trajectory. Curt, running into the middle, saw the ball flopping his way. He stretched out his hands, bobbled the ball, and then held it between his hands. Curt had intercepted.

"That's it, Quake! That's it!" Dave suddenly yelled. It had been the first exclamation that had come out of him all day, and the whole team looked at him. Dave turned red, but he spoke again: "Thanks for dedicating last week's game, guys, but . . . we're winning this one for Dad as well, OK?"

Every member of the Quake felt the power in Dave's request. There was no defeat here. Now, all of a sudden, each of them felt they could pull off a victory. This would be their final hurrah. The energy that Ed and Bill had felt had spread to all. But this energy was more than inspiration. It was joy. The joy of being a Quake.

Jack threw a pass to Dave, who brought it up two yards shy of the first down. Marcus then ran it for a new first down. The time was ticking. Five minutes left in the game and two touchdowns back.

The Quake called a no-huddle offense, going straight to the scrimmage line after each play, making sure little time expired.

Jack connected on a ten-yarder to Al. They rushed to the line. Marcus ran it up eight yards. Again, straight to the line. Curt ran twenty yards out, then came back five yards for a fifteen-yard pickup.

First and goal. The ball was hiked. Ed, exhausted, missed a block on Steve, who came barreling toward Jack. Jack scrambled right and pitched it back to Marcus. Then Jack rushed ahead, putting a block on a Seahawks defender as Marcus ran it in for a touchdown.

Mitch scored on the two-point conversion, and now the Quake were down by only four points.

Three minutes to go.

The Seahawks called a time-out. The Quake fans were cheering. Mitch and Curt held their fists in the air.

"Stay focused now, y'all!" Marcus screamed. "We all gotta stay focused. Everything counts now, man. Everything!"

Mitch kicked the ball deep. It was caught by Rick, who scrambled past the blocks of Tom and Steve before Marcus pulled the flag at midfield.

The Seahawks lined up, their mouths in a scowl, their eyes determined. Now was their moment to show off their best.

The ball was hiked. Steve placed a block on Jerry, and then ran off the line of scrimmage and stopped in the middle pocket. Rick soared the ball to him for a twenty-yard pickup.

The Seahawks were thirty yards from a touchdown and the win.

Marcus and Jack felt the momentum change. Again they began to believe, as the other teams had said, that the Seahawks were just too good.

The ball was hiked. Rick backpedaled a few yards, eyeing his receivers while watching Steve hold off Ed. But Ed used his forearm shiver again, and soon Rick found himself backpedaling even farther from the line of scrimmage to escape his defender.

The Seahawks' Tom had drifted out short. He then noticed an opening in the middle pocket and sprinted there five yards out from the scrimmage line. Rick saw him, and before Ed could reach him, he let go a rocket pass to his running back.

Ed leapt, his arms stretched upward, trying to deflect the pass. Instead, the ball stopped instantly, locked between Ed's hands.

Ed fell down with the ball in his hands.

The Quake had the ball with less than two minutes to go and a seventy-yard drive to the goal line.

"We got it we got it we got it we got it!" Bill yelled. "Quake! We got it!"

But Ed still was on the ground. Bill and Mitch ran up to him.

"Damn!" Mitch exclaimed as he inspected Ed's hand. "I think you broke it."

The referee called a time-out, and Ed went to the bench to get his little finger splintered. Dave was called in from the sidelines.

Now came the last series of the league and, for many of them, their lives. First down and seventy yards to go.

The ball was hiked. Jack used all his best players. Marcus sprinted down the left field line as Curt slanted a post pattern and Mitch ran up the right field line. But Tom, Ken, and Rick were waiting for the bomb. Jack threw the ball. Marcus and Tom leaped together. The ball touched Marcus's fingertips, but only for a moment as Tom knocked it out of his hands.

Second and ten. Exactly one minute to go.

They lined up on the left side of the center, all but Bill that is. It was Bill's signature play again. The ball was hiked. Everyone slanted right and Bill slanted left. But Steve had stayed back this time, and he stayed right on Bill's tail. Jack had to find another open receiver. He threw it low to Curt, but the ball hit the ground first.

Third and ten. Thirty seconds to go. The Quake called a time-out.

"Man! Thirty seconds!" Marcus exclaimed. "They know we'll be throwing to Curt or Mitch deep. They're going to stay back. Do we got another time-out?"

Jack shook his head.

"This is it. We can't stop the clock after this play."

A stillness fell in the huddle. No one could decide the play. No one, that is, until one voice spoke softly.

"I know the play."

The team turned their heads in Dave's direction.

It was unfathomable. Dave was suggesting a play. Never, ever, had Dave suggested a play. He had always left that up to his teammates. But as the Quake members stared at Dave, never before had they seen such intensity in his eyes.

"Mitch and Curt will run deep and cross, while Marcus runs up the left sideline," Dave explained, his voice growing more assured with each sentence. "That will cause their deep men to go with them, and the third deep man will follow Marcus. Bill can stay back and block, because he's the biggest of the rest of us. Then, when Mitch and Curt cross, both of them will run as fast as they can back to the scrimmage line. Their men should follow. And then . . . I'll streak out. There will be no one on me. I'll be wide open up the right sideline."

"You!" Jack cried. "We're going to trust the last play of this game to you?"

Dave stood up to him with confidence and resolve.

"Because they won't expect me. I've caught only one pass all day. A simple five-yarder. That's all. And I *will* make this catch, Jack. Never have I been surer of anything in my life. This is the game. I know it, Jack."

Jack looked over at Marcus. Marcus was fingering his lips, questioning the play.

"He's right," Bill spoke. "That's the play."

Al nodded. He looked over at Dave and smiled confidently, giving Dave a push on the shoulder. "Yeah. That's the play."

They came to the line. It was now Bill who hiked the ball. Jack took two steps back as Steve approached. Bill's eyes were staring down the approaching rusher, his feet square and planted. Then Bill lunged, stopping Steve's forward motion.

Curt and Mitch were flying straight up the sideline. Fifteen yards out, they both slanted at the same time. Marcus then emerged from the backfield.

The Seahawks defensive secondary played twenty yards off the scrimmage line. They saw the cross coming.

"Stay in your zone, men!" Rick called. "Stay in your zone!"

Mitch and Curt crossed.

"I got the blond guy!" Rick yelled. "Ken, their running back! Up the sideline! He's yours!"

The defense backpedaled, staying in front of their men. Then, in unison, Curt and Mitch put on the breaks and ran back toward their quarterback. Tom and Rick ran back with them, while Ken followed Marcus down the left sideline.

Then Dave flew up the right sideline. He darted past Tom and Rick. Rick tried to change his motion, following on Dave, but only after Dave was three strides ahead of him.

Steve finally was able to slip by Bill and was coming down on Jack. But Jack had spotted Dave. He now brought his arm back. He threw the ball as hard as he could.

The ball soared high, over the heads of Bill and Al, above Curt and Mitch. Dave looked back, seeing the trajectory of the ball ready to come down over his shoulder. He heard the thuds of his defender's cleats, but then, everything was still. There was only himself, the ball . . . and a still peace.

The ball floated into his arms.

Dave ran as he had never run before. He felt the strength of his body, of his legs. He felt unstoppable.

Rick took one last lunge and fell, missing Dave's flag by a fingertip.

Dave ran into the end zone.

The Quake had won the West Los Angeles Flag Football Spring League Championship.

Dave fell on one knee, facing his teammates as they approached him with outstretched arms. Still, there was silence. Dave looked up into the sky, into the heavens. There, above him, floated a cloud with golden rays shooting from every edge. He felt its brilliance and, at that moment, he felt his father, looking down on this game, finding favor in his son, not only for winning the game, but for becoming a confident, self-assured man, one who knew how to love, one who understood the meaning of God, family, and team.

The Quake ran up to Dave. Jerry and Mitch raised him onto their shoulders. Next to them was Tony, slapping Dave on the shoulder, laughing so hard.

"I can't wait to play with you in the fall league. What a team!" Tony exclaimed joyfully.

Ed had also come off the sidelines, running toward his teammates, his two smallest fingers on his right hand now wrapped together in a splint. But before he could join the celebration in the end zone, Bill turned around and ran into him with a chest butt.

"What an interception, Ed!" Bill cried. "What a game!"

Ed laughed, seeing Bill's tears. Bill stared at him with his watery eyes and then clasped onto Ed with a strong and warm embrace.

"I'm sorry, Ed, but it's been an honor playing with you all these years. I mean . . . what I'm saying . . ."

He let go of his embrace, his tears streaming faster, looking straight into Ed's eyes.

"I've waited for more than four years, and I've tried and tried but I couldn't, trying to figure it all out. But this is it, Ed. I got to tell you. I got to tell you . . ." He broke into a sob. "Ed, I'm in love with you."

Bill quickly wiped his tears.

"I'm sorry," Bill said, "making a fool out of myself like this and all."

They were the words Ed had always wanted to hear. And now they had come.

"Bill, I . . . I wanted to say it first."

Bill saw those brilliant light blue eyes approaching him, blurring into an iridescent azure, melting into him. He felt Ed's lips, the warmth of his tongue. It had come. Finally, it had come.

Curt ran from teammate to teammate, embracing each one. Suddenly he noticed Ed and Bill in a deep embrace. Without a thought, he searched for the man he loved and found the bouncing light brown hair of Al, who was celebrating by hopping up and down in laughter. Curt ran to him and took him into his arms.

Mitch and Jerry let Dave down, allowing Tony to approach his man with a loving kiss. From the sidelines, Holly and Brenda watched those on the field, and so they turned to each other and embraced.

Marcus then took a deep breath and turned to Jack, who, seeing Marcus's intentions, made an ugly scowl, which eventually turned into a smile.

"Well . . . All right, Mother, but just because we won the championship."

And with Jack's words, Mother approached him and gave him a big, wet kiss.

The Quake shook hands with the Seahawks and ran to their bench, picking up their bags, but not ready to depart from their comrades. Not allowing the moment to end, Mitch placed his arm around Bill and gave him a smile. They then walked over to Ed, and Bill put his one free arm around Ed. Soon, a chain began to build, Ed wrapping his arm around Jerry, who wrapped his around Dave, who wrapped his around Marcus, who wrapped his around Jack.

"Can you believe this?" Jerry exclaimed. "It's like the ending of a Hollywood movie."

Side by side, their arms clasped, the Quake walked off the field and into the sunset.

ABOUT THE AUTHOR

Dan Boyle, a native of Tacoma, Washington, moved to California and wrote for a variety of small newspapers before becoming a reporter for the *Los Angeles Daily News.* He currently works in health care marketing and public relations.

SPECIAL 25%-OFF DISCOUNT!
Order a copy of this book with this form or online at:
http://www.haworthpressinc.com/store/product.asp?sku=4887

HUDDLE

_____in softbound at $12.71 (regularly $16.95) (ISBN: 1-56023-459-8)

Or order online and use Code HEC25 in the shopping cart.

COST OF BOOKS_____

OUTSIDE US/CANADA/
MEXICO: ADD 20%_____

POSTAGE & HANDLING_____
*(US: $5.00 for first book & $2.00
for each additional book)
Outside US: $6.00 for first book
& $2.00 for each additional book)*

SUBTOTAL_____

IN CANADA: ADD 7% GST_____

STATE TAX_____
*(NY, OH & MN residents, please
add appropriate local sales tax)*

FINAL TOTAL_____
*(If paying in Canadian funds,
convert using the current
exchange rate, UNESCO
coupons welcome)*

☐ **BILL ME LATER:** ($5 service charge will be added)
(Bill-me option is good on US/Canada/Mexico orders only;
not good to jobbers, wholesalers, or subscription agencies.)

☐ Check here if billing address is different from
shipping address and attach purchase order and
billing address information.

Signature_____

☐ **PAYMENT ENCLOSED: $**_____

☐ **PLEASE CHARGE TO MY CREDIT CARD.**
☐ Visa ☐ MasterCard ☐ AmEx ☐ Discover
☐ Diner's Club ☐ Eurocard ☐ JCB

Account # _____

Exp. Date_____

Signature_____

Prices in US dollars and subject to change without notice.

NAME_____

INSTITUTION_____

ADDRESS_____

CITY_____

STATE/ZIP_____

COUNTRY_____ COUNTY (NY residents only)_____

TEL_____ FAX_____

E-MAIL_____

May we use your e-mail address for confirmations and other types of information? ☐ Yes ☐ No
We appreciate receiving your e-mail address and fax number. Haworth would like to e-mail or fax special
discount offers to you, as a preferred customer. **We will never share, rent, or exchange your e-mail address
or fax number.** We regard such actions as an invasion of your privacy.

Order From Your Local Bookstore or Directly From
The Haworth Press, Inc.
10 Alice Street, Binghamton, New York 13904-1580 • USA
TELEPHONE: 1-800-HAWORTH (1-800-429-6784) / Outside US/Canada: (607) 722-5857
FAX: 1-800-895-0582 / Outside US/Canada: (607) 722-6362
E-mailto: getinfo@haworthpressinc.com

PLEASE PHOTOCOPY THIS FORM FOR YOUR PERSONAL USE.